Fate and Faith

The World War 2 Novel

GW00644830

William Wood

ISBNs:
Paperback: 978-1-80227-028-0
Hardback: 978-1-80227-030-3
eBook: 978-1-80227-029-7

Published by PublishingPush.com

For my beloved Federica who has joined in the journeys
needed to make this book.

To my dear friend Jonathan Keates who has helped
and encouraged the writing. He was never shown
the dreary dialogue, nor the pretentious footnotes,
let alone the purple passages.

Thank you to Sophie at Publishing Push for her
efficiency and help. For Sophie, every error by the
author is an opportunity.

Contents

List of Characters

Author's Note: This novel is not quite War and Peace, but it may help to have a summary of the characters we meet as we follow Ruth's journey.

Those marked with an asterisk are intended to appear again in Volume 2 of a trilogy.

Ruth Neueman	lovely Soprano who leaves Toul in France to teach music in Krakow
Conrad Neuman	father of Ruth. Head of a Jewish household and porcelain manufacturer
Sophie Neuman	mother of Ruth, who converted to Judaism to marry Conrad
Jakob Neuman*	brother of Ruth who joins French army
Vivien Neuman*	sister of Ruth who leaves for education in England
Michel*	boyfriend of Vivien, who joins army with Jakob
Adolf Breuer*	Violin teacher with designs on marrying Ruth who is much younger
Viktor Auerbach	successful entrepreneur in Krakow and old friend of Conrad
Melchior Neuman	elder brother of Conrad, running the family printing business in Strasbourg
Josefz	loyal chauffeur to Viktor Aurbach

Hainski	anti-Semitic landlord when Ruth begins her life in Krakow
Agnieszka Zeleski	friend of Viktor Auerbach who helps Ruth in Krakow
Piotr Zeleski	husband of Agnieszka. Senior lecturer at the Krakow school of medicine
Witold Zeleski*	son of A. and P. Zeleski. Schoolboy and then pilot.
Lukas Zeleski*	son of A. and P. Zeleski. Schoolboy and then pilot
Maria*	nurse in Krakow. Friend of Witold and Lukas
Bruno Berling	school teacher in Krakow and then flight commander in Polish air force
Halina Berling	wife of Bruno, from the distinguished Kutzreba family
Archibald Hillman*	British civil servant
Vlad Glast	schoolboy, plays timpani. Of German origin in Poland but anti-Nazi
Stefan	In choir with Agnieszka and friend of Ruth. Resistance fighter.
Lutoslawski	Polish Composer and conductor
Emil Mendler	German officer in charge of logistics Krakow
Henri	Romanian landowner of German ancestry
Valeria	Sister of Agnieszka Zeleski, married to Henri

Chapter 1: France 23rd May 1940

Groupe de Chasse III/1 operating from Toul Cross Airfield was transferred to Le Bourget on 23rd May 1940.

Pilot Officer Witold Zeleski of the Polish Air Force was delayed because on the previous day, his plane had been damaged by machine-gun fire. The Morane would only take a day to repair, and then he was under orders to re-join the Groupe de Chasse at Le Bourget. The truth was that the pilot was in no better condition than his machine. But the cause was the actions of his ally rather than the enemy. After a slow and dangerous journey, Witold had reached France, one of over a thousand Polish airman who were determined to continue the fight after the defeat of their own country. But there were long delays while French bureaucrats decided whether the Poles should be allowed to defend the skies above their offices. The morale of the Polish pilots fell like a bright coin tossed into a well.

During his escape from Poland through Romania, Greece and Northern Italy, Witold had been focused on reaching France where the war must continue. But after his arrival, waiting and inactive, he reflected on the defeat of his own nation, his parents left in Krakow, his home city occupied by the enemy, the loss of his brother and his small hope of once more seeing the woman he thought he loved. She had told him to keep a secret. Witold, building castles in the air, imagined that she might accept him if he returned. After selection and training to fly in defence of

France, he learned that his Groupe were to operate from Toul Cross Airfield. Toul was the home of Ruth Neuman, and he began to persuade himself that his posting to the city of her birth must be a sign that they belonged to one another.

While the fitters were at work on his plane, Witold walked into the city. The two towers of Toul cathedral dominated the stone streets. He was extremely unhappy about the recent orders to retreat. Sitting in the cool gloom of the cathedral, he was alone, except for a trapped pigeon which flapped sadly in the vault. Witold's eye was drawn to a stained-glass window brightly shining in the afternoon sunshine. Jesus was in Heaven surrounded by angels. He was placing a yellow crown on the head of his mother. He stared at the Coronation of the Virgin for a long time. He remembered hearing Ruth singing to herself in Krakow. When she caught him listening, she had touched his cheek. It was the only time she had caressed him and it was, therefore, unforgettable. An additional memory returned to him; she had told him that this music was her first public performance in the cathedral at home. He had been right to come here, to think about Ruth in a place important to her. Witold stood up to walk, slow and thoughtful, between the tranquil Gothic columns of the nave. He opened the main door and turned to look back at the window. The pigeon, seeing the light, swooped overhead into the freedom of a sunlit afternoon.

On 23rd May, Witold met the Polish ground crew in the early morning.

"She's in great shape. You can bag another three today, Sir."

They were proud of his record in the air war.

Witold took off soon after 7.00 am for his final flight from Toul Cross. The engine bellowed as if the pilot were prodding an angry beast. Gathering pace over the bumpy runway, he revelled in the sound, the increasing speed, then the easy control as the rear wheel lifted just before take-off. Free from the ground, the plane and pilot were together in exhilaration and independence. The airfield was only a kilometre to the North of the city. For the last time, he flew past the towers of the cathedral which had been a familiar and valuable marker ever since the Groupe de Chasse had been stationed there.

On the flight to the South, Witold thought over his resentment that the Groupe were not now flying North to attack the Germans. The invaders had forced their way across the French border at Sedan and Dinant. They were now heading North-West to separate the allied armies in Belgium from the French reserves to the South. Long lines of communication extended from the German border and along these they must bring their supplies. The front was somewhere between Amiens and the English Channel, or "La Manche," as the French called it. Witold was sure that the aim of the airmen at Toul should be to disrupt these supplies, cut the communications and harry the reinforcements. He fumed to himself as he sped South away from the enemy.

Witold brought the Morane in to land at Le Bourget, expecting to find his Polish colleagues there. He was directed to see the Commanding Officer. The Group Captain was a small man of sallow complexion and with deep-set, sad eyes below his dark oiled hair. His sorrowful expression was reinforced by a heavy and drooping moustache extending to the sides of his mouth. On his desk were a coffee pot and an empty cup. As Witold walked in, he stood and saluted. His highly-polished boots and well-pressed uniform gave no indication of any hurry, emergency or even war. Witold, conscious that his own uniform was stained and he had not found time to shave this morning, felt no sense of inferiority.

"You speak French?"

"Yes, Sir."

"I am pleased to see you in such good time. You have had an uneventful flight from Toul, I trust? May I offer you a decent cup of coffee?"

"Thank you, Sir."

"Very good. Please, do take a seat. I gather the Boches had made it more of a sieve than a Morane. After such a scrap, you did well to bring her in at Toul."

The senior officer was offering his eager male friendship as if he needed support.

"The damage was nothing serious. The machine can take a lot of punishment."

The Group Captain came to the point. It seemed to require an effort of will to pass on an order. He reached for a file on his desk, reading from it as he spoke.

"You will be required to fly South to Plessis-Belleville to join the rest of the Groupement de Chasse. I have arranged for your fuel tanks to be replenished."

Witold was astonished. His mind raced; further South? Who was this pathetic rat? Why was he telling him to fly away from the enemy? Again? What timid escape was he talking about? There were invading forces to attack and they would be ideal targets. Witold controlled himself. He was speaking to a superior officer.

"But why should we not attack the Germans now, while they are trying to force the armies into the sea?"

The Group Captain looked surprised.

"These are the orders. They are not to be discussed because they will not be changed."

"But...."

"Not even for one Polish pilot who disagrees."

The moustache seemed to tremble as the officer worked up a sense of resentment, even bordering on anger. Witold was infinitely more furious. He must control himself and make another attempt to reason with the man behind the moustache.

"Surely we can be over their lines of communication within an hour. We can disrupt them, slow them down, support the armies."

"We need to conserve the Air Force. We are re-equipping with faster planes. Then we can take on the Messerschmitts."

"And you have all these faster planes magically ready just now?"

"Please do not use sarcasm to a superior officer."

"Sir, I have fought those German planes with an aircraft much inferior to the Morane Saulnier 406."

"Forgive me, but with what result?"

Two pink spots had appeared beside the sallow cheeks of the senior officer, now using sarcasm himself. He had not expected to argue with a Pole.

Witold continued in his slow but accurate French, well taught by Ruth Neuman only a few years ago.

"I have come from my country with great difficulty to help defend yours. I insist on being allowed to take on the Germans."

The pink spots grew increasingly red. The Group Commander was also angry now. Witold made another, more determined, attempt to appeal to reason.

"The enemy will not expect us. The Morane cannon will hit hard even against Panzers. Their lines of communication extend at great length to the North of this airfield, and we cannot fail to find them. We can pick and choose what to attack. I have seen Messerschmitts firing on Polish troops who could do nothing to defend themselves. Strafing them. Now their troops are in your country and will make excellent targets for us. Once a few vehicles are burnt out, the whole column is immobile on the road, and is again vulnerable for hours."

"Our orders are entirely clear. We must retain our men and preserve our machines."

Witold, for all his anger, knew this was a losing battle. He must not give way to his temper. He swallowed, thought hard and paused for a moment. Witold regarded himself as a man of honour. He did not lie. Now, perhaps he would.

"Very well, Sir. I will take off as soon as the airfield control permits. My chart shows the position of Plessis-Belleville."

The Frenchman returned to his original placatory manner. "Let me know if there is anything else I can do for you." He stood up to indicate that this unfortunate exchange was now over.

When he went out onto the grass airfield again, the fuel line was being retrieved from the plane. Before the engine started, Witold studied the map on his knee. He found Plessis-Belleville, to the West and then turned over the map to look North towards Amiens, where he would find the German invaders and then the English Channel. These were his alternatives. He must decide. The plane roared over the grass runway. The Group Captain did not watch the impeccable take-off nor see the course set by that difficult Polish pilot.

Witold had needed a moment of calm to make his decision. He remembered the window in the cathedral. Surrounded by angels, Jesus was placing a crown on his mother's head. The Coronation of the Virgin. But surely, Jesus had brothers, so it made no sense to call her a virgin when Jesus was crowning her in heaven. Why did his religion emphasise virginity? A woman who lived a fulfilled life would not pass through the real world as a virgin. His fixated mind returned to Ruth. He was sure that she too had seen the same window with bright daylight shining through it. This renewed connection with Ruth increased his confidence. Witold's emotional world was founded upon tales of solitary knights who would champion a lady, preferably in distress, then set off to war, and return in triumph. It was inevitable that he would turn North.

By coincidence of time and place, at this moment in Krakow at the door to her flat, where Witold had last seen her, Ruth was welcoming a visitor. His complete kindness, sympathy and sincerity must surely be more attractive to her than the unexpected arrival of an impulsive Polish airman. The German colonel, a logistics expert, watched her slim figure as she led the way up the stairs.

As a practical pilot, Witold considered his options. He was flying a fighter armed with a single cannon, fired centrally, and wing-mounted machine guns. The best place to hurt the invaders would be close to the battle front, somewhere well to the West. If he could find Stuka dive-bombers to attack, he knew how to deal with them. If they were protected by Messerschmitt 109s, he would have a fight on his hands. With a full tank, he had a range of over 450 miles, so that he could afford time to attack and then escape. The engine pulsed steadily. The regular beat restored calm and confidence in the pilot. Witold realised he was smiling. For all his anger, frustration and doubt, the joy of handling the Morane-Saulnier and his complete control of his machine remained a comfort. Whatever might be wrong with the world, Witold was, and knew he was, a fine fighter pilot possessed of courage to match his determination.

On the 23rd May 1940, General von Runstedt had ordered one wing of his advancing forces to halt. He wanted the others to catch up. One leading unit protruding from the main body was vulnerable to be attacked from many sides. On the 24th May, Hitler visited von Runstedt's headquarters and agreed with him that the "Halt order" should be confirmed and must continue. Militarily, the leaders' purpose was to consolidate their gains and to allow supplies to reach the advance units. It is possible that a British counter-attack at Arras from the 21st to the 23rd May led to this cautious approach. Subsequently, the Führer told Rommel that he had been concerned for him when he heard what had happened. At that time, Rommel had been pressing on, perhaps too fast and too far. But despite the set-back at Arras, the General was certain that the High Command was making a mistake. He was just as sure that it would do him no good to argue with Hitler. The Panzers would reach the coast soon enough. Victory was certain. But if it had been left to him, there would have been no delay and Irwin Rommel would be the leader who would drive the British into their famous channel.

Witold, flying North, found the columns of German supplies proceeding steadily through Amiens. Some vehicles were horse-drawn, most were covered lorries but he could not tell which of these were carrying valuable supplies or troops. If there had been tanks or petrol tankers, he would have attacked, but he saw neither. He kept high above the columns and followed them, flying West towards the front. Then he saw to his right a flight of Stukas moving in from the North. His pulse quickened. There were eight of them and they would normally be protected by Messerschmitts at a higher level. He searched the sky but found none of the enemy fighters. Looking down again, he could see their target. The Stukas were heading for a line of guns which must have been set up to hold the German advance. He knew that the Stukas would continue until close to the guns, then drop onto them. Diving at speed, they would be almost impossible to hit. The Stuka was designed to withstand extraordinary forces as the plane levelled out directly above the target. For Witold, the dilemma was to lose height in order to catch at least one of them at the end of the dive, or to continue the hunt towards the front. To lose height was against his training and his instinct. He would be vulnerable to any German fighter, but here he was, above this battle, and with his chance to strike.

Two Stukas dived and dropped their bombs before he could attack. Then, as the third descended, he moved in from the flank, waiting until the plane had slowed and levelled so that it would become a sitting duck. To bring his path to converge with the Stuka required skill and patience. It compared with football, when he was approaching the goal with his brother Lukas on the wing, ready to send over a high cross. He knew when to sprint, just as Lukas swept the ball upwards, to find it and score. In truth, this had happened perfectly only a few times. But when it did, his memory retained the personal delight as part of a store, kept to maintain his sense of confidence, his self-belief. The plan, the expectation, the execution, the exhilaration combined in his recollection. Now again, he was in the right place at the right time. He would use no more ammunition than he must. His bullets raked the hull of the Stuka. Almost as soon as the Morane recovered from the recoil, he turned to attack the next dive-bomber. Again, he must make the calculation, but this time it was not good enough, and he passed ahead of the descending Stuka.

The third plane pulled out early and dropped no bombs. Its pilot bravely flew ahead of the Morane to allow his rear gunner a shot. Witold cursed. He should also have been ready to fire, but he was in mid-turn. The next Stuka descended as if performing a demonstration in a flying school, perfectly aligned for the target. The performance did not include the possibility of an enemy fighter lying in wait. As the German pilot levelled the plane, he saw, above his starboard wing, the Morane coming in. The Stuka seemed to wriggle in the sky as the bullets struck the tail and the pilot lost control. Witold missed the final Stuka, and decided not to follow it South, away from his destination. He needed to gain height while he could.

A cannon shell burst through his starboard wing. He had climbed into danger where he had been seen by the pilot of a Bf 109. The Morane could withstand such damage provided that a shell did not burst in the engine, or hit the pilot. Witold knew the enemy must be diving from somewhere behind him. He banked and turned. Craning his neck, he could not find the "Hun in the sun." Then the Messerschmitt flashed past close beneath the Morane. Witold pushed the joystick forward, turned slightly and steadied the Morane. He must dip just enough to let the gunsight drop onto the enemy cockpit. He checked the turn and bank indicator to make sure that he was not skidding in the sky and fired a short burst. The canopy crumpled and the machine dropped out of view. Even if the pilot was still alive, his plane was out of control.

Following his own training and practise, Witold immediately turned away, well aware that where there was one Bf 109, there were likely to be three more. Banking, he suddenly

saw a bright tracer just ahead of his own fuselage. The turning
Morane was a difficult target and the machine gunfire missed.
He tightened the turn, looking for the enemy. There, well to
his left, something glistened. The weak sunlight caught the flat
Perspex canopy of his adversary. The German had overshot,
and was now below him. The advantage of height more than
made up for the slower speed of his plane, and Witold turned
again heading down for the Messerschmitt, now at about 150
feet above the ground. The pilot was pulling right for all he was
worth, but Witold hauled hard on the stick and followed. The
Morane turned faster than the Bf 109 and, although he was close
to blacking out under the G-forces, Witold knew where he was
in the sky and where he would find his opponent. His aching
eyes saw that the German had now steadied, no longer turning
so much, and Witold caught him in his gunsight. The Morane
was still turning. Check the needle on the turn and bank indicator. Adjust the rudder. Squeeze the button for a long burst.
There was an explosion and the plane went straight down.

At a low level again, Witold was anxious. There was heavy
cloud to the North. Perhaps he was nearer the coast than he
thought. Repeatedly turning his neck to see if there was another
plane behind him, he reached the cloud. Roaring up into the
denser air, this was like the run back to his place after a successful
shot at goal. He allowed himself a moment of triumph.

"You can do this. You know you can," BB used to say. It had
been proved true.

He was now following his compass due North, but in the
cloud, he did not realise that he was now over the channel. His
map extended to La Manche, but did not include England. In
his ignorance, he flew further North than he intended, and
when he came down below the cloud, he saw, for the first time

in his life, the grey-blue sea. He must head West and he would find the only ally in which he placed his confidence; England.

The chain home line of RDF radar masts, 250 feet high, had been constructed along the South and East coast of England. Whether they would work as well as Air Chief Marshall Dowding hoped was a matter of speculation. There were also teams of spotters recruited to watch the sky and trained to differentiate the British Hurricanes and Spitfires from the enemy. These were the components of Britain's air defences. 447 fighter planes had been lost in the unsuccessful battle for France. Of the 52 squadrons of fighters, which had been regarded as the minimum required to defend the nation, there remained only 36. The watchers on the ground and the radar spotters were well aware of the danger to their homeland, and were alert for any foreign plane approaching the island on the 24th May. The Morane was a blip on the radar screen. It was coming in from the East where no Spitfire or Hurricane should be. From air fields to the South of England, six squadrons were operating over France in support of the French and British armies, but they would be returning from the South. The incoming plane from the East must be an enemy. Hurricanes were ordered to intercept and vectored in by ground control until their pilots would see the incoming plane.

Witold's last human contact had been with one of Poland's defeatist allies, and now the other ally was sending up a flight of Hurricanes to destroy him. The Morane was just over the coast when he saw the planes approaching to attack in standard RAF V-formation. There was plenty of time to think. He should not fight back against his allies; indeed, he had little ammunition left to do so. His mind moved on. He had intended to give to Ruth the silver cup he had won at the Deblen flying school when judged superior to both his brother and his commanding officer in aerobatics. He had found his answer. He would show the British Hurricanes what could be done in the air with a French Morane 406.

Returning to the coincidence of time, at this moment, as Witold stood his plane on its tail and then began to rotate into a perfect barrel roll, Ruth took up her violin to play the music which the colonel had brought her. The bow descended and softly drew forth the first sounds of a beloved Bach Partita. Admiration may displace action. In Krakow, the German colonel held his breath in fond attention. In the sky over Suffolk, the British flight commander exhaled in astonishment.

PART ONE

Chapter 2: More Than Six Years Earlier

10th November 1933 - Hitler's speech at the Siemens plant in Stuttgart Germany.

> *"It is a small rootless international clique that is turning the people against one another...Jews who feel at home everywhere.... My only interest is for the German people".*

On the same date as the German Chancellor made his speech, Ruth Neuman was walking through the city of Toul in Northern France. She was eighteen, slender and well aware that she had a pretty oval face with delicate features surrounded by black curly hair. She was the oldest of three children in a loving family and she was a gifted musician. But she considered that she had three problems. First, she had agreed to sing a solo part in Handel's Messiah which was to be performed in Toul cathedral. Second, her violin teacher seemed to like her too much. Third, she had just learned that her younger sister Vivien was the cleverer of the two. Returning from the first rehearsal of her part in The Messiah, Ruth had identified these three problems so that she could occupy her mind with them during the long walk home.

She loved Handel's music and she found it thrilling to sing her part. She had been overjoyed when Madame Endrigkeit suggested that she should audition for it. But the facts were that this was a Christian work, to be performed as part of the Christmas celebrations in the City, and Ruth was Jewish. She told her mother about the audition. Sophie Neuman loved music and was naturally proud of her daughter's singing voice. "What do you think, Mutti? With this title, it must be all about the Christians' Jesus." Her mother sighed. "Of course it is. If only they were doing Haydn's Creation. That has lovely parts for your voice too, and must apply to both Faiths. But it is wonderful to audition for The Messiah, and if you get the part, we can say it's a sign that you are meant to do it."

The audition went well. The young conductor appreciated her singing, and said that her voice was perfect for the cathedral. Madame Neuman told Ruth that she would talk it over it with her husband. So, the rehearsals proceeded. As the weeks went by, Ruth twice asked her mother what her father had said about it, because she would have liked to tell him about the rehearsals and discuss the music with him. He was an enthusiastic violinist, and he also encouraged her singing in his own quiet way. When she had played a violin solo at school, he had listened to her practise, encouraged and helped her. She knew that music was of great importance to her father and that he took deep delight in her playing. She was less sure of his attitude towards singing as a soloist. She never talked with her father about The Messiah and he never mentioned it.

Conrad Neuman detested ostentatious behaviour. He was highly critical of anyone who "put himself forward," and Ruth was concerned that this might include performing in public. Meanwhile, Sophie Neuman told her daughter that she just needed the right moment, and so Ruth had left the matter where it was. She knew her father had an open mind and generous nature; she had her mother's permission and she was enjoying the rehearsals. But just today, she had seen the proofs of the programme, which explained much about the origin of the work and printed out all the words. On the front cover, her name appeared with the other three soloists in very large letters. Ruth had also seen the yellow notices which would be pasted up around the town. These referred to the orchestra and conductor and the famous tenor soloist. She concluded that there was no chance that her father could remain unaware that she was singing. If he wanted to forbid her, he had left it too late.

The second problem related to Herr Breuer. He had been teaching her violin for six years since she was eleven when her father said that she now played the instrument better than he did. Conrad Neuman knew many members of the Nancy orchestra and, with their advice, he proposed Herr Breuer. Her mother said that he was the best dressed gentleman in Toul. Conrad replied that this was not the main qualification for a violin teacher. As the lessons proceeded, Ruth found that she liked him very much. His strong German accent seemed appropriate when he discussed violin music, which was often written by German composers. He was enthusiastic, keen to demonstrate how he would play and always most encouraging to her when she followed his advice.

Herr Beuer obtained free tickets to the concerts in Nancy where he played in the orchestra. Ruth went with a friend, Helga. When she pointed out her teacher amongst the violins, Helga said she admired his tailcoat, high collar and small moustache. However, Ruth had been surprised that in the last few months, Herr Breuer sometimes congratulated her on some difficult playing by putting his arm around her shoulders and squeezing her right arm just above the elbow. This was her bowing arm, and she thought he might be testing the muscle strength there.

But he should not need to do this most times she went for a lesson. Perhaps the gesture was just meant to congratulate this arm on its skilful exertions in music. But this was not what was going on. She knew it when he stroked back her hair from her cheek. She blushed, turned away and then, when she looked back at him, saw that he was as red as a beetroot. Ruth did not tell her mother about this, partly because it was embarrassing and partly because she was not sure whether she minded at all. She was eighteen. No one had kissed her yet. Helga had been kissing for over a year, or said she had been. Although Herr Breuer had freckles on his pale skin, and his forehead was shiny and bald, he had a lovely smile, pale blue eyes and whenever she saw him, he was beautifully dressed. His violin playing was heavenly.

Six months ago, she had noticed that the tooth behind his right incisor was missing. This had rather spoiled his smile, but then it came back, slightly whiter than its neighbours and he smiled more frequently and more enthusiastically than ever. How old was he? She knew that her father was five years older than her mother, who was still under fifty. She decided that Herr Breuer was probably in his mid-forties. When she told Helga about the squeezing of her arm, her friend replied that if that was all that he was squeezing she had nothing to worry about. With her experience, Helga must be right. She continued to imagine what it would be like if he kissed her until she reached Rue Jeanne d'Arc.

Ruth was now halfway home, and decided to consider the last problem, her clever sister. Only yesterday, Vivien had told her that, in the autumn, she was going to be moved up one academic year. She had been given some physics books to study in the holidays, and she wanted Ruth to help her with these. Ruth did love her sister, who was a calm and thoughtful child of fifteen. She had always known that Vivien was bright, but so were all the Neuman family. Initially, Ruth found this sudden proof of high intelligence seriously annoying. After careful consideration, she now decided that she must dismiss this thought. It was pure jealousy, a mean and contemptible emotion. She could be proud of Vivien, just as she was proud when her brother scored a goal at football. She neither needed to compete with her sporting brother, nor her brain-box of a little sister.

The streets of the old town were superficially similar, with cobbled roadways and stone pavements. But beside these flat surfaces arose a wonderful variety of walls, gateways, shuttered windows and ancient doorways. Lights burned behind some shutters but the side streets where Ruth walked were empty. The city had stood for centuries, sometimes powerful and prosperous, occasionally besieged and impoverished. It was the seat of the Bishops of Toul who had constructed a palace of huge dimensions and grandeur, as befitted the Head of State. When necessary, these worldly bishops had led their own troops into battle. They would then supplement the armour of God with heavy plate which would more certainly withstand the arrows of the enemy. All this was shown in stained glass and statues recording the martial attitudes of these proud Christian Lords. Since those medieval times, Toul had been absorbed into the French state. Under Louis XlV, the ubiquitous military architect Vauban had constructed a series of fortifications to protect the city against an attack from the warlike Prussians who then controlled the German-speaking land to the East of Metz. The varied history of the city left its mark along the old pavements. Here, a niche in a wall contained the Blessed Virgin, there, a doorway had been changed to a window, but leaving in place the original steps leading up to it. Some Renaissance stone decoration ended abruptly where the old elegance had given way to the need for an extension of a building into its former courtyard.

Ruth enjoyed the jumble of these old stones which distracted her from pursuing her intended thoughts about Handel's Messiah. The grey sky was lower and darker than it had been when she began her walk home. Pigeons flying in an unruly formation conducted a thorough tour of the air above the buildings. It was the end of the afternoon daylight and she sensed that a light drizzle might set in. Ruth increased her pace and turned a corner.

She saw a familiar figure on the far side of the road. It was Madame Dubois walking slowly and carrying two heavy bags, from one of which there protruded the feathery green tops of carrots. Ruth quickened her step, crossed the road and came up behind her.

"Madame Dubois, may I take something for you?"

"What a good chance to find you here just at this hour!" replied Madame Dubois, smiling broadly. "I always come this way from my sister's greengrocer's shop, but I have never seen you here before. You are too old to have been given a detention at school, I am sure!"

"No, Madame, not too old, but far too good," replied Ruth cheerfully. She went on to explain that she had been doing some extra music practice and that was why she was coming home so long after school had finished. Ruth lived near the Dubois' home. She offered to take the heavy bag there.

"No, my dear, it would be out of your way, but please, take it to your house and Marcel will pick it up from there. I think he is at my home with your brother and sister, and he can fetch it when he walks over with Vivien before your Sabbath supper."

Marcel was two years younger than Ruth, and a great friend of her brother Jakob. Now that she thought about it, Marcel seemed to spend as much time with Vivien as he did with Jakob. She walked home quickly and avoided the rain. In the Jewish household, her mother was at work on the challah bread, and told Ruth to prepare the candles and set the table for the Sabbath meal. The family assembled, the traditional prayers proceeded and Ruth reflected that she had little to worry about. Indeed, there was no point in pondering the few troubles she might have. Her chair was close to a warm stove and she was surrounded by a loving family.

Chapter 3: The Messiah

"Arise, shine, for thy glory is come, and the glory of the Lord is risen upon thee."

Christmas drew near. Yellow posters for the cathedral concert were on display, as it seemed to Ruth, on almost every public space. They advertised the fact that the work was to be sung in a German translation which most music-lovers in Toul would understand. Ruth knew that Handel was a German composer who worked mainly in London. The Messiah had indeed been written and first performed at Handel's direction for audiences in Dublin, the capital of Catholic Ireland, then under the control of the British Protestant government.

Although her father never mentioned the oratorio, Ruth guessed that he must be aware of the performance and had chosen to say nothing to her. She did not want to make him angry or resentful and wondered what might be in his mind.

When a young teenager, Ruth discussed religion with her father.

"In this country, most people are Catholics, but across the border in Germany, they are mainly Protestant Christians. What can they be arguing about when they all believe in their Jesus Christ?"

"I am not sure of their differences, Ruth. But in the Middle East there is Islam, still based on our God, but worshipping Him very differently. Further East, more religions. Each generation brings up children to follow the parents' religion. We are exactly the same, I suppose, and it is just not sensible to argue about who is right or wrong. The important thing is to behave well and to respect one another, don't you think?"

Her father had gone on to speak of anti-Semitism, which all Jews knew was a recurring problem. "And although it is said to be rising again, I find that at work my colleagues treat me as they find me. So do customers and anyone I get to know. You will find the same, I trust."

The preparations for The Messiah continued, generally with a local chorus master who was rehearsing the choir. There were two further rehearsals with the young conductor of the Nancy Orchestra who would be responsible for the performances in the cathedral, on the 20th and 21st of December. Ruth found the music constantly running in her head. Sometimes, when her father was out, she would sing her favourite aria, "I know that my Redeemer liveth". Her mother might clap when she finished and then laugh at Jakob who generally put his fingers in his ears. The young conductor had told her that she sang this with complete sincerity. She was uncertain what he meant.

Sophie never did find the right moment to talk this over with her husband. Conrad was a sincere Jew, but did not practise his religion with great vigour. Sophie had converted to his faith in order to please him, and indeed, because he and his parents had made this a condition of their marriage. In the first ten years of married life, they went regularly to the synagogue where both were welcomed and Sophie made many new friends. Some became customers at her little dress and haberdashery shop. They chose to name their first child Ruth, after the biblical character who was not Jewish. In the Jewish Torah, the Old Testament, this Ruth was a Moabite who married into the Jewish race, and was an ancestor of the great King David.

The children went to two local schools, which retained many characteristics of the Catholic religion. From childhood, all three of the Neuman children attended the synagogue on Saturdays so that they understood Hanukkah in December, while at their school, they learned about baby Jesus born in Bethlehem. In the synagogue, they learned of The Passover and its importance to their Faith, while at school, everyone focussed on the Easter story of the Passion of Jesus and the Crucifixion. Ruth was awarded a little prayer book for excellent study of Hebrew. When the children reached teenage, the parents' attendance at the synagogue became less frequent, and on many occasions, the children were permitted to participate in useful or sporting events on a Saturday.

Ruth sometimes felt regret that her parents took less interest in the Sabbath. She always enjoyed the tradition, the candlesticks and the Sabbath plate with loaves of challah arranged on it. The ritual within her own family brought a sense of reassurance, warmth and belonging. The family celebrated the Jewish Festivals, especially the Passover and Escape from Captivity, with the traditional meal, wine, the bitter herbs and the reading from the Torah. Conrad still took pride in his position as the Head of a Jewish household. Even as he said the prayers and broke the bread, he also knew that his family were going through the forms of their fine and ancient faith without ardour and perhaps without belief. He was, by nature, a questioning scientist, used to demonstrating in the works' laboratory the validity of any proposition. Even in the synagogue, he knew that he held onto his religion because he loved the tradition and the old forms of worship. His final analysis was that religion was an option for all men, a matter of choice. He had simply chosen to follow the same one as his forbears. This was not a matter of conviction; only preference. He did not find this a satisfactory answer and would not have liked to defend it amongst his friends in the synagogue.

On the day of the first performance in the cathedral, Ruth went to the fine old building very early. She saw the chairs set out for the orchestra at the East end of the nave, the benches for the choir behind and the seats for the four soloists between them. She had a moment of self-doubt. Could her voice alone fill this great space? Would she come in on the right beat and at the right note? She found a corner at the back and composed herself. She was wearing a long black and grey dress with a silver necklace lent by her mother. She was entitled to hope that the dress was on permanent loan since Sophie had taken it in and made specific alterations so that it only fitted her daughter.

"I had two to choose from, the navy blue or this black one with grey details. Your father always liked this one the most."

"Mutti, it's lovely, even if it does make me look like a school mistress."

At mid-morning, there was a full rehearsal, in which the famous Nancy conductor said almost nothing. But he nodded with evident satisfaction when Ruth completed each of her solos. Ruth stayed with the other musicians over lunch. The Bass, rotund and bearded, said he needed at least a glass of Burgundy before the performance.

"The vocal cords need oil just like a sewing machine," he said. Then, looking at Ruth, he added "But you, my dear, should just carry on as you have been doing so far. I reckon you are getting better every single time you sing."

At ten to two, the orchestra took their seats. The choir walked in as the clock on the church tower chimed the hour. Ruth and the four soloists entered from the vestry and took their places facing the congregation. Ruth immediately saw that her mother and Vivien were in the second row. They grinned at her. Vivien made a small thumbs-up gesture. Not wishing to smile at her family, Ruth looked away from the audience and up at the stained-glass window showing Jesus surrounded by angels in Heaven. She concentrated on the window, brightly shining in the afternoon sunshine. Was he placing a yellow crown on the head of his own mother? She stared at the Coronation of the Virgin for long enough to distract her until eventually, the conductor took his place. When the applause stopped, he set the work in motion.

The performance began smoothly. Ruth sang the simple recitatives about shepherds in the fields. She found that she could hold a note for fraction of a second longer to catch the echo from the stone vault. The conductor made direct eye contact with her, he nodded, and slowed the little orchestra to allow her the extra time. Towards the end of the oratorio, Ruth began the aria, "I know that my Redeemer liveth." The conductor reduced the pace of the music further. The phrasing and the biblical language were sublime. As she began to sing the words, "For now is Christ risen," Ruth saw, to her astonishment, her father, calmly sitting beside a pillar halfway down the cathedral. His eyes were shining bright and he was concentrating only on her, but Ruth must look away and focus on her singing. Her voice swelled as she reached the higher notes, and she almost choked with emotion on the final, low and beautiful words, "For now is Christ risen, the first fruits of them that sleep." Sitting down as the aria concluded, she now looked at her father again. His face was flushed, he was nodding, smiling wildly and, with a green handkerchief, he was mopping tears from his eyes. She had never loved him so much.

Chapter 4: Adolf Breuer

"Duplicity is necessary in daily life in that it covers many things from sight so they may not disturb the pleasure of others." Edouard Renee de Laboulaye.

Ruth went to bed early after the performance. There was a knock on her door. It was her father.

"I have come to say good night and well done today, Ruth. We are all proud of you."

"Thank you, Papa. I was not sure whether you wanted me to sing in the Messiah. I wish you had told me you did not mind."

"I am sorry. Some things are best left unsaid." He paused, then added, thoughtfully, "Perhaps I would have said..."

She interrupted him. "You mean you might not have allowed me if I had asked?"

"Possibly not. I am not sure. But now I am very glad about it. I was going to say perhaps it was just meant to be so."

"Thank you, Papa. There is one thing I have been thinking about as a result, and I would like your help. The Christians, they worship the one true God, don't they?"

"They do worship Him, in their own way, yes."

"So, the coming of the man they call the Messiah has resulted in millions of people finding the one true God?"

"Yes."

"Which can only be a good thing. Perhaps the best thing ever."

"I see your point, which is a good one. Those words you sang, "I know that My Redeemer Liveth" are words from our Torah. They are not part of the Christians' Gospel. The question is not whether there is one true God. The question is only whether Christians are right to say that the Messiah has come. We say we are still waiting and the true Messiah will come to us at the End of Days."

"Yes, Papa. But he has come. I mean he has come for them."

"Ruth, it is the end of a long day. Sleep well now."

Although the many congratulations she received from all her family seemed to solve problems one and three, Ruth remained unsure about Herr Breuer. The violin lessons resumed in the new year. He told her that he had gone to the Saturday performance but chosen a seat well to the side in case he put her off. One spring afternoon, he asked her to play through one of the Schubert sonatas which were his favourite pieces. He said he would not interrupt, and sat silently at his desk.

"Ruth, I am not certain I have anything more to teach you."

"No," she answered, "I have a lot to learn."

The trouble with Herr Breuer was not what he said or did with Ruth. It was what he thought. He had a mistress, Yvette, who he visited every Thursday evening. He had met her when she was discreetly advertising her services many years ago. Although he paid her for each visit, she was no longer a prostitute. She often cooked dinner for him, and they had become very good friends. As the economic slump gave way to better employment opportunities, she had found work in a jewellers' shop in Nancy and only saw a few regular customers such as Breuer. He helped her to find a better job in the concert hall office, and sometimes he considered marrying her. Breuer never asked whether she had any other admirers, nor whether she continued to receive visits from the owner of the jewellery business. His selfish mind considered that it would appear very proper if a prominent violinist in the City Orchestra should marry a fellow music-lover from amongst the staff of the concert hall. But whenever he toyed with this idea, he eventually decided against it.

Breuer was a fiercely competitive man who wanted to make his way in the world and needed his marriage to help in that direction. He imagined that he might be a composer. After Ruth had been attending his violin lessons for over a year, her French teacher asked her to learn a poem by Apollinaire, about the First World War. She had told Breuer that because she found it hard to learn poetry but easy to remember songs, she had decided to write music for the verses.

"I hope that it is at first engaging and then becomes sad like the poetry," she told him.

Intrigued, he asked her to play it. When she did so, he realised that if a child could write music of such sensitivity at the age of fourteen, he must give up any such ambition himself. When they discussed it, she wanted to write the parts of a woodwind section as well as the violins. Breuer was reluctant to talk about this, because it annoyed him that she had a precocious talent in a field normally dominated by men. Having abandoned composition, Breuer decided to become a famous conductor, like Gunter Klein. When he attended a rehearsal by Klein, he faced the fact that he had neither the insight nor the charisma to conduct at a professional level. Breuer was reduced to hankering after the place of "First Violin" in the orchestra, but when old

Felix Krol retired, the committee decided to advertise, audition and to appoint young Siebel. Breuer hated Siebel secretly, while copying as much of his technique as he could. Siebel smiled prodigiously as he played, and indeed smiled whenever he discussed music with his colleagues. Breuer was soon doing the same.

He had been born to an impoverished and unmarried woman who worked in one of the factories near Toul. As a boy, he had been supported by a schoolteacher who recognised his aptitude for music and lent him a violin. From this background, of which he never spoke to a soul, he needed to make his way into the cultured classes of Nancy and Toul. To marry the elder daughter of Doctor Conrad Neuman, the Head of Research and Development and Board Member of the porcelain works just outside Toul, would be entirely satisfactory to Breuer. Further, the younger the bride, the better able she would be to care for him in his old age. He was approaching fifty and it was only wise to think ahead. When enjoying his Thursday evenings with Yvette, he sometimes imagined that her body belonged to Ruth. He usually found this helpful, and so it seemed did Yvette. He did not often allow himself to reflect on this aspect of his life. When he did, he concluded that it demonstrated that he would do well to marry Ruth. When the time came, he would work out what to say to Yvette.

In the winter of 1932, Breuer gave Ruth a ticket to hear the Nancy orchestra perform a programme including two works by Maurice Ravel. He was the most famous French composer of the period and it was hoped that he would attend and possibly conduct the performance. Ruth had seen photographs of the handsome face of the composer and thought she would recognise him. Unfortunately, he had a motor accident in

October and could not come. Ruth was captivated by the Pavane for a dead Princess, with its simple tune, repetition and varied orchestration. At her next lesson with Breuer, she explained that she was interested in adding to her original music for the Apollinaire poem. She was working on a second movement which would be repetitive and lyrical like the Pavane, and followed by a third which would be in the form of a Requiem. Breuer did not want to hear more about this. "My dear Ruth, we are meant to be studying the violin, and I am reluctant to spend time on a composition intended to revisit the Great War. Let us try out that Schubert once more."

Ruth played the Schubert accurately and with a fluid enthusiasm but faster than Breuer would have wished. He preferred to avoid any spoken comment, and so he demonstrated on his own violin a slower and more languorous approach. She appreciated the difference and, following his example, achieved a superior performance. They played some more Schubert in this way, and when the lesson ended at 4.30, he again put his arm around her shoulders, squeezed her upper arm and said to her, "That was as beautiful as it could ever be."

Then, he turned to face her and held her in an embrace. His mouth was beside her ear as he whispered,

"And so are you, my dear, as beautiful as could ever be."

She blushed. Looking at him, she saw his visage with its pale eyes and smiling mouth was like a curtain behind which a fire was raging. The evidence of that fire was his flushed face. As they stood together, Ruth could feel something pressing on her abdomen. He must have something there in a front pocket of his trousers.

"Thank you so much," she said to him, as she turned in embarrassment for the door. Down the stairs and out onto the street, she found it was drizzling but decided not to go back for the little umbrella which she had forgotten in her haste.

After fifty paces, there was his voice, "Mademoiselle Neuman," and he hurried after her, still red in the face, to hand her the umbrella. "I must speak to your father," he said. Ruth walked homeward thinking over what had happened. She decided not to mention to Helga anything about this experience, because she seldom kept a secret. She did have a conversation with her mother. "He called me 'my dear' and said I was beautiful as could ever be."

"Now Ruth, so you are, and it is hardly a surprise that gentlemen should like you. But he is your teacher, much older than you and I will have a word with your father about it all. Now, dearest, do you feel upset with him, or would you be happy to go on with his lessons next term?"

She asked this because Ruth had to take her examination in the final grade at the end of that summer term.

"I don't know," replied her daughter. "I don't know what I should think, nor what I really think. He is a lovely man, and always so kind to me. And he plays so well; I sometimes think that together..." She did not finish the sentence, but her mother knew now that her daughter was unsure of her feelings. She also knew that this romance must go no further.

Before Sophie Neuman had found the right moment to raise the problem with her husband, Breuer located him in his office and asked him if he had time to talk something over whenever he finished work that day. He returned at the agreed time, and made a formal request to marry Ruth.

"But my dear Breuer, our family is Jewish both in race and in religion, while Ruth is only 18 whereas you are well over forty. Although you say you have some reason to think that she would be willing, she has absolutely no experience of life and I could not allow..." Breuer interrupted before the refusal was spoken to answer quickly.

"She will be nineteen in October. May I just ask you to think this over until then? As for the religion, the way the world is going, I thought a father might think it could be helpful if she were married outside the Jewish Faith. I have been told that it will be very difficult for a Jewish girl to obtain a place in any music school in these times."

The ease and speed of these words suggested to Conrad that Breuer had expected his answer and prepared this response.

It was indeed true that when he had made enquiries about his daughter's wish to study music at the highest level, Conrad Neuman had encountered only negativity and pessimism. There was an unspoken reason behind this, but like every Jew, Neuman was aware of the problem. Anti-Semitism was seldom expressed openly in France, whereas it was part of the political programme of Adolf Hitler in Germany. Indeed, Neuman had recently been able to recruit two German experts from the Royal Porcelain Manufactory in Berlin. The institution was a symbol of German technical skill and good taste, but its most famous designer, Marguerite Friedlaender, had chosen to emigrate because of anti-Semitic prejudice. Two assistants, one of whom was also Jewish, decided to leave in protest. When they discussed the situation, they explained why they were very pessimistic about the future for Jews in Germany. He avoided telling his wife about his new assistants, nor did he ever mention it to Ruth. Neuman was walking alone beneath a sinister dark cloud. He did not imagine that it would blow away.

Breuer was continuing: "And whatever may happen, my dear Conrad, please be assured that I value our own friendship so much and wish only the happiness of your daughter." Neuman could only reply politely to such fulsome remarks and the two men took their leave of one another as if there was nothing between them. As he walked slowly home through the calm but severe stone streets of Toul, Neuman knew that his friend, if indeed he really was his friend, should never be permitted to marry his daughter. He would talk it over with his wife. Sophie would surely agree that the proposal was impossible. However, before Neuman found sufficient strength of purpose to raise the issue with his wife, a letter from Krakow arrived.

Marguerite Friedlaender moved first to The Netherlands, but left for America when the Germans invaded. Her husband, who was of German nationality, was not permitted to emigrate and was later called up into the German Army. The couple were reunited only after the war when he joined her in the U.S.A.

Chapter 5: Krakow: City of Kings

Ruth first made the journey from Toul in Northern France to Krakow in Southern Poland when she was fourteen. The Neuman family had been invited by Conrad's great friend and fellow student at Strasbourg University, Viktor Auerbach. For all three children it had been an important experience. First came the letter of invitation, so suddenly arriving and so wholly unexpected. The family cancelled their usual trip to a guest house in the Auvergne and anticipated an adventure which would involve a long journey, a different country and a new language; Polish - not easy according to Madame Neuman.

The holiday began with the arrival of an enormous green motor car. Jakob saw it first and went outside to see the vehicle going around the bend and out of sight. He was about to come indoors again when he heard the sound of the same car returning. It was of a make and size he had never seen before and was driven by a youthful chauffeur in uniform. He spoke in slow German, "My name is Juliusz. Mr Auerbach has sent me to collect the Neuman family." As soon as they were ready, he would load the Adler. Juliusz had recently taken delivery of the car at the Adler works in Frankfurt and was full of enthusiasm for the vehicle. Within an hour, the chauffeur had shared the

From 1928 to 1933, the Adler works produced a powerful Standard 8 limousine, which had an engine of 3887 cc with 8 cylinders in line.

Neuman's midday meal and the family's luggage was strapped onto the rear rack. The journey began. Unfortunately, the chauffeur was separated from the family by a glass division. Behind this were two smaller seats facing rearwards while the larger, higher and most luxurious leather seating was at the back of the passenger compartment facing forwards. There was room for three on the rear seats which were taken by Monsieur and Madame Neuman, and the children took it in turns to sit between their parents.

The route took them through Germany, where they stopped at Munich. The following day brought them to Vienna. They stayed outside the city but in the morning, Ruth was deeply impressed by the grand avenues and fine bridges over the Danube. Then, they turned East for Krakow, which they reached with bodies tired, clothing creased but minds full of this new geography. Viktor was expecting the Neumans. His eyes sparkled as he shook hands with them all, enquiring about the journey, the route, hotels and the comfort of his new car. The housekeeper provided a late dinner for them. She spoke only Polish and with her help, Ruth made a small start on the language. Good Night, and Good Morning were learnt ready for tomorrow. Vivien shared a bedroom with Ruth. They scrambled into a high bed and then sank, giggling with pleasure, into a deep feather mattress.

Viktor's spacious home was a three-storey building set back from the road and constructed in grand symmetrical style. Its stone front was darkened by soot but relieved by large sash windows. There were five bedrooms on the first floor, and the Neumans were surprised to learn that Viktor had a separate bathroom for himself. The housekeeper lived on the top floor, as did Juliusz, the chauffeur. There was gas heating, which

Viktor could control from a series of taps in the hall. "Can't let the staff blow us all up," he said, as he turned off the heating to the third floor. Like many a wealthy man, he was careful about small matters of expenditure. Conrad had known that after working for an employer in the chemical industry, Viktor had established his own chemical business. He now explained very simply that he had also started a separate business in aluminium and bought another which made agricultural machinery.

Viktor used to say that Conrad was one of the most amusing men he had ever met. Conrad was more serious than entertaining within the family but Viktor seemed to bring out a more comical side of his character. Indeed, the two men shared the same sense of humour. Ruth knew this because they wrote to one another twice a year, and Conrad would read out the wittiest parts of Viktor's letter, and then work hard on his response. The phrase "good enough for Viktor" in the Neuman family meant that an incident was funny enough for Conrad to include it in his next letter.

Throughout the stay in Krakow, Viktor placed ,at the disposal of the family, the new Adler car and the chauffeur. He did what he could to show them around the city but he was generally busy in his offices during weekdays. Once, when he was able to leave early, he arranged to meet the Neumans at a café in the main square. Viktor arrived after his guests, and as they turned and waved to him, Ruth noticed a woman at a nearby table doing the same. She was accompanied by a young man. Viktor exchanged a few words with her as he moved on to join the Neuman family. Did he perhaps notice that Ruth had seen the young man? For whatever reason, Viktor invited them to join the table and introduced them as Therese Berling and her son, Bruno. He was dark-haired, with high semi-circular eyebrows above large brown eyes. He was happy to practise his French. "This gives me an excuse to talk a lot," he said, as if anticipating his mother's instruction to let the others into the conversation. He had been at the Jagiellonian University for a year and was enjoying a stage and style of education very different from the schooling of the Neuman children.

At the end of the week, Viktor and the Neumans shared the traditional Sabbath meal and prayers. The chauffeur, Juliusz, joined them, but spoke only when Viktor encouraged him to join in. They read through Psalm 91, taking alternate verses. Viktor read beautifully, while Juliusz was halting and following the words with his finger on the text. For the children, it was a demonstration of the continuity of their Faith. The very same celebration was going on in every Jewish household, in millions of homes, hundreds of towns and dozens of countries.

Later in the evening, Viktor told a joke he had picked up recently.

"One proud Jewish mother said to her friend, "My daughter-in-law is pregnant. I am so pleased to be able to share this with you."

"My congratulations. I can now tell you that my daughter-in-law is also expecting. The gynaecologist says he believes it will be twins."

"Since you mention it, my daughter-in-law is also expecting twins. Both are boys."

"I am so pleased to hear that because our daughter-in-law is also expecting twin boys, both professors."

On the second weekend of their visit, they all went to a concert, in which the City orchestra first performed a modern work by Messiaen. After the interval, a Chopin piano concerto was played by someone who had been taught by Chopin himself. They met elegant Polish citizens who knew Viktor well, and gave the impression that he was much respected in the City. On their last evening in Krakow, Viktor organised a party, attended by about twenty guests, most of whom could speak French and shared his interest in music. These included Bruno and his mother who they had met at the café in the main square. Another couple, Piotr and Agnieszka Zeleski, brought two boys who were plainly on their very best behaviour. They had similar yellow hair, carefully combed. The older one, Witold, had had more Slavic features, while the younger, Lukas, had very bright blue eyes and the toothy smile of a boy aged ten. Ruth was with her brother Jakob when he began asking them questions about their school. Speaking in very slow French, both could give good answers. Viktor introduced the mother of these boys. She was a tall woman with fair hair and gold-framed spectacles which gave her an academic appearance. He mentioned that Agnieszka belonged to the St Andrej choir. She asked if they had been to see the church of St Andrej.

"No, we have spent a whole day at Wawel and admired the cathedral there."

"Going to St Andrej so often, I loyally recommend it as the finest church in Krakow."

"I am sure it has the finest choir."

"You are planning a career in the diplomatic service. The choir is one of the few escapes for the busy wife and mother. When I am there, I must forget about whether we have any food in the larder, who has done his homework or most likely not, and just concentrate on the music. It is a wonderful distraction."

"I wish it was the same at my school in France. I am often made to conduct the choir while the music teacher plays the organ. The chorister who is concentrating on the music is a rare specimen at school!"

"But I thought Viktor said you played the violin."

"Yes, I love the violin and singing too. And what about your sons, are they also musical?"

"No. It's just football at school and fighting at home."

Sophie had joined the conversation. "Football seems universal, I agree. It is almost the same thing as fighting, and older boys enjoy it for the same reason, I think."

Indicating her son, she continued, "This powerful young man, Jakob, grew out of fighting at the right age, but even now he is fourteen, he refuses to grow out of football."

Jakob made a patronising comment about women failing to understand the real pleasures of life, and his mother pretended to agree with him.

After dinner, Viktor said that he had heard Ruth practising her violin, often repeating the same music. Was it a Bach violin sonata? he asked her. Ruth smiled happily. "Yes. It is one of his Partitas. I am glad that you could recognise the composer of any piece played by me!"

"You are just fishing for compliments," said Viktor. Then, seeing Ruth blush, he said, "Now, have you had a good time with us in Krakow?" A mischievous smile was accentuated by the expression in his deep brown eyes.

"It has been truly wonderful," replied Ruth.

"So, were I to ask a favour it would be impossible to say no?"

"I am already beginning to guess what this might be," said Ruth. "Perhaps a performance for this demanding audience is just what I need before I have to play it for my exam next term."

The party formed a semi-circle around Ruth who made only one obvious mistake at the beginning of the piece and then completed the Partita. The adults praised her performance. Bruno did not say anything, but had been listening intently while watching every movement of the bow and the vigorous motion of her slender figure. The two small boys had not pretended to have any interest in music while chatting with her, but now seemed impressed. She did not know that the Head of Music at King David's school was amongst the guests. This portly gentleman with a generous white beard below a rubicund face decided that he would only embarrass the young musician if he told her who he was and how much he appreciated her performance. Agnieszka did come up to her.

"That was a delight for us all. It has been such a pleasure to meet you, Ruth."

After two weeks in Krakow, the family were once again in the Adler motor and driving West to France. Taking a different route because Viktor thought the children might like the mountains, they descended into France from the Swiss Alps. Reaching Colmar, they had difficulty finding an hotel in the town, but Juliusz, the chauffeur, was able to help. He found them lodgings at the Pfeffel, which was unlike any establishment they knew in Toul. It was a tall old building with rooms to let on the upper floors, beneath which were a beer stübel and restaurant. At dinner, they found that most of the local delicacies involved pork, but the waiter was able to produce boiled lamb which was intended for the lunch menu. The last part of their journey followed the road up the valley of the river Rhine which, in the sunlight of early autumn, seemed to welcome them back to their own country. "La Belle France," said Madame Neuman.

Chapter 6: The Letter From Krakow

After their holiday in Krakow, Viktor twice visited the family in Toul. Once, he was on his way home from business trips to a German manufacturer in Frankfurt. He arrived unexpectedly the day before the Passover Festival. Sophie begged him to stay in Toul because he would be unable to return to Krakow in time for Passover. There was to be another guest, Conrad's brother Melchior, who ran the family printing works in Strasbourg. Sophie warned Viktor that Melchior was very quiet, and, since his experience as a prisoner of war in Russia, spoke with a stutter.

During the Passover meal, Conrad referred to the significance of the sweet charoset. It was delicious but represented the clay bricks made by the Hebrews when enslaved in Egypt. Jakob, who was twelve, wanted to talk about whether the Jews had been involved in building the pyramids, which were stone not brick. Viktor said that this was part of the tradition. Melchior, who had been silent for much of the meal, now joined in, stuttering as usual.

"Pyramids are made from blocks of limestone. The problem is to work out how they could move such heavy materials over the desert sand. Wooden wheels would sink in. The best I can do is to imagine an immense number of slaves pulling broad sledges over the sand."

"So, these pyramids are really a monument to the slaves not the Pharaohs," said Viktor.

There followed a discussion about conquered civilisations, in which Melchior joined, gradually losing his stutter. "I should know. I fought in The Great War for the Kaiser, but was not allowed to become an officer because I was Jewish. Although I was taken prisoner, the Russians were defeated. I thought that we must be the victors. But by the time I got home, I found we had lost. Strasbourg became French again. That is the confusing story of how I became a Frenchman."

Conrad explained to Viktor, "It's a bit more complicated than that. Melchior had to take over the family printing firm. Printing presses are huge and unmoveable. You either give it away or get on with your business, even if the border has moved and you find yourself in a different country!"

"Fascinating," said Viktor. "As for me, I was trying to defend Krakow from the Russians at the same time as Melchior was defeating them in the West. We were luckier. It was the end of the partition of Poland between Russia and Germany, so we got our country back. To me, this was wonderful. Before I joined up, I had heard the rousing speeches of Pilsudski and became a Polish patriot. I would have fought to the death for Poland, and the outcome has meant a lot to me. But if I had stayed in Germany like you, I would have fought on the losing side."

Melchior went on, "I have to say that when a war begins, all the cards are thrown up in the air. You cannot tell where they will land, which side will win."

"Too true, and it's not just the war which is a complicated sort of lottery. The peace process is another exercise in gambling with states and citizens."

Melchior agreed. "No part of life is predictable. You start off on one course, like learning type-setting and business. You promise your Papa that you will carry on his firm, whatever happens. Then you have to become a soldier. Back to business. To support your widowed mother, you must print French newspapers and magazines instead of German. The umlaut stays in the print case! Now I am becoming a philosopher. As for you, brother, if Strasburg had been French when we were young, you would never have studied chemistry in Germany nor found your delightful friend Viktor. I would not be meeting him this evening. It's all for the best where the cards fall."

Melchior had said all this with no trace of his stutter. Conrad looked at his wife. She stared back at him. Conrad turned to his brother. "Perhaps I shouldn't say this with the children here, but this is wonderful, Melchior. It is the first time since the war that you have been enjoying a good conversation with us. You aren't stuttering at all."

Melchior blushed, then grinned. "It's the good company."

Victor agreed to meet Melchior at his printing business next time he was near Strasbourg. Viktor was shown over the works like a visiting celebrity. Over the years, the two men became firm friends.

On Viktor's second visit to Toul, the Neuman family put on a musical evening in his honour, and Ruth made a considerable impression both as singer and with her violin. She played a piano duet with her sister Vivien. Viktor, with his usual warmth and directness, told Conrad how much he envied this happy and successful family. It was Vivien who replied to him, "I must ask Papa to remember these kind words next time he is going to tell me off for making a noise or keeping him waiting!" Sophie, also smiling, said, "Well, Viktor, there is still time for a wedding and all of the consequences, good or bad!" In response, Viktor said that he thought of his business as his family. He nurtured it as it grew, and was proud of the number of employees who worked for him. He had also joined the City Council at Krakow, supporting a Jewish deputy Mayor of Krakow. Viktor's work as Head of the Board of Governors of King David's Jewish School absorbed much of his spare time. He admitted that he had acquired the nick-name "The puppet-master" amongst other members of the school council, because of his ability to call in the right person for the school, whether it was an architect, Head Groundsman or coach driver who might be needed.

Viktor also talked over with the whole family a problem he had with a German business. He was dealing with a father and son who had very different methods.

"The father is an absolute rogue, and I have never trusted him. He cheats his own employees, and overcharges on state contracts. But he has made the mistake of sending his son to excellent schools where he has acquired much better standards. Emil is in charge of all transport and deliveries. He is highly effective and is winning more orders. But he is thinking of leaving the family firm because he disagrees with his father's way of doing business. Yesterday, Emil told me that he has been encouraged to join the German army. So, the Wehrmacht will gain a highly efficient officer and I foresee trouble for the family business."

Viktor mentioned the name Emil in this conversation but, at the time, Ruth did not have any reason to remember it. She did, however hear her mother asking Conrad if he had noticed Josefz using Auerbach's first name when speaking to him. Viktor had made a rapid sign to him, and Josefz did not repeat this indiscretion.

Letter from Krakow

2nd June 1934

My dear Conrad,

I trust that you and the family are all prospering and progressing as busily and successfully as ever. I wonder whether you would consider the following as an opportunity for Ruth, who must be finishing school this summer. Unless she is determined to pursue an academic career in music, I believe that I can offer her a temporary position teaching music at King David's. You will have heard me mention the school, which is flourishing. The music department has only one full-time teacher. The choir has improved in recent years. We badly need someone for the autumn term. One person who would really bring out the potential of the choir is your daughter. She would also teach violin and piano.

On a slightly different note, you have told me of your concern about anti-Jewish feeling where you are, and about its proximity to Germany. From my own travels, which take me to Germany very frequently, I entirely agree with you. Fortunately, here in Poland, our race seems to be more welcome, and indeed Krakow elected a Jewish deputy mayor not so long ago. She would be most welcome amongst us. It would be a pleasure to have her staying with me and to help her to enjoy a busy social life. She already has a small circle of admirers in Krakow, namely everyone who heard her play a few years ago, especially Agnieszka Zeleski who has asked to be remembered to you all.

When I mentioned Ruth at recent Board Meeting, I took the liberty of advancing her age to 19, while knowing that her birthday is in October.

I enclose a copy of an application form which the school would ask her to complete, if she is interested in this position. Please do not be too concerned about language. Most of us speak French or German, but if Ruth could find a Polish teacher during the Summer holidays, this would be worth doing. I know one or two Polish people in Nancy and can try to fix this up too.

Yours ever
Viktor

Ruth filled in the application form, increasing her age by one year, but accurately setting out her qualifications in violin and piano. She stated that she had been conducting the school choir from the age of 15, and would be interested in helping King David's School to maintain its choral tradition. She decided not to mention that she had sung solo soprano because she thought that a boys' school would have no use for a soprano and might guess that she would be looking for solo singing opportunities outside the school. She added that her command of the Polish language was limited, but she was keen to learn and spoke French and German.

The governors accepted her application for the September term. Ruth went to Nancy to learn Polish three mornings a week with Madame Krimpty. When she arrived at her house, the Polish lady presented her with a small parcel. It contained a biography of the Polish composer Chopin, which Viktor had ordered from the bookshop in Nancy. Two things, he proposed: Write a short letter to him in Polish every fortnight, and ask Madame Krimpty to work out a specific vocabulary of musical terms. Ruth followed both suggestions.

While she was packing her two new suitcases, Sophie came into her bedroom.

"I want to say something to you."

"Yes?" replied her daughter who was busy folding a dress. Ruth thought it might be something about not letting Viktor down, or an instruction to ask his help if in difficulty. But it was not.

"I have been content to be Jewish. I have been very happy to be married to your father. But I had the choice. I could have decided not to marry him and not to become Jewish. Also, in Toul, we are different from the strict Orthodox Jewish community in Krakow. I am anxious that there could be trouble. You know what I mean. I think you now have a choice similar to mine. You might decide not to emphasise your religion when you are in Krakow. Your father and I will not pester you with questions about attending the synagogue there. Anyway, my dear, you think it over."

"I have plenty of time to think while I am on the trains," replied Ruth. She was surprised to hear her mother speak in this way and guessed that she had heard something about the Jews in Krakow.

Chapter 7: Two Schools

Ruth arrived in Krakow on a cool September evening. At the station, she found a horse-drawn cab in which she was driven to Viktor's house. The same housekeeper welcomed her, and was delighted with the new Polish phrases which Ruth had been practising. In the week before the school term began, Ruth enjoyed looking around the city of Krakow in the September sunshine. It was autumn weather. When in the sun, it was pleasant enough, but on a cloudy day, she often needed to warm up in a coffee shop. She learned how to use the tram system and was surprised to find that it continued to function until late in the evening. She enjoyed the grandeur of the city far more than when she had come as a young teenager. She appreciated the spacious squares and fine buildings which she now had time to study and enjoy. She was also interested in the sophisticated restaurants and bars which suggested a more colourful way of life than she had experienced at home. Beside steps leading down to a basement, she noted an entrance marked "Cabaret," and a notice stating that it would open in the late evening. She wondered what might happen inside but decided not to pose this question to Viktor.

On her second day in the city, Ruth found herself in Kazimierz, a long street much of which was given over to Jewish businesses, many with living accommodation above. The Old Synagogue stood at one end, near to a busy square, the teeming centre of Jewish commercial life. She did not enter the Synagogue, preferring the bustling atmosphere of the square outside. Ruth recalled her mother's reference to the Orthodox Jews whose traditional appearance set them apart. They were distinctive, perhaps even elegant, but she did not appreciate the dark tailcoats, the hats and straggly grey beards which predominated. She caught snatches of Yiddish spoken between the shopkeepers, their staff and the Jewish customers.

Well-educated Polish people spoke French and had great respect for her home country, which Ruth much appreciated. However, she was determined to learn Polish, and she gradually improved on the basic language she had learnt with Madame Krimpty.

On the day before the school term began, Viktor was able to set aside an entire morning to show her the way to the school and to help around the building. She saw a fine Bosendorfer grand piano bearing a discrete plate announcing that it had been given to King David's school by Viktor Auerbach in December 1931. The school was modest in size and the atmosphere amongst the teachers was friendly. The children were not troublesome, and she soon mastered enough Polish sentences to be able to teach music, whether to a class or to an individual who was learning the violin or piano. She worked out in advance some Polish phrases of encouragement, and would decide which to use while the pupil practised on piano or violin. Then she might demonstrate some improved technique on the instrument. The boy would nod and try to copy her. Thus, music itself solved the language barrier. She enjoyed taking her lunch in the school refectory. She encouraged the boys to speak more slowly, and to teach her two new Polish words every day. Walking home to Viktor's house, she decided that on balance, her first weeks of paid employment had been a pleasure. Ruth posted a letter home in which she explained that she was content, Viktor was well, her Polish improving and her pupils not troublesome. She felt she had nothing exciting to report.

At the prestigious boys' school, St Xavier's Krakow, the Head of Music was sixty-seven years old. He enjoyed his work so much that he had continued beyond the usual retirement age. In late September, he experienced sharp chest pains. The school doctor was summoned and diagnosed a serious heart condition. He must be admitted to hospital for observation.

"But we have the school carol concert in two months' time," expostulated the High Master, as if it was extremely careless to require hospital treatment just before an important event.

He instructed the school secretary to make rapid enquiries. Agnieszka Zeleski had recently been invited to Viktor Auerbach's to meet Ruth again. She suggested to the school secretary that they might find out about her progress in her position at King David's.

St Xavier's School, Krakow

"Dear Miss Neuman,

The High Master would be most grateful f you would come to see him this Wednesday at 9.30 AM. He has had a discussion with the Headmaster at King David's School and believes that you may be able to help us at this time. We have just lost our Head of Music, through ill-health and urgently need someone to replace him. I look forward to seeing you on Wednesday morning if you would please come to the main office and I will take you to the High Master, Colonel Padnieski.

Yours truly,
Secretary to the High Master

When she received this summons, Ruth's reactions were twofold. She was surprised by the peremptory tone of the letter, with its assumption that she would be willing and available to attend at the time specified. However, she had heard of the establishment which had a fine reputation as a leading boys' school in Krakow. Although she had never entered the school, she had noticed the extensive stone buildings and boys wearing their distinctive uniform were conspicuous in the late afternoon around the town. It would be typical of the establishment to confer on its headmaster the title High Master. Ruth also knew that Agnieszka's sons attended St Xavier's. She decided not to discuss the impending meeting with Viktor. It was difficult to put her finger on the reason for this. Partly it was because she did not know what lay behind the request, which might lead Viktor to try to find out. Further, if there was to be an offer of employment, she would prefer this to be on her own merit and not as a result of some behind the scenes manoeuvring by "the puppet-master".

Ruth found the school office and was taken into the large study of the High Master.

"This is Miss Neuman," said the timid secretary and departed. There was an overpowering aroma of pipe tobacco. Through a blue fog, Ruth saw a heavily-built red-faced man in his late fifties. He made up for the bald and close-cropped hair with a hedge of eyebrows, a heavy moustache and thick beard.

He wore pince-nez glasses, behind which searching blue eyes stared at the slender music teacher. She was invited to sit in a hard chair opposite him, and he offered what he intended to be a smile. It was the sort of distortion of the mouth seen in those whose habitual expression is a frowning grimace.

"Thank you for coming so promptly, Miss...er Neuman. I won't take up much of your time. We have sadly lost our Head of Music, Holzer. He has been taken into hospital with some sort of heart condition and cannot carry on with his work here. This is a serious problem for us, because we have our carol concert in December and for us this is a highly important occasion. I have been told that you can make the most of a school choir and, if you have the time to give to it, I would like to make you an offer to take over from Holzer. I have had a word with the Head of King David's and have his agreement to discuss this with you. I do not have the power to make a permanent appointment without the Governors' approval, but we badly need to find someone very urgently.

I know that you are committed at King David's for this term in any case, but the Headmaster there has agreed to reach some mutually convenient arrangement which will not disrupt your teaching there. Simeon and I go back a long way and he is very understanding."

Again, there was something in this commendation of a fellow Headmaster which implied that compliance should be expected from King David's whereas St Xavier's would only co-operate if it was advantageous to do so.

"We need to knock our Christmas concert into decent shape. You will appreciate that this is one of the few occasions when we expect the parents to participate in school life, and it will be disastrous if we cannot put on a good show for them."

The High Master had spoken without pause, but the words of his loud and commanding Polish were easily understood. The sense was more opaque. To Ruth, it was not clear whether the High Master had already made an agreement with King David's or whether the matter was left to her own decision. She did not quite dare to ask him to explain. He was continuing.

"You will find the boys here are generally well-disciplined. They enjoy their music and will want to make a success of the concert."

She was disconcerted when he said that she should report any "ill-discipline or slacking" directly to him. She wondered if he had ever been inside a school music room.

The discussion ended when Ruth had said that this was a most unexpected and generous offer, and was formulating the correct Polish words to ask for time to think it over. Before she reached this request, the High Master looked at his fob watch, extended his hand to Ruth and thanked her with warm words, a firm hand shake and another fearsome smile.

"I will ask the secretary to write to you at King David's," he said.

When she left, somewhat dismayed and anxious about how to put together a Christmas event, she realised that the High Master had failed to say any word of welcome to her, given her no encouragement nor indeed an indication that he had any appreciation of music. It was only with difficulty that she found her way back through the dim corridors to the school office.

Returning to King David's, she continued with her usual music lessons until the late afternoon. Ruth felt exhausted by the events of the day, and was delighted when the housekeeper said that Viktor would not be home for dinner until later in the evening. Ruth retired to her bedroom to consider her position. She told herself that she should be pleased to receive an offer, whatever it might be, from a much more prestigious school than King David's. Although she had found the High Master to be completely insensitive, and he had not said anything about it, she realised that someone from King David's must have recommended her for this position. She hoped that it was not Viktor. When he came home, she asked his opinion and he expressed a very similar judgement.

"Congratulations, my dear. I am proud to say that all this rapid progress has absolutely nothing to do with me, and I promise that I am too fond of my dear friend Holzer to have poisoned him in order to get you the job! In fact, I saw him a few days ago, when he had just been discharged from hospital. He will be out of action as a teacher, but seems to be in much better health now. He is a good man and a great musician. At King David's, we use many facilities such as the swimming pool and some sports fields which belong to St Xavier's. If we have been able to do them a favour by offering your services, the Board will be very pleased."

"I cannot quite understand what the arrangement is. Am I being offered the position as Head of Music at St Xavier's? What do you think?"

"This is the High and Mighty High Master wanting to keep all his options open. He is probably correct to say that he needs the Board to approve an appointment, but of course he could get their approval very rapidly if he wanted to. His idea is to see how these nine weeks work out and if all goes well, then he will give you the post. But this is not so bad for you, Ruth. You can decide whether you like it or not. If you do, then I hope you get an offer you choose to accept. But if you don't, you are under no obligation to start in January at St Xavier's. You have your options open too!" Ruth had a glimpse of the successful businessman within Viktor Auerbach's intriguing personality.

The arrangement was that on three days per week, Ruth continued at King David's, but on the other days, including Saturday mornings, she would teach at St Xavier's. On her first morning at St Xavier's, Ruth started very early to make sure she could find her way to the school, which was on the far side of the city from Viktor's house. It was a bright but cold morning in Krakow. Although nervous about her work, Ruth was feeling optimistic. She enjoyed the Hapsburg grandeur of the city, very different from Toul. An electric tram rattled past, and made her jump. Following her route, she could see at the end of one street, a spacious and formal city square. She glimpsed bars, restaurants and cafés with colourful awnings. When she reached St Xavier's, she was impressed by the fine buildings at the edge of the City. The main double doors were closed, but she found another entrance and went to the school office. It was not quite 8.00 in the morning, but the secretary showed her to a music room and gave her keys to its cupboards where various instruments and music stands were stored. Then, she took her along brown corridors and stone steps to the assembly room, explaining that the school would meet there at 8.45, "for Notices and prayers."

She met the Head of Middle School, who, after a few words of welcome to Ruth, produced timetables, explanations about the buildings, the Fire Drill and again referred to the carol concert in nine weeks' time. She was told about the location of "The Senior Common Room." When, later in the week she found it, Ruth thought that the elderly schoolmasters were competing in the amount of tobacco smoke they might emit.

She noted a separate "luncheon room" where this meal was served to the staff at a long table, but decided not to enter it. She would concentrate on her teaching and preparation for the carol concert.

The carol service would take place in the local church of St Xavier, after which the school had been named. Ruth felt confident about working with the school choir at St Xavier's. First, she had to try out the younger boys for places amongst the trebles. Two promising trebles would take solos, and another keen boy was given a place as "First Reserve" as if the choir was a sports team. The rehearsals for the choir took place after the school day had finished. Some of the choristers were plainly tired and reluctant to try hard. On one occasion, Ruth suggested to a difficult boy that he did not have to remain a member of the choir if he did not wish to. This specific choice produced an immediate increase in energy and co-operation. Even when she had to teach music to a class of thirty boys, Ruth found that the boys were generally well-behaved and happy to learn. Instructing the entire school might be more challenging.

On the four Friday mornings before the carol concert, the normal school assembly was replaced by music practise in the church. Working out the ingredients of a Polish carol service was easier than Ruth had feared. She was given service sheets for previous carol services. She also found a battered hymn book when clearing out a cupboard. It must have been at least a hundred years old and contained several carols with simple tunes which would allow an interesting experiment. She tried different choral arrangements, using the old Polish words and tunes as a basis for her own ideas. There were some more sophisticated parts for the choir and the final verses would be sung by the entire congregation with choral descant.

At the Friday morning practises, the church organist would play over the tune and the entire school would sing, led by the choir. Ruth directed the school from the steps of the chancel and the "Captain of the choir" took over her usual task of conducting the choir. They knew their parts well and the trebles had been practising descants in many of the carols. Although she was nervous, Ruth won over the boys by saying that what everyone wanted to hear was a big noise. Surely they could achieve this. "Most of us will then be in tune, and those who are not will be drowned out."

Boys laughed. "Let's begin with Adeste Fidelis, and when we get to the last line, don't let me down. It's the punch line and I will punch the air as you sing it." When they got there, she was poised to do just this, punching out the words Venite adoremus with her clenched fist.

"Why don't you try this to see if it gets you any louder?" she said. "Once more, please, from the first Venite." The whole school now punched the air; "Venite adoremus, Dominum."

"That was just brilliant," said Ruth. "And I think all of you were in tune too. So, as we go through these carols, remember what my punch means. But also, we need some contrast. Some quiet whispered singing. Do you think you can do that?"

Some boys called out loudly, "Yes!" Ruth laughed and asked them all to whisper it. The school was beginning to enjoy itself. The boys became willing participants in her experiments with the old carols. They liked the foreign teacher, and perhaps they had a sense that the outcome would be spectacular.

Little by little, Ruth was making her mark. On the last of the school practises, she explained about the descants which would be sung by the choir while the rest of the school followed the basic tune. "The choir are formidable. They sing with the tongues of larks and the lungs of lions. Can the rest of us keep to the right tune while they soar above us? It's going to be tough."

She completed her work with the older carols, choosing one for the school to sing and two for the choir. She was pleased with her musical arrangements, which she hoped would bring new life to the original tunes. Ruth found that she was expected to read part of the Gospel, and she enlisted the help of Agnieszka to improve her accent. It was a demanding phase of life, as she told herself at the end of another week.

Chapter 8: Christmas at St Xavier's

By mid-November, Ruth was finding the walk to and from St Xavier's extremely tiring. A heavy fall of snow left the pavements slippery and her journey took even longer. On another morning, she faced gusting sleet and arrived drenched. When Agnieszka visited her at Viktor's house, she could see that Ruth was exhausted and encouraged her to look for lodgings close to the school. Ruth soon found a promising place. The house, close to St Xavier's, was also near the tram stop which would take her in the other direction to King David's. It was the home of a middle-aged couple called Hainski. Ruth agreed on a rent which would include breakfast and supper. The arrangement would last until the end of the school term, and then would be extended if her work at St Xavier's continued. The lady of the house rattled away in rapid Polish. Ruth was able to tell her that she had only been learning the language for three months, and could only understand it when slowly spoken. Mrs Hainski showed her around the house, telling Ruth where the bathroom was, when she might use it and where and when to join her host and hostess for her first supper. Her bedroom had a small coal fireplace and simple furniture. There was a crucifix over the bed.

Following the instructions of Mrs Hainski, she went down the stairs, where she was introduced to the head of the household. Mr Hainski had a forbidding face surrounded by vigorous facial hair and an aroma of tobacco. They stood behind their chairs in the dining room, and Ruth naturally copied them. Mr Hainski then uttered a series of Latin words, which were incomprehensible to Ruth. She realised that this was a Christian Grace before the meal, and joined in saying Amen when the words ceased. Mrs Hainski smiled in approval. The meal began with a thick vegetable soup, but Ruth was dismayed to see, laid out on the table, a plate of cold meats and sausage which could only be pork. She avoided this, and went to bed early. Living close to St Xavier's, Ruth found an easier routine, concentrating on preparation of school and choir for the concert. When her dinner included pork, she pretended that she had no appetite because she had eaten too much at midday. Then, in her own bedroom, she cheerfully consumed food which she bought at the local grocers.

In the last week before the concert, Ruth began to feel unwell. Perhaps the strain of preparations for the event, the lack of support and the cold weather combined to affect her health. When the day arrived, she forced herself to take her place; she contrived to conduct as she had in the rehearsals, and when the concert concluded, she felt utterly exhausted. She had sensed an atmosphere of intense excitement within the school and the parents. The old carols which she had rearranged proved entirely successful. The choir sang even better than they had in practise, and the boys' faces showed their pride in their performance. But on the following day when the High Master wanted to see her, she had returned in a cab to Viktor's house. There, she went to bed and accepted every offer of help and care from the housekeeper. Viktor told her to stay in bed, eat as well as she could, and "sleep all the hours God sends." Taking his advice, she remained in bed for three days. Viktor did not invite her to participate in any of the Hannukah services at his synagogue, but he spent many evenings with her until he had to leave for a business trip at the end of December.

As her health improved, Ruth became concerned to know whether she was to continue at St Xavier's. She knew that the High Master spent this holiday with members of his family near Lvov, but could not write because she did not know the address. Fortunately, she met Agnieszka Zeleski in the city. She now learnt that Piotr Zeleski was a governor of St Xavier's. Within two days, Ruth received a message from Agnieszka. The Board had been impressed with the concert and the conduct of the young music mistress. They were not looking for any other music teacher. It followed that she could have the position if she chose to accept it.

In the New Year, Ruth returned to the Hainski's house and to St Xavier's at the start of the term. She followed her usual timetable. Perhaps some of the boys were more responsive in her music classes, but none of the staff made any specific contact with her. There was no official letter from the school office, nor any word from the High Master. The first week of January proceeded slowly. Ruth became disconsolate. She still found that she had to concentrate hard to understand the Polish language, and often she felt tired and lonely at the end of the school day.

She ventured into the luncheon room, and sat next to an elderly schoolmaster. She offered to fill his water glass from the jug. She did not understand the Polish words in which he asked her to fill it only half full. When he tried to drink, his hand trembled so much that he was spilling water over the table. A younger teacher saw the problem and quickly poured off half the glass into his own.

"We all have our little peculiarities, but you can't know them from the first day with us," he said. He was one of the younger teachers. Ruth had seen him occasionally and he had once given her helpful directions when she was lost in a corridor. She had noticed his semi-circular eyebrows, deep brown eyes and ready smile. She also had a vague memory that she had seen him before.

"Congratulations on the carol concert," he said. The man with the tremor cut in, "BB, you have a tone-deaf ear when it comes to music, as we all know from standing next to you at Assembly!"

As she walked back to the Hainski's at the end of the week, she reflected that the only one of her fellow teachers to say anything welcoming was BB, the one with the distinctive eyebrows. She could not communicate well in the Hainski household. On the Friday evening, when Mrs Hainski offered brown sausages of unknown content, Ruth said that she had eaten too much at lunchtime. Then, she suddenly thought about what would now be happening at home in Toul. The family would be together, there would be a sense of calm, of warmth and often there would be gentle laughter. They would eat supper which they all enjoyed. Here, she was lonely, refusing food she could not eat, and unable to participate in conversation even if she could find a fellow human to talk to. She bent her head to look down at the vegetables which Mrs Hainski had served onto her plate. Better to concentrate on the parsnips, carrots and potatoes than be overcome by self-pity. Mrs Hainski was complaining that the best butcher could not sell any topside of beef. Her husband replied: "Ah, the Jewish one. They will be keeping it back for their own kind. They are all the same." Ruth could understand this anti-Semitic observation, but there was no point in making any response. Perhaps it was a good thing that her Polish was still too limited for her to enter into a discussion.

After this dull weekend, on a grey Monday morning, she received a note from Viktor Auerbach.

"I am sorry to have been so neglectful. Your uncle Melchior has come to stay. Would you be able to come to supper on Wednesday? Bring violin, if you can. No need to reply. If you come, we will be delighted to see you, and if you don't come, then I know you will be too busy - also a good thing!"

The day seemed brighter already. In the early afternoon, Ruth walked past snow-covered buildings to the market square. She looked up at the statue of the Polish writer Mickiewicz, dominating his corner of the huge space. Further away, she admired the irregular towers of St Mary's, the Mariacki, as the locals called this fine Gothic church. There was an aroma of roasted chestnuts in the air, more fragrant than the baked potatoes which street vendors used to offer in Toul. She bought a present for Auerbach, chocolates, from a fancy shop where elegant women were taking tea. A trumpeter began a short tune, played from high in one of the Mariacki towers, marking the hour. "Krakow is a grand city, and I am lucky to be part of it," she thought.

On the Wednesday evening, she took a tram which rattled through the city in the direction of Auerbach's house. She was pleased to see her uncle, and found him much more amusing here than when he had been with her family in Toul. When Ruth asked him about his printing business in Strasbourg, Melchior joked about the care taken to lay out and print perfectly whatever disagreeable rubbish the editors might commission. He was now producing and distributing two newspapers. Although his business was successful, he was gloomy about the political situation. His work force was largely Jewish and it was difficult to retain his skilled staff against an undercurrent of anti-Semitism.

The other guests were old Holzer and his younger sister. By the time they had finished supper, Holzer had enjoyed too much red wine to play the piano with accuracy, but Viktor found the sheet music for a Haydn violin sonata which Ruth knew and wanted to play regardless of the unreliable accompanist. The music and conversation continued late into the evening, and Viktor insisted that his driver should take his guests home.

The grand green Adler limousine was waiting at the steps as she left the house. She knew the chauffeur, Juliusz, who had brought her entire family to Krakow four years ago. He was pleased to see Ruth and spoke better German now. After the Holzers had been taken to their home, the chauffeur became more talkative.

"So much has happened since your visit here. Mr Auerbach and I have travelled thousands of miles in this car. We have been to Germany frequently, so that we know the road as if it were on our doorstep, and choose different hotels only if we are looking for a change."

Juliusz was describing these journeys as if they were a pleasure shared with Auerbach.

"Who would guess when I said good bye to you in France that I would have the pleasure of driving you again as a resident of my city?"

"My family are most grateful for everything you did for us," replied Ruth, and then thought that she was being condescending and unnecessarily formal with the chauffeur. She added, "It is a great pleasure to see you here again. Do you remember once when we could not get into an hotel in Colmar? They were all full, but eventually you found us rooms above a beer stübel? You were my hero that night!"

The chauffeur was smiling broadly when he opened the passenger door for her. He waited until she had entered the house before driving away. Ruth had the happy sensation that she belonged in Krakow. Her usual confidence and optimism had returned. An evening like this was an experience which would never have happened at home.

Correspondence with Herr Breuer and Vivien

25th November 1934

Dear Miss Neuman,

I write in pursuance of our usual friendship and to enquire how is your important work progressing. I feel confident that your enthusiasm for all music will bring you success in your post, and you will happily experience the reward which we all feel when encouraging youth and aptitude.

This brings me to remark that I have enjoyed teaching you more than any other pupil. I trust that you shared in much of the pleasure from so much excellent music.

And now, there is spring in the air and I am considering some travelling during the Easter break. We have been playing Brahms, and have achieved noted success with the first two symphonies. Now, we have two more important concerts, and thus we will complete all four. Then I will take two weeks of holiday. As you know, I have never been to Krakow, nor any part of Poland, and I am considering a train journey to Vienna and then travelling down to Krakow.

With every good wish,

Adolf Breuer

9th December 1934

Dear Herr Breuer

Thank you for your letter with its good wishes and news of the concerts in Nancy.

It is kind of you to say that you enjoyed teaching me. I am sure that I would never have reached this situation at St Xavier's without your guidance. As for me, I am extremely busy with teaching both music and preparing for a school concert.

Forgive me if this is a poor excuse for writing no more about my occupations here.

I could not encourage you to visit Krakow in April. It is generally cold and windy at that time of year. I wish you every success in the concert programme.

Best wishes,

Ruth Neuman.

3rd January 1935

Dear Miss Neuman,

Thank you for your letter which I received last week. I trust that there was no misunderstanding as to my motive in considering a visit to Krakow. My circumstances have much changed in recent months and, to my delight, I have made a proposal of marriage to Mademoiselle Ouvrier, who works at the concert hall. I was considering whether we might go to Vienna immediately after our marriage and then to Krakow, if the train times permit.

We have now completed all four Brahms symphonies, and I believe that all were well-received.

With every good wish...

Ruth did not reply to the second letter.

10th January 1935

Ruthy darling,

How are you? You have written to Mutti and Papa but no special page for me. Why is this? Surely you have important secrets and matters not to be made known to our parents?

I can tell you that I am having a very hard time at school. The trigonometry is not the problem. It just appears difficult on the page but really is not. We are also going to start mechanics next term and I think I will enjoy this too. My trouble is that in German, we are studying Goethe whose idea of a description, whether of a country, a place, a people, or a person is that woolly generalities, long explanations and discursive asides seem to last until the end of time. It is so dull that I can scarcely sit at a desk with Goethe for longer than ten minutes. But the lesson lasts for three quarters of an hour!

The entertaining gossip is that Yvette Ouvrier who was [according to a Wicked Tongue] a friend of Herr Breuer, has agreed to marry the manager of the Victoire jewellery shops in Nancy. I don't know either of these people, but I thought you would be amused. According to Wilfreda Teniers [the Wicked Tongue], our friend, the famous violinist, bought a beautiful bonnet in a well-known store in central Nancy. Then Mademoiselle Ouvrier was seen wearing it next day, which was her birthday. Wicked Tongue guessed that he gave it to her. But her engagement to the Victoire manager was announced at the end of the same month. Don't tell me that the jeweller might have been bought another hat just the same. Lightning does not strike twice in the same place. But the arrows of Cupid, they do…

I have had a big success with Marcel. I told him that if he mentioned a football team again, I would not speak to him for the next hour. It worked really well. I was out with Jakob and Marcel last Sunday. The boys began talking about a match reported in the Saturday paper and I maintained complete silence until Jakob had set off for home! This was two weeks ago, and since then, Marcel has not spoken a word about this stupid game!

Missing you, dearest and most favourite sister! Vivien.

The morning after Ruth received the letter from her sister, she found herself laughing ridiculously as she walked to St Xavier's. She had been relieved to find that she had no sense of jealousy when Breuer had told her of his plan to marry, and now she knew that his scheme had come to nothing, she merely laughed at the folly of men. Turning in at the entrance gate, Ruth had to stop sharply in order to give way to a blue car which was noisily entering the school ahead of her. The driver waved, but was unrecognisable in his goggles and leather motoring helmet. As she was about to enter the building, she heard running steps behind her. Taking off his helmet, the driver spoke.

"Miss Neuman, I am so sorry. I should have stopped and waited for you! Instead, you only just avoided becoming the first victim of my disgraceful driving by jumping back in the nick of time!"

All this was said with a huge smile. It was the young schoolmaster who she had met in the luncheon room. Since then, he had offered her some help when she was carrying an armful of musical instruments along the school corridors.

He had an attractive, resonant voice, and when he spoke to her in clumsy French, his Polish accent amused her. Everyone called him by his initials, BB. Ruth realised that the driver was not nearly so embarrassed as he was pretending, and so she replied in kind.

"Ah, BB, I am pleased that you missed me this once, and will concentrate on keeping out of your way in future."

Chapter 9: Bruno Berling

"You can do anything if you have enthusiasm."

Henry Ford

BB was, above all, an enthusiast. As a schoolmaster, he seemed to be in his element. His happy marriage into a wealthy family meant that he had no need to worry about his modest salary. He had met Halina at a hot and stuffy concert in Krakow, where he had seen a well-dressed girl looking at him. He had also noticed her plentiful fair hair and slender figure. During the interval, he made sure that he happened to be at the bar nearest to her seat. She was with an older lady who Bruno assumed was her mother and they were struggling to be served in a welter of taller customers demanding iced drinks.

"Allow me to get these for you. These bars are so understaffed and you may die of thirst before the barman notices."

He said this to the older lady, but it was the girl who laughed. He affected to have taken no notice of the daughter and was merely keen to help her mother. They enjoyed only a few minutes' conversation, in which the older lady failed to introduce her daughter. However, when the concert resumed, he looked boldly across to her, caught her eye and she raised a gloved hand in acknowledgement. Her smile was a perfect crescent. Until roused by a crescendo of Rimsky Korsakov, he worked on a poem about the young lady:

When she smiles it's like half a moon
Shining from the sky at night.
If I make her laugh it's the bright sun
Dancing out behind a cloud.
The brilliant day needs the unnamed girl
And my heart hopes for her delight.

Bruno thought about her as he walked slowly home, remembering the calm face, the pale blue eyes, her smile and the hair thick like compressed straw.

In the late 1920s, Krakow had a small social elite to which Bruno Berling did not quite belong. He made enquiries but could not find out the names of the ladies he admired. Then, he saw the girl again, leaving Kebbels' book shop. Bruno treated this chance encounter as a meeting of long-lost friends.

"Wonderful to see you again," he enthused. "And what have you just bought from old Kebbels?" It would have been rude for her to make no response and before long they were in discussion about Sienkiewicz' historical novels, and how much his pupils enjoyed them. He asked after her mother as if he knew her and was rewarded with the information that they were meeting for lunch in the market square at half past twelve. Bruno joined them there. He learned her name, Halina Kutrzeba. Although her mother was plainly a dominating lady, Bruno was invariably well-dressed, had old-fashioned good manners, ready conversation and he made no mistake as he pursued the daughter.

Visiting their home, he offered fulsome admiration for a flower arrangement, a narrow field of artistry in which the mother took great pride.

"Did you really conceive this delightful arrangement and then create it only this morning?"

"You are too kind. The florist delivered these irises when I had asked for something else, but I did my best with them."

"That is the hallmark of the real artist. You succeed even when something has gone wrong, like a violinist with a broken string. They are wonderful, the whites set against the deep blue."

Bruno knew that the mother was enjoying every moment inside his folly of flattery. But Halina caught his eye and winked at him. Bruno was completely wrong-footed by Halina's reaction and finished the conversation in a subdued tone.

When they were alone together, Halina explained, "We want her on our side, Bruno. I need her agreement nearly as much as you. We both have honourable intentions."

She kissed him swiftly on the cheek. It was an indirect reference to their marriage. Of course, this was his intention, but it was the first time that either had referred to it.

Because Halina liked riding, Bruno submitted to a series of lessons, telling no one, so that when he went to stay with her family, they could ride together. He avoided riding with Halina's older brother who was a cavalry officer. He was seldom at home, but whenever he met Bruno, he made it clear that he also approved of the match. When he left, he said one sentence to Bruno, "Go on and ask my father. I know he will say yes." Seven months after their first meeting, Bruno and Halina were married in the great church of St Andrej.

On their wedding night, he joined her in the hotel bedroom. His wife was in bed wearing a nightdress. Moving beside her, he held her tightly, kissing her mouth. This they had often done in recent months, and both enjoyed. He shifted his position, raising his body so that he could start to undo the buttons at the front of her nightdress. Then he felt misgivings about this. He would enjoy seeing her breasts but it would be a gratification for him, perhaps an embarrassment to her. Instead, his right hand moved beneath her to a place where he had never touched her before.

"Tell me to stop if anything is not a pleasure for you."

She kissed his lips and continued to do so while he again drew slightly away from her and moved the hand so that the palm was first on her stomach and then went down to the little mound. He did not move for a time while his tongue continued its loving probes. He raised his mouth from hers, and looked down into the wide-open blue eyes.

"For me you are the perfect woman." She made no reply and he continued this thought.

"I would forego all art, every sculpture, any painting and representation of the female form for this reality, being with you, my Halina."

"That sounds like poetry."

"It is true. My sincere feeling."

Gradually, the hand moved lower. The fingers found the entrance. She drew in a rapid breath and arched her back. They kissed with fresh ardour, until he spoke again.

"If you are ready, I will try now, but if it is difficult, tell me to stop."

She said nothing, but the thighs opened more, as he moved on top of her body and began to enter. The pressure was gradual but continual. There was a moment when she gasped, but she kissed him with yet more passion. The penetration proceeded until he filled her body completely. It was the end and also the beginning. He lay above her, and inside her, inactive, stiff. Then he began a slow movement hoping that her body would react.

With infinitesimal responses, Halina joined his rhythm, and they continued in gentle motion.

He took his face from hers to look into the pale eyes. He kissed them and she smiled in response. It was the perfect crescent which he had adored since he first saw her. This encouragement was too much for Bruno. A sudden rush overcame his determined care and control. He had done his utmost, but passion would not permit such restraint. Deep desire, long denied, possessed the man. He raced to the end, panting and shuddering. He finished, and held her again in a loving embrace. He hoped he need say no more. He should not speak of regret nor apology for he had done all he could. He guessed she understood. He was right. He knew because she stroked his head until he slept.

Halina loved her husband dearly and their early married life was a delight to both. Her parents financed a honeymoon which included a long visit to Western Europe staying in comfortable hotels in Paris and London. She revelled in showing Bruno around Paris where she had spent some months in her early teens. The scale of the Louvre museum astonished him. Then they walked to the Isle St Louis where Halina wanted to show him Sainte Chapelle. She had first seen this space aged thirteen, when she had been mesmerised by the experience. The deep blue painted vaults were decorated in gold. The high stained-glass windows poured a stream of coloured sunshine onto the stone floor creating patterns like a kaleidoscope. There was an overwhelming incensed atmosphere. When she had first seen it, she had thought this was her own personal experience. Her husband now stood still as if enchanted. Only his eyes moved.

"I never knew this. I should have come before. It is wonderful."

Halina knew that her husband had the same appreciation of this space. She took his hand.

"We feel the same," she said. He turned to look into her face. "Yes, we do."

The channel crossing was another event. Bruno had never seen the sea before, but found himself amid grey waves, rolling with the ship, watching the empty horizon until there was the hint of a shape, dead ahead, which must be England. He could speak the language, albeit slowly, and had his own vision of the British nation, learnt from those parts of its literature which he had studied. He thought that the people had the same sense of patriotism as his own countrymen, but had the good fortune to live in their own island. They were thus protected from the troubles which so frequently befell Poland, caught between the sledgehammer of aggressive Germanic powers and the huge anvil of the Russian Empire.

He was in a state of heightened emotion as the shape of England enlarged and grew into the forms of the white but hefty cliffs outside Dover harbour. The little steam ship drew closer to the entrance where her rolling stilled and she moved slowly to the jetty. On that grey afternoon, the couple stood together on the deck. Above them stood the strong Norman keep of Dover Castle and the high clouds of a windless day. Seagulls, circling expectantly above the ship, called noisily, their cries also a sound new to him. They stood face to face, and as he looked over her shoulder at the massive old walls above, he felt another swell of sensation, a mixture of excitement and recognition of his own good fortune. His body shook slightly, whether a shiver of cold or emotion.

Looking into her pale eyes, he said "Thank you for this."

She raised her eyebrows and smiled at his reaction. "It is my pleasure," she replied.

In London, they met Bruno's only English friend, Archibald Hillman. Bruno had met him when he had visited Krakow as part of a delegation from the British Foreign Office. Hillman was making more progress than most of his colleagues with the Polish language, and had demanded that he practise speaking in Polish when he invited Bruno to spend the evening with him. Thanking him for putting up with his hesitant conversation, Hillman insisted that whenever Bruno should come to London, he must look him up, and had presented his visiting card. This showed two addresses, "My family place in Sussex and the little flat in town."

After an exchange of letters, Halina and Bruno found Hillman at the London address in Wimpole Street, not far from The Albert Hall. His friends called him "The AH" which were also the initials of the famous Victorian concert hall, where his family had a permanent box. Many of his friends might tell their parents that they were going to the AH, then skip the concert and enjoy his stock of port and Armagnac instead. The AH did indeed love music of all sorts, but if his friends preferred chatter and alcohol, he was always willing to "Go with the flow," as he put it. AH affected a racy manner and admired Noel Coward. Like a hero in one of his plays, he arose not long before lunch time at the weekend, and wore flamboyant dressing gowns of his own design.

Halina was most intrigued by Archibald Hillman. His manner was a mixture of genuine warmth and affectation. His sense of humour was always self-deprecating. The three laughed constantly. They spoke French together most easily. Hillman told Bruno that his Polish had never been so go good since their happy evening together in Krakow. He made it clear how much he admired Halina.

"Are all Polish girls so beautiful?" he asked gallantly. "They certainly are," replied Bruno who was now adopting the AH style of humour. "And that is why I have been able to make the most careful selection and chosen Halina for her character alone. In general, the Polish young lady is snobbish, stupid and obstinate. If it were not so, we would ask you to visit and find you a wife."

Halina laughed at this nonsense, while thinking that few of her unmarried friends would admire this quaint and slightly plump English gentleman. He could not be more than twenty-eight but his curly ginger hair was already receding and his chin seemed lost in the fleshy folds of his neck.

The AH took them to a Henry Wood Promenade concert. He introduced them to his friends in the adjoining box. Another evening was spent at the D'Oyly Carte Opera watching The Mikado. After the performance, AH found the sheet music for the opera and on his upright piano he strummed through some of the songs. They had enjoyed something to drink and collapsed with laughter as they all tried to sing "Three Little Maids From School Are We", complete with the bobbing curtseys which had been part of the performance.

The visitors saw the sights of London including The Tower, the Crown Jewels and then Buckingham Palace and The Mall. They had agreed to meet AH at the Travellers' Club, where he often took his luncheon with colleagues from the Foreign Office. The AH knew many other members to whom he introduced his

Polish friends with much pride. They enjoyed the atmosphere of discrete conversations, the occasional snatch of laughter, and the coffee taken in deep leather armchairs close to the library doors. When these opened, Halina could see two gentlemen surrounded by cigar smoke. One was asleep and snoring vigorously. An hour later, as AH showed his guests down the steps, he had to motion them to one side, out of the way of some running footsteps. Halina was astonished to see that these belonged to the snorer who dashed down to a waiting cab. "House of Commons, Cabbie, quick as you like!" AH explained that this was the Under-Secretary of State for the colonies, late for a Parliamentary committee after a good lunch.

That evening, Halina asked AH about his work. "I have pretty much decided to make a move," he said. "They won't mind. They have spotted my talent for laziness and given me a glowing reference for the Air Ministry." Halina asked him to explain and AH told her that he had been learning to fly, which was, he said, an absolutely splendid sensation.

"Love it as much as I do, I know I will never have the skill to fly a warplane of any sort. Nor navigate one either." He saw his future career in the procurement of the best planes for the Royal Air Force. He expounded on the progress made in aircraft design with a surprising level of knowledge for a professed dilettante. "Your PZ7 fighter is up to the minute too," he said after extolling the merits of mono-wing planes against the biplanes operated by most Air Forces. BB had only read about aeroplanes and followed the progress of the nations competing for the Schneider Trophy. "Speed is valuable," said AH, "but to me, the greatest need is for improvements to radio. When we can give reliable directions to the pilots, and they can keep in communication in the air, this will give more advantage than just speed. So, I will be liaising between the RAF and the technical suppliers."

"I see your point. The prestige of winning the Schneider Trophy is not enough. You need to build planes as fast as an opposing Air Force. And to get them to the right place."

"If I can convince my old Polish friend, I must be on my way to persuading my government!"

The conversation moved on to motor cars. Bruno had an enthusiasm for the appearance of a modern automobile but had seldom driven one. AH began talking about independent front suspension, then he paused, put a hand over his mouth and said, "Us chaps never know how boring we are, especially to the ladies we are most eager to please."

"It's all educational for both of us," replied Bruno easily. Halina smiled to herself at this stage, because she knew that her parents were planning a surprise wedding present for Bruno.

Apart from the sight-seeing and the friendship with AH, the London visit offered another advantage to the Polish tourist. BB bought an enormous quantity of Durex Featherlight condoms, which were not readily available in Krakow, saying, "We can have a lot of fun together before children slow us down." Halina agreed with this, and was herself pleased with another demonstration that she made him happy.

The international Schneider Trophy was won by the British Supermarine entries three times, so that the trophy was awarded to them permanently in 1931. In winning the series, a record speed of 400 m.p.h. was achieved.

Chapter 10: Married Life and Loss

At home, Halina's family provided a house on the Kutrzeba estate and for Bruno himself, a small blue motor car in which he could drive the six miles to school every morning. When this generous wedding present was being discussed, Bruno did not like to ask for the more powerful version of the little Lancia, but secretly paid for the larger engine to be installed. The vehicle took them on touring holidays in the second and third summers of their marriage. They drove over the mountains to Bucharest and then followed the Danube West towards Vienna.

After nearly two years of marriage, BB developed his own enthusiasm for flying. He joined a flying club and took lessons in a two-seater biplane. When Halina complained that this must be dreadfully dangerous, BB answered that her passion for horses was not much safer. When she disagreed, he persuaded her to go up with his instructor. She loved this experience, and when the engine was switched off and the little plane was allowed to glide down, she told BB that she could see why this meant so much to him. The couple discontinued the condoms, BB saying, "If I fall out of the sky, you may have someone to remember me by." Halina laughed with him, but in her heart, she was anxious for her husband and secretly wished that the aeroplane had never been invented.

Halina knew she was pregnant. She told BB at once.

"Wonderful. You will be the perfect mother and have the most beautiful children. If they are boys, they will be my star pupils, and if girls, I will love them all the more."

But it was not to be. At nearly six months, Halina became anxious that her baby had ceased to move within her. She made an appointment with her doctor. BB went with her.

"Just to stop you getting bored in the waiting room," he said. Before the consultation, the nurse used a stethoscope and made no comment. When Halina asked if she could hear the baby's heart-beat, the nurse would not give a direct answer. The doctor arrived, repeated the examination and said that he had sad news to give her. He went into far too much detail about the unborn child. It became clear that the foetus would never be born alive. Halina would have to wait for nature to take its course. Bruno had attended with his wife and when the doctor had left the couple alone in his consulting room, he stood, raised his wife from her chair and took her in his arms. He kissed her tear-filled eyes.

Bravely, she smiled up at this troubled face. "I always enjoy trying again," she said.

There soon followed a second pregnancy. Initial optimism gave way to anxiety again. There was another consultation and now grave news about the prospect of any successful pregnancy. Halina must carry a baby throughout this pregnancy but no living child could be born. BB was always supportive and never said that the birth of his children was important to him. In truth, he knew that he would have made a good father, but in his mind, family life was for Halina to control, and he saw his part as supporting her. They went to the main hospital in Krakow to discuss the situation with the most experienced gynaecologists there. He confirmed the worst news which BB had partly understood at the previous meeting. If Halina were to conceive again, the same result was to be expected.

When they were alone, Halina took her husband's hand.

"I am so sorry," she said. It sounded as if she was apologising to him. BB held her in a long embrace, swaying on his feet with her. "It is just not a matter to say sorry for. Family life is what we have already, between you and me. It is more than I ever imagined. I am truly concerned only to make you happy. If there were to be children, you would have loved them, and so would I. But I have you to love which is enough for me."

They had to tell Halina's parents. They arrived after dinner on a dry autumn evening. Halina tried to put a brave face on it, but somehow, she found herself in tears when she had only got so far as to say that this pregnancy had failed. After a pause, her father said something to the effect that there might still be children. She shook her head and left it to her husband to explain. The couple went to stay with Halina's parents over the remaining weeks of the pregnancy. During this time, BB developed a sympathetic relationship with his father-in-law. In the past, he had seemed remote, but at this time of adversity, he offered firm support. When dinner was finished, the two would sit together, the older man smoking a cigar.

One evening, after some French wine and then liqueur, Jezioro began:

"It is my opinion that my wife suffers from snobbery, Halina from kindness and you suffer from charm. Now, Bruno, what do I suffer from?"

"That is a most unfair question to put to your son-in-law, especially when you accuse him of being charming, which can often mean grovelling!"

"All right, I will provide the answer. I suffer from an over-active mind. It's not that my brain is brilliant or original. It just never stops working. Here I am in retirement, living in the country with every opportunity to maintain an empty mind, but mine continues to pester me!" As if to prove his point, the father-in-law embarked on a discussion of international affairs which he followed with close attention. Jezioro was concerned by the development of a Nazi regime in Germany. He doubted whether the treaty which the Polish foreign minister had just negotiated with Germany would be of any value to Poland. "We know that Hitler has a huge rearmament programme. These new weapons are intended either to make war or to threaten war. Hitler must fear that France and Britain may strike before his programme is complete. That is the only reason why he has signed a treaty with us. He will break it whenever he feels secure in the West."

BB was by nature optimistic and expressed confidence in the French. After the First World War, Jezioro had been an officer in the army which, trained by the French, had defeated a serious Russian attack on Warsaw. He told Bruno about a young colonel, Charles de Gaulle, who had assisted in Polish military training. He had been on "very friendly terms" with another of Jezioro's friends, the Countess Czetwertynska. "When the colonel was returned to Paris in August 1920, we were all very relieved. He must have been twice her size!" Jezioro spoke seriously about de Gaulle and his latest ideas. He lent BB his most recent book called Towards a Modern Army, published in 1934. Jezioro said that de Gaulle's ideas, in favour of mobile warfare and tanks, were unpopular in France but he was trying to persuade his former colleagues to adopt them. "Although I have no influence these days, I keep telling my friends in the

Ministry we should invest in tanks. Since they were all in the cavalry, they prefer horses. My son is just the same, refusing to grow up."

BB read the book, taking special interest in de Gaulle's proposals for the use of war planes capable of operating at a distance and in support of ground forces. Subsequently, they discussed the Polish Air Force, BB repeating to his father-in-law what AH had said about the strength of the Luftwaffe.

"Your English friend will be right. They will try to catch up with the Germans, and so should we. Planes and pilots, tanks and mobile forces are not just the way to attack. They provide the only defence." At this stage, BB found these military theories fascinating. Saying this to his father-in-law, he added, "I hope all of this is just theory, and we never put it into practise".

"It had better just be theory," replied Jezioro grimly.

Speaking privately with Halina in their bedroom, BB said how much he appreciated her father's company.

"He is a thoughtful person," she replied. "Whereas my mother is the complete opposite. She does not mind adding to my own disappointment by showing that she is somehow aggrieved and blames me."

"I am sure she has no intention of giving you this impression," replied BB. He had always found it easy to get on with his mother-in-law, who required of him only deference and polite conventional conversation. These were demands he could easily fulfil.

Both Halina and BB were surprised and touched when her brother secured leave from his Commanding Officer to come home from Poznan to spend time with them both. On the evening before he returned to his duties, Halina commented to him that it was now even more important that he chose a wife and secured the future of the family by having children of his own.

"Not me," he answered. "I am more than content with my officers in their Mess, my horses in their stables and my men in their barracks."

There was a silence between the three of them. Something had been left unspoken. The way he had made his answer did not invite any further discussion and BB adroitly diverted the conversation away to the pleasures of Poznan. When they were alone, Halina asked what BB had made of it.

"I think he might be one of those men who will never like women. But whether this is fear, lack of confidence or something strange, I could not possibly guess. You know him much better than me."

"I am not so sure that I do. I hope that he is just too lazy to think of adding some real responsibilities to his life."

As the time passed, Halina carried the dead baby through every long day. When her husband came home, she appeared to be calm, resigned and appreciative of his concern for her. But when the time came for her to be delivered of the infant, she was kept in hospital for several days. She looked pale and was subdued whenever Bruno visited her. She was plainly depressed and there was nothing her husband could do but sit beside her bed, holding her hand.

When she returned home, this deep disappointment took its toll upon her. BB supported her through it all, and faced the new reality that his apparently perfect life also included a tragedy. Halina took months to recover, if she ever really did. The first thrill, the subsequent anxiety, the grim news and the long-drawn-out loss of two babies in a short time forever damaged a young woman for whom life thus far had been uncomplicated.

She had given away her beloved riding horse when she found herself pregnant and felt too demoralised to replace her. She had little to do in the house; she started smoking again, then tried to engage more with her religion and her parents. The old priest offered a formula of prayers and ritual. He could not explain her loss nor give comfort for it.

In 1933, a modern play, The Cuttlefish, by Stanislaw Witkiewicz, was to be performed at the Cricot theatre in Krakow. BB encouraged Halina to come.

"It may be absurd and incomprehensible, but it should give us something new to think about."

Halina had agreed with some reluctance. As they set off for the Cricot, Bruno was saying, "The more you dread any event like this, the better it turns out."

"True, my dear, and just the same if you really look forward to a party it will turn out boring and disappointing. The only logical answer must be to dread going out all the time."

She said this with a wry smile, and Bruno was pleased to see that she was beginning to make fun of her own state of inertia. She never lost her determination to please him and he loved her for it.

The play, about creative art in a totalitarian state, made both of them laugh and did indeed give them much to discuss. All the way home they talked over the purpose of the theatre and whether the performance of a play might be a work of art in its own right, achieved mainly by the director, as opposed to the director's interpretation of the playwright's intention. BB was bringing his wife out of the small shell into which she had crept.

They attempted to continue this topic of conversation with Halina's parents but failed to attract any interest until Halina mentioned the name of the playwright. Her mother knew his family. She had perfect recall of the names, ages and prospects of all the local nobility. If any of them also distinguished himself in any cultural fashion, his place in her private pantheon was assured. The father, well known as an architect, resided in Zanopane, where the Kutzrebas had met him on a shooting weekend. She had also known his son when he attended the Krakow Academy of Fine Arts.

"He wore the most bizarre clothes then, so if he is now a playwright, I am not surprised his play was so strange."

"Mama, this a new play, which we are lucky to see here in Krakow, and it would be better if we could discuss something more profound than someone's choice of clothes."

It was rare for Halina to stand up in front of her mother's steam-rolling style of conversation, and Bruno was quick to mollify his mother-in-law. He had given up any thought of an interesting discussion about the play.

"How intriguing that you knew his family. His father was also a painter, wasn't he?"

"Yes, Bruno. They have exactly the same names, father and son."

Jezioro joined in the conversation to complain that the father had given his own names to the son.

"The point of assigning a name to anything or anybody is so that we can easily identify what we are talking about. If a man gives his son his own names it strikes me as self-absorbed foolishness!"

Jezioro was, as always, kind, but his innate self-control and sense of order made it difficult for him to express himself to his

---

Witkiewicz was a brilliant Polish artist and intellectual. There will be a footnote about him when we reach 17th September 1939.

daughter and to relate to her loss. His attitude was that brooding over troubles should be avoided. "Put it behind you," he said, not perceiving that his daughter was quite unable to do so.

While her parents were of little help, Halina could take comfort in the solid support of her husband. She tried to find out more about his days at school and the pupils for whom he worked with such enthusiasm. She agreed to his suggestion that the Zeleski brothers should come to dinner. When they arrived, she noted that Witold was wearing a long scarf just as her husband did. It was a new insight for her to watch their response to Bruno, hanging on his every word, but drawn out when he put a proposition for them to discuss. They were keen to answer, as well as they could, any question he might pose. Seeing how he encouraged and stimulated them, she also took an interest in these young men, and was rewarded with the obvious admiration of both brothers. Gradually, she was emerging from a state of depression.

When the new music teacher had arrived, BB recognised her as the teenager who had played the violin at Auerbach's reception many years ago. Thinking that she might be embarrassed, he chose not to mention this. He knew that she had difficulty with the Polish language and he spoke in French when he offered help. Assisting her with an armful of musical instruments or chatting about how to deal with pupils of different abilities, he noticed that she was an attractive young woman. But his interest in her was that of an established teacher wishing to support a newcomer from another country.

However, when the new music mistress made a brilliant success of the Christmas carol concert, he would normally have told Halina about it. But a small voice in the deepest recesses of his mind meanly told him not to mention Ruth.

Chapter 11: Lukas and Witold Zeleski

Piotr Zeleski taught physiology at the medical school in Krakow. His work, which included research, was his main interest in life but he was also a careful husband and father. His wife, Agnieszka, was the romantic one. She was artistic, loving and chaotic. She was an enthusiastic mother of two boys and would have loved to have a larger family, regardless of the expense, a factor she seldom considered. She had inherited a modest sum from some aristocratic relations and felt entitled to leave mundane financial matters to her husband. She made sure that her family were well fed, that her children had good warm clothing against the cold of winter in Krakow and that the boys had every book which she had enjoyed as a child.

On winter evenings, the brothers were willing to go to bed early because they loved the atmosphere she created as she read in her resonant voice about Teutonic knights, daring horsemen and triumphs in battle. Agnieszka sat beneath the dim light of an oil lamp with the book on her knee, while the coal fire threw strange shadows on the bedroom wall. They learned to love the historical novels of Henryk Sienkiewicz and Adam Mickiewicz. This translated into the games they enjoyed in the garden at home or with friends in the park. They played "knights in armour" using sticks as swords, dustbin lids as shields and bicycles as horses. They jousted enthusiastically, often finishing their afternoon bruised or bleeding. Their mother provided sticking plaster, iodine and advice to be more careful another time.

Witold and Lukas made bows from willow branches and scoured the woods looking for straight lengths of ash for their arrows. Birds' feathers were easily found, but fitting them so that they would flight the arrow was a task they never mastered at the ages of nine and eleven. They devoured, old stories about Polish hussars, the cavalry of the 16th century armed with lances, sword and pistols. They learned about the hollow lance which allowed the hussar to carry a weapon even longer than the foot soldier's pike, and the great Polish victories such as the Battles of Chokim or Polonka. Sometimes in their imagination the brothers were side by side on horseback, wearing the great eagles' wings which spooked the horses of the opposition. They studied the success of the Polish cavalry, riding in a loose formation and at great speed. Opposing archers had difficulty finding a target. Just as they reached the enemy, the knights closed up tightly and struck them with all the force of massed cavalry.

The boyish interest in Polish military success was reinforced by visits to Wawel castle. The complex had been the royal palace when Krakow had been the capital city. Polish Kings had been crowned in the adjacent cathedral. Their tombs led to more research in the history books which Agnieszka gave or borrowed for them. Like all children, they were delighted to see the bones of Krak's dragon hanging by one of the cathedral doors. There was unlimited food for the romantic appetites of imaginative boys.

The wedding of a cousin led to the boys' first meeting with their aunt and uncle who came to visit from Romania. Agnieszka often spoke of her beautiful younger sister, Valeria, who had fallen in love with a Romanian student. The parents were against the match until they learned that Henri would inherit extensive lands in Transylvania. He was descended from a line of Saxons who had lived in this part of Romania since the Middle Ages, retaining their German language, religion and customs. Lukas pestered his parents separately about these foreign relatives. Piotr described his brother-in-law as an erupting volcano of endless ideas and constant conversation. He knew that Henri had lost swathes of his property in the recent agrarian reforms in his country. But he had changed his farming methods and was now using machinery so that he was more prosperous than he had been in the days of dependant peasants. Piotr discussed this with his sons, suggesting that Henri and the Saxons might have a more scientific approach than traditional Romanian landowners.

Having exhausted his parents' knowledge, Lukas looked forward to meeting his uncle just as much as his elegant aunt. He was not disappointed. Speaking in slow German, Henri apologised because he was borrowing the boys' bedroom during his visit. Henri noticed the models of armoured knights and books about early battles and started a serious conversation with his nephews. He was surprised to learn how much the boys knew about the Saxons of Romania, and the land reforms recently introduced.

"Did you not dispute it when your property was given away?" asked Lukas.

"It is much better with us in Romania than the Revolution in Russia. We have all benefited from the warning sounded by Trotsky and Lenin. Much better to agree to these reforms than lose everything. Also, as you said yourself, Lukas, I can be a better farmer now, and this seems to be working."

Henri was enjoying talking about himself, which, in truth, was one of his greatest pleasures.

Henri and Valeria had arrived in Krakow with a beautiful tall dog, which they introduced as Greig. It was some sort of setter with glossy chestnut hair. The animal behaved perfectly throughout its visit, except that when they took him to the park and began playing football, he always took possession of their ball. Eventually, they had to tie him to a tree. Witold spent much time brushing the chestnut coat, so that Henri called him "Greig's Groom."

The wedding took place in the church of St Peter and St Paul. On this cool September morning, the congregation entering the church breathed an atmosphere of incense and flowers. The organist playing Bach added to the sense of expectation. The bridegroom waited, elegantly dressed, but plainly nervous. The bride arrived, face veiled. The congregation sang the Magnificat in Latin. Lukas was standing next to his uncle during the ceremony. He was surprised to see that during the service, Henri took and held his wife's hand. When the couple said their vows, he heard Henri take a sharp intake of breath and, looking up, saw tears coursing down the face of his uncle. Lukas was astonished, but was reassured when Valeria joked about it during the wedding reception. "Henri, as usual, had to borrow my handkerchief. It happens at every wedding. As for funerals - you would not imagine the quantity of salt water this grown man can produce!" Henri did not seem to mind this banter, but said one thing which Lukas always remembered. "It's just these big family occasions. I love them. They remind us all that there is nothing more important in the whole world than our family." Agnieszka agreed with her brother-in-law, saying she appreciated that they had come all this way for their cousin's wedding. "We would never have missed it, neither of us," said Valeria.

Before they left, Henri made Agnieszka promise to bring the boys to stay with his family in Transylvania in the following summer. The invitation was repeated and since Agnieszka was determined to see her sister whenever she could, the visit was arranged. For both boys, it was a formative experience, not least because they found in Henri an adult who was completely different from their father, noisy and talkative, adding a zest for political discussion which they had never encountered before.

Chapter 12: The Brothers at St Xavier's

When in his first year at St Xavier's, Witold surprised the teachers with his knowledge of history and enthusiasm for literature. Lukas, arriving a year later, appeared less studious at first. Once he gained an interest in a subject, then he showed good concentration. Many of the teachers were elderly gentlemen with huge moustaches and traditional black attire. Two of them had been injured in the Great War, one wearing an eye patch over his missing left eye, and the other limped about leaning on a stick. The youngest of the school teachers was Bruno Berling, who taught French and English language and History in the middle and senior school.

Before he reached the middle school, Witold had taken note of BB, as the boys and other teachers called him. A master had sent Witold to collect a notebook from his classroom, just before morning prayers. Returning from this errand, Witold saw BB drive his blue Lancia through the gates of the school. It was a bright autumn day and extremely cold, but BB drove with the roof down, wearing blue leather goggles. He was only just in time. The school teacher leapt from the car, slamming the driver's door as he made for the assembly hall steps which he took two at a time. Witold ran up after him. To the boy's surprise, BB opened the door and held it for Witold while he took off his goggles. The teachers stood along the side of the hall, and as the last to arrive, BB was at the back. Having delivered the notebook, Witold found no room in the usual rows for boys of his seniority and took a place just in front of BB. The deep voice was unmistakable as BB sang the responses to the prayers, the Ave Maria and the hymn selected for the day. Witold noticed that BB failed to miss out verse 3, as was shown on the board and was singing his way through most of it before he realised he should be on verse 4 like everyone else.

When he was with his classmates, Witold tried to make fun of BB describing this mistake, but his friends sided with BB. His wide smile and encouraging approach made him the most popular schoolmaster at St Xavier's. Amongst the other teachers, only the High Master owned a car. The boys were aware that he went to a local flying club. BB was sometimes seen in the city with his wife who was the daughter of one of the local land owners. It was also known that BB and his wife had travelled to Paris and even London. Many of the schoolboys regarded him as a role model.

Alongside the blackboard in BB's classroom, there was a notice which read:

1. Your life is important to you and to the world.
2. It is all you have for yourself and to offer to others.
3. Choose the right targets and then work hard to achieve them!

BB was in charge of the under-16 football team. Perhaps it did not take much to inspire teenage boys to play football, but BB also taught them enthusiasm for their team and how to work out tactics which left one of them ready to score and others able to feed him the ball. In defence, the entire team ran back to regain the ball, take the initiative and push forward again. Both brothers were keen footballers. Lukas was fast and although short, he was a muscular boy. His speed and powerful right foot made him a natural choice for the right-wing position. He revelled in this. On the wing, he would face the opposing full back and could often get past him by pretending to move to one side and then pushing the ball to the other. He learnt a method of dealing with defenders who would be racing back to tackle him when he was sprinting down the wing. He became adept at the sudden stop, trapping the ball and leaving the other to go past, so that he could either continue his run or pass to one of the forwards in the centre. This might well be his elder brother, Witold, and they became known as the heavenly twins because of Lukas' miraculous ability to send a high pass across the field to Witold.

The brothers did indeed look similar, but were eighteen months apart in age. Lukas was shorter than his brother but they had the same skin tone and straw-coloured curly hair. In the previous year, the team captain was a boy who irritated them both. He was annoyingly good at German, but since his family were German and spoke the language at home, this struck them as unfair. On the football field, he showed a flair for control of the ball and accurate shooting. He demanded that Witold should pass to him, even when Witold had his own chance to score. Witold soon learnt that it was better to pass to Vlad than to try himself. If he missed, he would be reminded of his failure for days after the match.

In the following year the brothers were in the school under-16 team. They also played for their school house, St Peter's, in the final competition against St John's. Agnieszka concealed her reluctance and came to watch. She arrived at the sports' field wearing a fur coat, hat and riding boots, but without an umbrella.

The High Master was already smoking his pipe upside down as he sat on a shooting stick staring out though his pince-nez spectacles. "Pass the ball!" he bellowed occasionally when he thought one of his pupils was too keen to retain it. When the rain increased, he was able to turn his complicated shooting stick into a substantial umbrella and gestured to Agnieszka that she should join him beneath it. Then the wind caught the umbrella as the High Master was using his other hand to tamp his pipe. The match had to be interrupted when it went cartwheeling amongst the footballers. The High Master first swore, then apologised to Agnieszka. He looked out from under his fearsome eyebrows. "Don't know much about this game," he confessed, "but my staff tell me that your lads are darned good."

"We are not a sporting family," replied Agnieszka. "I am astonished they have any talent for this."

"Brothers are naturally competitive, which is a very good thing. Competition makes for determination, which is a fine quality. I wish we could teach it here, but to brothers, it often comes naturally." The eyebrows moved downwards in a forceful frown, to emphasise the words spoken.

This discussion was interrupted by excitement amongst the crowd as another goal was scored against St Peter's. The match ended and the teams gave three cheers to one another. Then, covered in mud, they departed for the changing rooms. Witold and Lukas emerged clean and contented. Their side had played well, but lost to a stronger team.

They found their mother waiting in the school porch. The three walked home through the wet streets of Krakow in an atmosphere of autumnal twilight, rank with the odour of coal fires. "Mother," said Lukas, "did you see how heavily they marked me? I only got in one cross in the whole game."

"You were brilliant," said Agnieszka. She had seen how a burly full back was always getting in Lukas' way, but she had missed the one occasion when he slipped and Lukas achieved this cross, landing the ball neatly onto his brother's head. Witold managed to head it, but the wet ball was difficult to control and he missed the goal mouth.

Inevitably, it was the star footballer of their year, Vlad Glast, who made both goals for St John's. They reached their house and while the boys changed out of school uniform, Agnieszka set the table. When her husband came home, he paid full attention to the boys as they recounted the story of their defeat. "If only Glast had been in our team, we would have won by five goals," said Witold.

"Or if we had been in St John's," said Lukas.

Both brothers admired BB. Witold did his best to copy his choice of clothes; a straw hat in summer, and in winter, a long scarf and an overcoat open like a cloak. Lukas took the words beside his blackboard to heart. He added a sense of responsibility to his boyish enthusiasm. He asked penetrating questions during lessons, and had to put up with accusations from his friends that he was too serious. They nicknamed him "The Professor."

When Bruno and Halina happened to meet the brothers in the city one Saturday afternoon, they invited them to supper. Over dinner, Bruno told them something most unexpected about Vlad Glast.

"He was the outstanding player in the under-15 team last year, and I knew how important he would be to us. So, a year ago, I had written out what I hoped to say in my end of season report on the team." He went to fetch it and returned with his handwritten note. "Glast has played at centre-half throughout the season. In every match, he was the most accomplished player on the field. He has always passed to the strikers even when his own ability might have tempted him to take on defenders and get to the goalmouth himself. Thus, in a season where we scored an impressive number of goals, he scored none at all. Instead, he created them for his team. Because the forwards knew he would do this, they ran into gaps in the defence, where he would repeatedly find them. His contribution to our success is only partly attributable to his own skill but more to his magnificent generosity and fine teamwork."

BB went on, "At the start of the season, I asked him to come for a chat about football. I read this out to him and we talked it over. It was a joke, to provide him with my report before the season began, but I think it worked. He understood that this way of playing was far more valuable than goals he might score himself. He has well-earned the praise by now."

When Lukas thought about this, he remembered the arrogance of Glast in the previous year, which had been transformed by his becoming an excellent team player now. Few other masters thought of praising the youngsters, whether for their academic work or ability in sports. They were expected to criticise harshly and frequently. Here was an example of praise given privately as an incentive and then repeated in the school magazine when it had been justified.

Lukas and Witold were much impressed by Halina. She took them both seriously, treating them as adults when they were both under sixteen. She asked their opinions about the school, the subjects they liked and their future plans. She was plainly interested in their answers. She was also dressed with an elegance which showed off her figure. The brothers were aware that she was childless.

It was partly as a result of the discussion with BB that Witold and Vlad Glast took to spending the school breaks together. Both boys also participated in the military training provided by the Junior Officer's Corp. This was obligatory at St Xavier's and involved marching, parading and polishing boots. Vlad became the drummer for the school marching band.

The arrival of the replacement music teacher had caused a ripple of interest throughout the school. She had arrived from France, a nation much respected in Poland. The boys were intrigued by her. She had a cloud of black hair, a youthful figure and spoke French and German, but was struggling bravely with the Polish language. The boys tended to snigger or to mimic her when she took the weekly school music practise. Some assumed that she was German, because of her name, and would sing the words of Deutschland Uber Alles to the tune of the hymn they were practising.

Chapter 13: Ruth: Calm Before the Storm.

In Germany on 30ᵗʰ April 1935, a Nazi decree forbade Jews from displaying or carrying the German flag.

One January afternoon in 1935, Ruth looked up from her desk and was surprised to see the face of the timid school secretary looking cautiously around the door of the empty music room.

"Miss Neuman, I am so glad I have found you. The High Master would like to see you this evening in his study at about six o' clock." It was not so very long ago that Ruth had herself been a schoolgirl, and she must have looked alarmed at this sudden demand from the High Master.

"No, No, Miss Neuman. I know that he wanted to congratulate you on that concert, and there is another matter, something even more important as well."

Recovering rapidly, Ruth got up from her desk and asked the secretary to join her on a bench beneath the chalk board. Ruth laughed, "I know you didn't mean to give me a fright. How wonderful to know everything that's going on here. I thought the concert went well and the boys seemed to love doing it".

"Yes, Miss Neuman and the parents...you could not see when you were conducting, but there has never been such enthusiasm nor so many favourable comments afterwards."

"It is lovely that you should say so."

"It was not just me; everyone thought it was wonderful."

"Can you tell me what you mean by those significant words "Something even more important"?"

The secretary blushed. "I am sure I should never have said that."

"I suppose I will learn at six o clock, but it would help me to know now, that is, if you are able to tell me."

Ruth wondered what the phrase "if you are able" meant to the secretary. It could mean "if you are permitted to tell me," but perhaps it meant "if you have the knowledge." Ruth guessed correctly that the secretary did know, ought not to say but that, after this friendly exchange, could not resist telling her.

"Miss Neuman, I took the minutes of the governors' meeting. They decided that the whole school should study German at the same stage as they learn French. Mr Auerbach said that you knew both languages and since you are already teaching French to the fifth form, you might be willing to accept the same position in German. Later, you would be the natural choice for Head of the Languages Department at the end of the year. It would be most exceptional."

The voice of the secretary faded. She had said far more than she should. But then, what was the harm? And Miss Neuman was looking at her with such surprise and modesty. Bringing good news was a rare privilege and the secretary would not have missed the chance for two months of her small salary.

All schoolchildren in Toul had studied German as their second language, and Ruth had enjoyed the intricacies of its grammar. Indeed, Herr Breuer frequently used his mother tongue when explaining finer points of musical expression. However, Ruth was anxious because when teaching French in the fifth form, the boys already knew the basics of the language and it had been easy for Ruth to take the entire lesson in French. If words needed to be translated into Polish, she would often have the chance to look them up before the lesson. But in German, she knew that the fifth form had not studied a word of the language, and she would have to teach in Polish. Having said goodbye to the secretary, who was most concerned that she should say nothing about their conversation, Ruth thought about her meeting with the High Master. What she really needed was some help with her Polish.

"Come!" came the order from inside. Ruth entered rapidly, and in time to see the High Master turning away from her in the hope that she would not notice that he was repositioning his false teeth. He turned back to look at her.

"Ah, Miss Neuman!"

His voice had only one setting for volume, namely maximum, but there were different tones, as Ruth knew very well. Now, the setting become buoyant and congratulatory. He could not, however, resist plenty of praise for himself.

"This school has had a fine musical tradition, even before I arrived. The links with churches, the enthusiasm of our parents and the standards I have maintained mean that high achievement is expected. I am delighted to say that your work with the school, as shown in the concert…"

Ruth allowed all of this to blow over her, while she smiled and looked appropriately modest.

The interview continued, with the High Master observing her over his pince-nez spectacles and from beneath his extensive eyebrows.

"There is a second issue, perhaps more important in the long run. The Board of Governors have recently decided to accept my recommendation that the German language should be given parity of importance with French. The problem is that they would like to start this now and we must find German language teachers without delay. Now, Miss Neuman, I am aware that you speak good German and I trust that you would accept the offer of a position to teach German in the fifth form."

"High Master, this is a great honour and opportunity which you offer me." Ruth had practised these phrases in Polish in the course of the afternoon. "I would be delighted to accept, and would enjoy helping the school with such an important transition. It has been a pleasure to teach music, which I manage despite weakness in Polish. In French, I mainly teach in that language. But in German, which will be completely new to the fifth form boys, I fear that I still have weakness and must improve my Polish."

She sat back, while the High Master absorbed what she had said.

"Sometimes, in the French class, I am so frustrated that the boys know all the Polish words and phrases I want to use to explain something. There are two boys who are perfectly intelligent but who are achieving less than their contemporaries in French. I do not like to give them a detention.... I had even thought of discussing with you what I should do to encourage them. They know exactly what I mean and yet…"

The High Master had a brain wave. He had seen the solution which she had placed in front of those gold pince-nez. "Why don't you get these duffers to have some French coaching with you and make sure that they perfect your Polish?" And so it was that she wrote a letter for Witold to take to his parents.

Dear Mr and Mrs Zeleski,

May I first thank you for your help in my preparation for reading the Lesson at the carol service. May I mention a related topic? I am concerned that Witold is a clever boy and is let down by his marks in French language. I fear that this may be partly my fault because my own Polish is still inadequate. I wonder whether you might agree to the following suggestion: Would Witold be able to spend a couple of additional hours on the French language every week, and also help me to improve my Polish?

I would be able to fit this in either on Tuesday or Thursday afternoons, at the end of the school day.

Yours sincerely,
Ruth Neuman

Dear Miss Neuman,

It is so very kind of you to offer extra teaching for Witold. My husband and I had indeed noticed that he seems to be making more progress in other subjects. We would be delighted to agree to your suggestion and feel sure that it will be a great benefit to him. Indeed, if there is a chance that you could help him during these holidays, I can assure you that he has plenty of time on his hands.

Whilst writing, may I congratulate you on the carol concert. There is something else which I would like to mention to you in person, and I will raise this when I collect Witold after his French lesson next Tuesday.

Yours very sincerely,
Agnieszka Zeleski

Agnieszka had a direct, quick manner but spoke in a refined accent. After a word of thanks to Ruth for the additional coaching, she went on to her request. Would she be willing to sing with her church choir on 20th January, when there was a special service in aid of a Catholic Mission? Ruth was happy to agree to this.

Vlad Glast played timpani in the rudimentary school orchestra which Ruth was trying to improve. She knew that he spoke fluent German at home. He joined Witold in the 45-minute sessions on Tuesdays and Thursdays, when they practised French and helped her to teach in Polish. Over a period of two terms, Ruth became much more confident in teaching a class of fifth-formers in their own language and both of the boys moved towards the top of their French class.

For Witold, the expectation that he should help Miss Neuman with her Polish was problematic. It upset the usual relationship between the schoolboy and his teacher. He did not mention it to Vlad, because he would have been unable to explain himself. Both boys admired her cheerful response to their suggestions in Polish and sometimes they developed a competitive attitude to helping her.

At the end of one school day, the two boys were waiting in the usual room expecting Ruth to join them. After ten minutes, Witold said he would go to look for her. He heard the sound of the piano coming from her music room, and guessed that she must be late in finishing a piano lesson. Then, he heard the soprano voice. He moved silently into the doorway. Ruth was accompanying herself as she sang alone for her own pleasure and satisfaction. The voice ceased, and she completed the piano part. Sensing that it was finished, Witold stepped back from the doorway, but she turned and caught him moving out of sight. Immediately, she remembered the lesson.

"Zeleski, I am so sorry. I have forgotten. It is Tuesday and extra French now."

She could see that he was embarrassed. She tapped him lightly on the cheek, and smiled.

"It's such a lovely piece. It was my first solo in public - in the cathedral at home."

To any observer, they appeared to walk easily down the corridor, but in Witold's mind there had been a shift as if winter had changed to spring with the sound of her voice and her caress of his face.

A month after her meeting with the High Master, Ruth received a brown envelope containing a message and a key. The message was from the school bursar. He had been instructed to offer Madame Neuman a small flat within the school. It was close to the main entrance, behind the caretakers' premises and the key would enable her to look at it whenever she had time. Ruth went to see the place immediately. The entrance was on the ground floor, where there was only a small hallway and staircase. Venturing up to the first floor, she found four rooms. There was a spacious living room with a fireplace, desk and two ancient sofas, a kitchen with dining table, a bedroom and a simple bathroom. It was perfect.

In recent weeks, Ruth had been increasingly concerned about Mr Hainski. Once, when she went to the bathroom, she realised that she had left something in her bedroom. When she opened the door, she was surprised to see Hainski immediately outside. It appeared that he had been bending down, but he now stood upright and moved away towards the staircase. Ruth was reluctant to consider the possibility that he had been about to look through the keyhole of the bathroom door.

Ruth noticed that some of her underwear, which she kept in her chest of drawers, was no longer folded in the way she left it. She also saw that the little book of Hebrew prayers which had been kept beneath this clothing was now the wrong way round. The book had been a prize awarded by the synagogue many years ago. In the present climate, she did not like the idea that the Hainskis might be aware that she was Jewish. She knew little of German politics, but she had heard of Adolf Hitler, the rise of the Nazi party and their hatred of the Jewish race. Following the discussion with her mother, Ruth had decided not to attend any synagogue and to avoid telling anyone that she was Jewish. The wisdom of these decisions was reinforced when she heard Hainski make occasional anti-Semitic comments to his wife.

"I wonder whether the new petrol tractors will make much difference to our cousins in the country."

"If they are buying them from the Jewish factory, they will break down and huge bills will be sent for the repairs," he would reply.

"Poles are patriotic and hard-working but the Jews just take advantage of us."

Ruth saw no logic in his attitude, but knew there was no point in disputing it.

When Ruth told Mrs Hainski that she would move out of her room into a flat provided by the school, she appeared to accept it. However, Mr Hainski demanded to see her, complaining that she had been expected to stay for at least a year and tried to change her mind. Eventually, she agreed to pay three month's rent. Some months later, she was surprised to see Hainski in the school courtyard. He had brought her a letter from her sister Vivien who had now gone to England. There was no reason for him to do so. He could have re-addressed it to the school. His manner was strange, looking at her closely without a smile. In the back of her mind, Ruth was concerned that she could not find the little prayer book when she unpacked her possessions in her new home.

Chapter 14: Ruth and Bruno

Rough winds do shake the darling buds of May
And summer's lease has all too short a date.

William Shakespeare

On 18th May 1935, the city of Krakow embarked on a day of civic solemnity, with processions of dignitaries, military parades, fanfares and church bells. Jozef Pilsudski, late dictator of Poland, had died and his body was brought home to his city to be interred amongst many other Polish rulers in Wawel Cathedral. This was an occasion not to be missed. It was a bright morning and the city, which had been subjected to much rapid repainting and cleaning, sparkled in the sunshine. A cool breeze carried cherry blossom from the trees as Ruth found her colleagues from St Xavier's. They had agreed to meet at a corner where some steps gave a good view. The High Master was standing stiffly in his best suit, with his shoes highly polished below his spats. He wore a tall hat and his First World War decorations shone beside his tie. On this special occasion, his pipe was in his pocket but he often checked nervously to make sure it was still there.

Old Ignacy Holzer found the schoolmaster's group and was warmly welcomed. BB introduced him to Ruth, not knowing that they already knew one another. Holzer responded, "Indeed, we first met when Miss Neuman came with her family to stay at Viktor Auerbach's house. There was a reception. I am sure your mother was there then."

BB agreed. "Yes, she was and so was I. But Miss Neuman would not remember me so I have never reminded her about it. I am not a very musical man, you see."

Ruth replied, "I wonder if Mr Holzer would agree with this. I always tell a class of schoolboys that the world is divided between only two types of human; musical people who say they are musical and musical people who claim they are not!"

"Lovely thought," said Holzer. "Very true. There is always a talent to be discovered."

Marching music approached the contingent of school staff. Down the flag-lined road paraded a band playing patriotic tunes and preceded by a corps of gorgeously uniformed officers. The High Master stood erect as any serving soldier. A flurry of cherry petals arrived to decorate his spectacles and the brim of his hat. Eyes front, he ignored them. When the band passed, the crowd cheered, as did other masters, including BB. More marching soldiers followed and then near the end of the procession came a team of eight black horses drawing the bier. At this, the crowd fell silent, some sobbing. Ruth, knowing little about the place of the great Pilsudski in the hearts of his people, watched this surprising spectacle of Polish emotion. A full hour later, when the complete cortege had passed, the school teachers were about to disperse. BB said goodbye to Ruth. He looked unusually hesitant.

"There is a mad idea I want to tell you about." He said this, but plainly changed his mind, saying that this was not the right time to mention it.

"Let me think it over and we might discuss it when we are not going to be jostled by all Krakow in full flood."

Ruth was unsure how to respond, having no idea what BB might have in mind. He filled the silence:

"The one thing Poland always does magnificently is a funeral for a hero or a martyr."

"Today was most impressive," Ruth replied.

The Summer Concert marked the end of every school year. While some of the most musical boys performed solos on various instruments, there were also rousing songs enjoyed by the different divisions of the school. In the past, a few schoolmasters would put on an amusing act, or sing a popular song. Old Holzer had often worked out an entertaining idea of this sort. The High Master seemed to approve of this levity on one occasion at the end of the school year.

The mad idea, which BB had nearly told Ruth about, was to sing "Three Little Maids From School Are We." He had seen The Mikado with Halina and AH, who had given him the sheet music. He mentioned the idea to Ruth and she checked with old Holzer to see what he thought of it. When he approved, BB worked with her to see what could be done. After a few false starts and rehearsals, the outcome was that BB sang in an alternating falsetto and bass accompanied by two hefty Polish youths, one, a full-back in the football team, and the other, more corpulent but an entertaining and popular rogue. They wore costumes which they imagined might have been appropriate for Japanese schoolgirls. Ruth lent BB a flute which he pretended to play. The boys were sworn to secrecy so that it would be a complete surprise. All of them added ideas as they practised and improved on the original song. For Ruth, the laughter of these rehearsals became the high point of her week, a contrast to the work which required serious concentration. Her natural sense of fun had found an outlet. BB and Ruth added an extra-high line to the song which BB pretended to sing in his falsetto, but which was really sung by Ruth at the piano. BB put on a look of elaborate astonishment as if he thought that these notes had come from his own mouth.

As a comic turn, the act was truly hilarious. They were the last item before the interval. The school erupted and even the High Master could be seen laughing, producing an enormous, braying guffaw which no one had heard before. He insisted that they repeat the performance as the finale.

It was after the Summer Concert that BB went to Ruth's flat to return a little flute she had lent him. She had felt his eyes upon her when they had practised for the concert. The two boys had always been present and his behaviour entirely proper. Whenever he had arrived for a rehearsal, she had looked at him with obvious pleasure. Ruth knew that he was married to a lady called Halina, and she had a vague memory that she had met his wife. If she were to see Halina now, she would have been interested to know more about her.

She had been to his classroom and seen his simple exhortation to his pupils:

1. Your life is important to you and to the world.
2. It is all you have for yourself and to offer to others.
3. Choose the right targets and then work hard to achieve them!

She liked these simple thoughts and his idea that they should be set out for schoolboys to note every day. If anyone had asked her, Ruth would have stated that she had a straightforward admiration for BB as a schoolmaster and colleague. But life was never so simple. She guessed that he found her attractive, and she could not deny that he was as good-looking as he was amusing.

When he knocked on her door, she welcomed him in and asked him to take the seat opposite hers. He looked directly into her face as he spoke.

"I keep humming that stupid tune. And remembering everything." In his foolish falsetto, he sang "Three Little Maids from School."

"That may be enough to drive it from one's memory," she said.

"No, I think it's part of me now," he said. "Ruth, you have had a wonderful year. I am not sure that you know how well you are appreciated. By all of us, I mean."

"It is so kind of you to say that. People are not very forthcoming here, but I have done my best and truly enjoyed it all." She was smiling up at him from her chair. He moved towards her.

"I will miss those rehearsals and all the fun we had."

He leaned in towards her, smiling. As he bent down, she suddenly realised he was going to kiss her. In the instant, as the unexpected happened, her reaction was simple. She turned joyfully towards his face. His mouth moved over hers. Gently, and after a short time, their tongues met and began a snaking dance in which hers had no practise. The movement became a rhythmic jive. Ruth felt saliva overflowing onto her chin. He held her face, looking into her dark eyes and seeing her response, and at last, he took his lips from hers.

He drew breath and spoke first, "I have a feeling that we should not have done that."

"No. We should. I have never done it before... but I mean it all."

"I feel the same. Please, Ruth, don't let's pretend this is just flirtation. It is too important. At least, it is to me."

"Thank you for saying that."

They kissed again and slowly moved to her bed to make love. Ruth had been apprehensive about the act, and was reassured by his tenderness. She held his shuddering body at the end, kissing again and again his fine face. He said to her, "To me, you are the perfect woman. All art, every sculpture, all painting and representation of the female form I would forego to be with you in the flesh."

"To me, it is all so new and strange, but very...." she paused, not wanting to say it was exciting, because the word sounded childish...."very good."

They stayed together all afternoon. Ruth told him about her family, their Jewish religion, and even about Monsieur Breuer. These were the factors which led her parents to decide that she should leave Toul. BB told Ruth about his marriage and his home life, the loss of their child, his travels and his love of driving and flying. When he thought of himself, he believed he was extremely lucky. But now he felt the need to be careful not to express his sense of good fortune. It might create a distance between his free-ranging way of life and her limited horizons. Today was not the time to explain that Halina had done no wrong and was a loving wife. Later, he would say to Ruth that he could not hurt Halina by telling her the truth, that he was infatuated with the younger woman. But in his heart, he knew he would not willingly upset his whole way of life because he had found this passion for Ruth. He would not say that this afternoon. It must be said and before too long, but not now.

He had used the same words of loving admiration to Halina, as a "perfect woman", on their wedding night, and he had sometimes thought about the phrase when recalling the intensity of his feeling then. To the woman, they should mean that her lover preferred her to the Venus of Milo or a beautiful Botticelli. But Bruno also thought that it would be a feeble lover who might choose sculpture or a painting in place of the physical love of a woman. He had meant the words when he repeated them to Ruth. He was enchanted by her slight physique, the oval face, the dark hair and eyes. Her joie de vivre and light-hearted contentment contrasted with Halina's more conservative and predictable personality.

For Ruth, the sudden rush of emotion and of physical delight made her see her world very differently. Since adolescence, Ruth had been defined by her music. She had this gift. Everyone admired it. Her role was to play or sing and be suitably modest about it. But it was not her music which Bruno admired. It was the personality, the body, the being who was Ruth Neuman. This realisation made her feel differently about herself, the woman appreciated by this man who embodied the joy of life for her. She had complete confidence in her own feelings and in Bruno. Her interest in Breuer had been a childish and uncertain fantasy when compared with this sublime sense of mutual fulfilment experienced for the first time. Ruth could not tell her parents or even her sister Vivien about it, but she had no thought that what she and BB did might be wrong. Their love was an absolute good. She told him so and he agreed, although he avoided saying outright that he loved her. He knew he loved Halina. They took precautions to avoid pregnancy, using the supply which BB had imported from London early in his marriage.

"What could go wrong?" she wondered, and initially, so did he.

Chapter 15: The Joy of Life

"There is only one happiness in this life, to love and to be loved."

George Sand

Making love came easily to them both. She loved his body and to Bruno, Ruth was utterly irresistible. When he was lying on top of her, she laughed at him because his right hand would hold both of her hands above her head. "You are the primeval male who has chased after that woman and now you need to hold her down. That is the male instinct, to catch, restrain, to violate and control!"

"I don't detect much submission in this woman," he answered, grinning. "The most demanding female I have ever had the good fortune to meet!"

"Now, now, Bruno! There is to be none of that showing off by the experienced man with his little girlfriend. I might tell you about all the advances which I have had to brush off in order to save myself for you."

"Were there so very many?"

"Not for a well-brought up Jewish girl in Northern France. No, there were not. But I can tell you about my Catholic friend, Helga, and the man on the bus, if you really need to know more."

Throughout the summer, BB went regularly for his flying lessons. Sometimes, he visited Ruth before going on to the airfield. More often, fresh from the joy of flying, he returned via the city, drove into the school and went to Ruth's flat. Once, when his wife was away, they spent the evening together and Ruth cooked the simplest of food. She also played a Bach violin sonata. When she played a second time, he stood behind her embracing her and moving with her body as she played. As his chest pressed into her back, Ruth could clearly feel the steady pulse of his heart, calm and healthy, she knew.

On another occasion, Bruno arrived at the flat with a cut to the forehead and a painful shoulder. He had crash-landed after making some sort of mistake which Ruth could not properly understand. He was shaken and so upset that he doubted whether he would continue flying. He was exhausted. She provided a warm bath, and he taught her how to massage his body. He lay face down on her bed, and she was to sit astride him, on his rump. She pressed all the way up his vertebrae from sacrum to neck and then worked more gently on the shoulder. She moved backwards. There followed a more sensual massage in which BB seemed to recover his usual self-possession, giving her instructions and revelling in her touch. It was inevitable that when he turned over, there followed love-making with her body on top of his.

"Magic hands," he said.

"For me, it was magic some other part."

Once, Ruth told BB that she had heard on the radio the principal violinist of the Polish radio orchestra playing a sonata for violin. "This position is held by a woman. I had never heard of her before, but in your progressive nation, a mere woman can be given such a position. It would never happen in France." Bruno noted the name, Grazyna Bacewicz, and three weeks later, presented Ruth with the music. "This is a gift for both of us," he said. "When you play it, I can watch and listen." The music he had found for her was a set of variations for violin and piano, composed in 1934. She found it difficult to play the violin parts of the Bacewicz, but eventually rewarded him with a performance of most of the work.

On the following month, Bruno arrived with a well-wrapped parcel in his arms. It contained an exquisite antique mirror. "This will go on your dressing table, and I will envy it seeing you when you wake up every morning."

He was standing behind her as she looked into the mirror, seeing her own face and above it his eyes smiling into hers from beneath the arching brows.

"Mirror, Mirror on the wall. Who is the fairest of them all?"

"Yes, that's it. The mirror has come to life and is judging the beauty contest."

She touched the veneered frame with its elegant boxwood inlay, and continued, "This must be very old, well over a hundred years. Just think of the variety of faces it has been reflecting back to their owners all this time. Some young, some old, some pretty and some less so. And, for the future of the mirror, I hope I can keep it all my life, reminding me of you."

In these words, she was telling him that she knew it could not last. He felt a sadness but also a relief, taking in her meaning. He replied, "Of course I want you to keep it always," and then he changed the subject.

Grazyna Bacewicz was principal violinist of the Polish Radio orchestra from 1936 to 1938. She was also a composer during WW2 and escaped from Warsaw during the Uprising.

In the evening, Ruth spent a long time looking at her face in the mirror. Was there a hint of a line beneath the eyes, perhaps also at the corner of her mouth? If so, she did not mind. But when she looked into her own dark eyes, she found there a brightness and a joy which she had never seen in the years before Bruno. This relationship could not survive forever, but it was a precious treasure now. It would be always there, in her memory, in her life. It was like an exquisite painting in an art gallery which is still there, on the wall and in your mind, even when you have left for lunch.

As well as the mirror, he gave her jewellery, including a ruby necklace when they spent a rapturous afternoon together on Christmas Eve 1935. She often cooked lunch for him, working with loving enthusiasm to make his favourite food. They told one another that these were the happiest days of their lives. They enjoyed a deep friendship alongside their sexual passion. He told her that he was trying to write a long poem which was to be Napoleon's reflections when imprisoned on St Helena, expressing both pride in his achievement and lamenting his failure.

"I can muster the thoughts, putting myself in his place and looking out into the endless Atlantic from the cold rock, but I am struggling with the words to express them."

She said she sometimes felt the same when composing music, but when she woke on the following day, a new idea for an arrangement or even a tune came quickly to answer her problem.

"I had no idea you are a composer."

"I cannot be. There is no such animal as a female composer."

"That can't be right. There have always been female artists in literature or painting. Thinking about it, I guess more women play musical instruments than men. Do you know whether a female student could enrol at the Warsaw Conservatoire?"

"I don't know," she replied.

She played through her musical arrangement of The Little Car, Apollinaire's poem from the Great War. It begins in a jaunty fashion, giving the date and names of people making a car journey when the war broke out. The poem concludes with the words:

We understood, my comrade and I
That the little car brought us into
A new age
And that although were both already fully grown men,
We had nevertheless just been born.

Ruth's music followed the initial cheerful tone but at the end it slowed became dark and foreboding. The last line of the poem was repeated with emphasis and at funeral pace.

"That is wonderful," said Bruno. "It adds so much to the words, and brings out the melancholy of the last sentence. I wish you could have trained in composition at The Paris Conservatoire. I have no real knowledge of music, but I have complete confidence in you, Ruth. We would have a female composer to join the famous gentlemen."

Ruth was pleased with his faith in her and returned to a more mundane view of her position.

"But teaching music here, I think I help the boys. They get something from their music lesson, all of them. And I have you."

Neither of them minded that their relationship must be kept secret. At this stage, Ruth had a very narrow circle of friends in Krakow. She knew the choir at St Andrej, and she went to the homes of a few parents whose children wanted a music lesson at the weekend. As a result, she was sometimes invited to join the family on social occasions. Her lover did not need to tell her that he would be ostracised by the social elite of the city if it were known that he, a man who had married into a well-known family, was in a liaison with a French schoolteacher. As for Ruth, she would lose her position at St Xavier's if found out.

Once, in the spring of 1936, she took the train to a little town to the South of Krakow where he met her at the station in the Lancia. She had packed a rucksack with a picnic lunch. They set off into the woods, walking along paths, surrounded by birdsong. Their footfall was quiet on the mossy track, and neither needed to speak. They were in separate but companionable thought. They found a green space where they ate quietly, not talking lest they disturb other creatures in the glade. They heard occasional rustling as small animals disappeared into the deep undergrowth. Then, they lay together, holding one another in a long embrace. This was a perfect idyll which they both knew, but would not say, could not last.

In the early evening, they drove back to Krakow, arriving when it was sufficiently dark for the occupants of the car to be invisible. In her flat, she expected that they would make love, but when they were undressed, he lay close to her and kissed her slowly.

"My mouth is like a boat leaving its harbour."

He said this as he stopped kissing her lips. His lips moved onto her left shoulder. "It is a missionary ship travelling to the West, hoping to arouse new places, found new congregations." The mouth went to her left armpit where it tickled her. "Now to the South East," where the mouth found her right breast. "Now to the West again.

Are the inhabitants looking forward to a visit from the boat?" The left breast seemed to be happy to welcome the mouth.

"Now we are steering South," and the mouth moved over her stomach to the dense forest of the mountain lower down. His tongue rasped there amongst the hair, then inside gradually. He remained in this place, worshipping her body.

"It is my turn now." Ruth said this boldly, but with no experience of this part of love-making. She moved now, uncertain, but he encouraged her.

One June evening, Lukas had been working late on a science project. As he left the laboratory, he took the passage to the school entrance. He saw ahead of him the figure of BB leaving the front door of the flat where the music mistress lived. Then, from the upstairs window, he heard a voice; "You have forgotten the car key, foolish angel!"

A pale arm emerged from the window, about to drop the keys to BB.

"It is tempting to keep them so you must stay all night!"

BB laughed and turned to catch the keys. As he did so, he saw Lukas now very close and well able to hear the words Ruth had spoken. BB was astonished to see Lukas and his expression showed both shock and embarrassment. He turned away and hurried towards the courtyard and his car. To Lukas, he could not have appeared more guilty.

After supper, Lukas discussed this event with Witold. Initially, his brother was keen to devise some innocent explanation, suggesting that Lukas must have misheard what the music teacher had said. Faced with Lukas' certainty, he agreed that there was no other deduction to make. The brothers had differing reactions to the revelation. For Lukas, it was appalling. There could be no excuse for BB. Witold saw it differently. Although he had shared an equal admiration for their inspiring teacher, he thought he knew the firm character of the music teacher who had helped him with his French and cheerfully sought his corrections to her Polish. She was an independent and attractive woman. If she chose to have a liaison with BB, this was her own decision and BB was a lucky man. Coupled with this thought, Witold also experienced a strong sense of jealousy. He tried to persuade his brother of this point of view, that Ruth had the right to make her own decisions, but his arguments confronted a granite cliff of moral certainty.

"What the pilot is doing must be utterly wrong. He cannot do this. He is letting us all down, not just his wife. He has been an example to us all. He knows he is. I just cannot ignore it."

For all his condemnation, Lukas was not sure what to do. Lukas' uncertainty was resolved on the following day. During the lunch break, BB sent a note to Lukas and they met outside the school hall.

"Zeleski, I must say three things to you."

"Yes, Sir."

"The first is this. I require your word as a gentleman that you will remain completely silent about what you saw last night. Second, I know you, and I have no doubt what you will have thought of my behaviour. You would be right to despise me. Third, I have decided to leave my post here. Indeed, I am about to apply to join the Polish Air Force. What I have done, I will stop and make amends for."

Lukas was astonished to be treated by his History teacher as an equal, but responded by giving his word, and added that he had already discussed it with his brother. BB had not considered this possibility, but replied:

"Of course, I should have expected you to do so. Can you give me the same assurance on his behalf?"

"Sir, when I tell him what you have just said, there can be no doubt about that."

A day later, Ruth received from her lover a kind but final letter. He wrote that he could not bring himself to meet her to discuss this. He would weaken and was determined not to do so. He wished to thank her for all her loving kindness, which, for him, must remain an unforgettable secret. If he remained at the school, he would find it a torment to see her every day, and so he had decided to leave. He trusted that she would understand. He wrote that with all her talents and qualities, it was fundamentally wrong to waste herself on a married man and he was sure that she would enjoy a fulfilling life in the future.

"You deserve much better than the relationship which I have so much prized and revelled in. I hope you will remember with sympathy your loving Bruno."

These words were an admission that he loved her.

Ruth knew she should not reply. However, in an antique bookshop, she found an old Bible. She found the words of Ruth, speaking to Naomi, and wrote the reference on a new bookmark.

She left this in BB's desk so that he would read the Old Testament words:

"Whither thou goest I will go; and where thou lodgest I will lodge; thy people shall be my people and thy God my God; where thou diest I will die and there will I be buried: The Lord do so to me, and more also, if aught but death part thee and me."

On the book mark she wrote, "And so I go with you always in spirit only. And in the very best spirit."

She accepted it should be the end.

When she left the book on his desk, she noted that the exhortation in his classroom no longer read:

1. Your life is important to you and to the world.
2. It is all you have for yourself and to offer to others.
3. Choose the right targets and then work hard to achieve them!

The last line had been replaced: **Seize the opportunities of every day you are given!**

He had changed these words after the summer term when he fell in love with Ruth.

The school was surprised to lose BB. It was assumed that his enthusiasm for flying was the only cause of his decision to join up. For Witold, this was his last term at St Xavier's. His parents had been expecting him to go on to the Jagiellonian University, although he had not stated which branch of science most appealed to him. They were most surprised when he told them that he had decided to pursue a military career. If he were accepted, he would join the Polish Air Force.

Chapter 16: Country Life

Agnieszka and Piotr Zaleski had recently moved out of Krakow to a small-holding at a little distance from the city. Witold was rather pleased to think of his parents as landowners, even if the extent of the property was not much greater than the garden of a large suburban house. The brothers helped their parents to move in the family furniture and each accepted his own bedroom. They took the aged dog, Griff, for ever-shorter country walks. In winter, they cut logs for the stove and in summer, enjoyed taking meals outdoors whenever it was warm enough to move the kitchen table onto the flagstones by the back door.

Witold returned to the Air Force, looking forward to the companionship and adventure of the Service and reflected with satisfaction that his parents had come to terms with his decision to join up. From the beginning, he had found the process of flying an absolute thrill. Although the training bi-planes were slow in comparison with modern fighters, they were more forgiving and manoeuvrable. When led by Bruno, the trainees must watch his plane until the moment when they must all "break" in different directions, diving and turning to avoid the notional enemy. Then, practising against one another, they must try to turn ever more tightly so that the pursued became the pursuer, on the tail of the other and able to shoot him down. Try as he might, Witold could not convey to his parents the delight derived from flying. His mother repeatedly told him to be careful and take no risks. Witold did his best to sound convincing when he claimed that flying a ten-year-old bi-plane was as safe as sitting in an armchair in an office. Lukas reacted differently. He asked theoretical questions which revealed a growing interest in the Polish Air Force.

Since the move into the country, Piotr now cycled from home to a village where he caught a bus to the medical school. In winter, when there was heavy snow, he sometimes stayed in rooms at the University. Agnieszka said that she enjoyed the romance of solitude, her books and a log fire. Piotr claimed that he was teaching physiology to the children of the doctors who had been his first pupils. At home, he occupied his evenings and weekends in growing vegetables and fruit. There were chickens in a run and rabbits in cages near the house.

On leave from the Air Force in the September of 1938, Witold brought a young nurse to lunch with the family. Maria arrived in time for a country walk with Piotr, Lukas and Witold. They followed narrow paths through the woods and were reduced to single file. Maria took the lead until they reached a clearing. Looking up, she saw tall sycamores, bright gold against the sky. In blustery weather, yellow leaves were losing their grip on the trees which gave them life. Giving way to a gust, a torrent of foliage was blown through the sky and then to the ground, mingling with drifts of their brothers already fallen. Maria came from Podgorze, a town which had been absorbed by Krakow. Hard roads and pavements were her experience of outdoors. As she entered the glade, she stopped suddenly in the sunlight, surprised by the mobile beauty of the surrounding trees in the wind and the wild foliage swept off and chasing around the walkers. Dancing in amongst the swirling leaves, Maria tried to catch them before they reached the ground. Witold joined in but Lukas, normally competitive, decided to leave them to their game.

On the way home, Piotr had discussed medicine with Maria and was impressed by her knowledge and enthusiasm. She asked about his research and worked out how it might affect hospital treatment. When they returned, Agnieszka was awaiting them. "Did you have a good walk?"

"It is a beautiful autumn," said Piotr, "And I think Maria enjoyed it even more than the rest of us."

"Why?"

"More of a novelty for her, I think."

"Is that right, Maria?"

"Yes. You always have this wonderful nature on your doorstep, but for me it's a complete surprise."

Lukas was restrained and left it to his brother to make the conversation both during the walk and the family meal. There was a moment of embarrassment when Maria saw the rabbit hutches, and assumed that the rabbits were family pets.

"How lovely to have so many. I have always been told they were good at breeding and this is the happy result! The babies are so funny. Do you let them come inside?"

Witold was reluctant to admit that they were kept to be killed and eaten. Lukas decided to tell her the truth about the rabbits, which left Witold looking somewhat foolish. Agnieszka moved the conversation onwards. She explained how she could never bring herself to kill either poultry or rabbits, and described her husband as the blood-thirsty physiology lecturer, murdering mice in the laboratory and rabbits at home. Maria laughed cheerfully at this. She was not going to be troubled by a misunderstanding.

Maria helped Agnieszka after the meal and joked about the impossibility of guessing where different items might be stored in another person's kitchen.

"Your mother has better ideas, I expect."

"No, it's my older sister, really. My mother died when my little brother was born."

"So, your older sister looked after you and the house, did she?"

"She did her best. If children have to take responsibility early, they just adapt to it, I think."

Agnieszka took to Maria. There was something so straightforward about the girl. Her blue eyes looked right into your face when she spoke to you. Her ready smile suggested that she was usually happy, and she had the knack of being neither too reserved nor seeking attention. Her snub nose might give the appearance of peasant stock, but she had a good figure and was nearly as tall as Witold. In her mind, Agnieszka was making a mistake common to mothers throughout all societies and generations that when her child introduces a person of the opposite sex, she should immediately prepare for a wedding. Thinking of Maria as a daughter-in-law, Agnieszka felt nothing but satisfaction. Had not Piotr just made some highly favourable comment about her?

In the evening, Witold told Lukas that he was very keen on Maria, and a month later, after the next weekend leave, he gave the impression that they were now a couple. Lukas may have been envious but this was not the reason why he did not congratulate Witold. There was something in his brother's manner which told him that Witold did not want to discuss this new relationship.

By this time, Lukas had also joined the Air Force and was in training at Deblen. BB had manipulated the system to bring

Lukas into the same unit. Witold had been flying for a year longer than Lukas, and was always superior in aerobatics for which he had a natural flair.

"You were dancing in the air with the plane as your partner," said BB, when Witold won the competition for aerobatics. But when they practised "dog-fighting" and gunnery in the air, it was the younger brother who had the exceptional determination to get close to the target, the more rapid reflex needed to shoot down another plane in mid-air. Tactics were a regular topic of discussion with BB who they now called by his Christian name. He had read everything available about the way the Luftwaffe had operated in the Spanish Civil War. They were working out how to attack the slow German bombers and to defend themselves against their powerful fighters. The three young men revelled in the Polish sense of patriotism, belief in courage and the success of the underdog, if only he is sufficiently bold and brave.

Deblen, Poland
*12*th *October 1938*

My Dear Archie,

Many, many congratulations on your engagement. I was delighted to receive your letter and the cutting from the Court Circular column in The Times. The Hon Jennifer can only be described as a "great catch" and I wish you and your fiancée every happiness.

The address will tell you that I have joined the Air Force. I really should have written to you at the time, because it is partly your enthusiasm for the air which led me to start flying a couple of years ago. Then, and this is an absolute secret between you and me, I got into a serious romantic scrape involving a lovely member of the staff at St Xavier's. I could not stay at the school where I would meet her every day, so I set off for the training school here. Since I was already a pilot, I was rapidly promoted. I have now been joined by two of my pupils from St Xavier's and instead of teaching them English and History, we are dashing about the sky in ancient bi-planes and more recently in PZLs. I confess that one of them is already much better in the air than I will ever be. Maddening, but I tell myself I should be proud of him!

Back to our fighters, the PZL is a good machine, as you will know. Some of us are working on a modification to allow us to retract the under-carriage. This should add more speed, but we are not going to keep up with your Hawker fighters. Do you think we can make a decent defence when our planes are so much slower than the enemy?

Tell me more as you get closer to the wedding.

All the very best,

Bruno

Wimpole Street
London

20th November 1938

Bruno, dear boy,

First thing: you Romantic Poles! Fancy an Englishman leaving his post because he falls for another woman! But you are who you are and I admire it all!

I confess that I discussed your case with the HonJen. She congratulates you, claiming that to serve your country in the Air Force will put you in pole position later. When hostilities are over, you must apply to become Headmaster at St Xavier's or anywhere else!

Jennifer is like this all the time! I want an easy life and a soft job, but the HonJen tells me that I must get into the Air Ministry and make better use of my languages. She says that I know half of the powers that be in Great Britain, and since she knows the other half, "we" have a brilliant future.

"It's not ability that counts," she says, "its affability!"

Now I must dash to meet her for lunch!

Take care not to be the test pilot of the plane with the folding undercarriage!

AH

Chapter 17: Krakow and Warsaw 1937 and 1938

Ruth had been careful to avoid any contact with BB for the remainder of his last summer term at St Xavier's. She felt hurt, but accepted his decision. She told herself that she had always known that she should not have allowed herself to become involved with a man who was married, a man who had married well and a man who was happily married. She would bear the loss alone. She told no one about the sadness which fate had inflicted upon her. Ruth was well aware of the vicissitudes of romantic life. She had read several novels on this theme. She needed no advice and was well able to retain her natural enjoyment of life. Sometimes, she would tell herself that the affair had been a blunder. It had been wrong. It had been bound to fail. It was contrary to the Ten Commandments of her own religion and was a sin in the eyes of the Christian Church. However, she could never deny that she sorely missed her beloved Bruno.

In the January of 1937, Ruth had been surprised when Agnieszka Zeleski asked her to sing a solo from Mendelsohn's Elijah in the church of St Andrej on a Sunday at the end of the following month. She was astonished that, two days after her rather vague agreement, the organist of St Andrew's sent her two pages from the score with a note to say that choir practises were on Tuesdays at 6.30 pm. "Come whenever you are free, or let me know another evening." Arriving at this 11th century church at 6.00 pm on a Tuesday in late January, Ruth found the main doors locked. It was cold, but the lights were on and she could hear the organ. Walking briskly along the flank of the old building, she located the correct entrance and found herself in a vestry amongst welcoming members of the choir who were chattering noisily. Plainly, she was in the middle of a group of old friends. She had the advantage that they were interested in her and the disadvantage that she had many new names to learn.

Agnieszka Zeleski arrived and apologised profusely that she had not been there to welcome and introduce her.

"But, Mrs Zeleski, I had not even told you I was coming today. Please don't apologise."

"You must call me Aggie."

At the far side of the vestry, a group of men were joking together, whispering and then suddenly laughing. Their conversation was unlikely to relate to choral music. Ruth knew this sort, men who enjoyed a joke and, when in a group, could take nothing seriously.

There was another loud burst of laughter.

"Don't take any notice of the nonsense from these youngsters. They'll calm down as soon as the boss walks in. You will be surprised to find that they take their choir practise as seriously as their football," said Agnieszka. In this combination of welcome, formality and ironic humour, Ruth was reminded of her mother, and took to her immediately. The sound of the organ ceased.

Zajak entered the vestry causing an immediate change in the atmosphere. The chattering choristers became orderly and committed. Forming a semi-circle around the piano in the corner, they practised the choral part. Zajak was both conducting and playing the piano, stopping frequently to instruct or criticise. It was a short piece, and, within twenty minutes, he seemed satisfied.

"Good enough," he said. "If Ruth is really willing to help us out here, let's go into the church, have the organ and give her a chance."

They left the vestry and the choir moved into their places. Ruth realised that she had left her music behind. She did not need it having learnt the words by heart when practising on her own. She was given a seat at the end of the choir stalls. Zajak's head appeared in the organ loft above them. The choir sang the short passage before the solo, whereupon Zajak stopped playing.

"Remain standing, everyone," he said and then, "I will take this very slowly, because the words are complicated and the music too good to hurry." The introductory bars sounded gently before Ruth came in slowly and softly. Zajak began to play more loudly, and Ruth knew he intended her to sing up. Her voice filled the church with the slow magic of the Old Testament words, well known to everyone. Ruth sang on, oblivious to the standing choristers who watched and listened. In the evening darkness, with the choir and soloist alone in the great building, a sense of timeless peace pervaded. When she reached the end of her part, Zajak also completed the organ passage. Then he stood up, looking down to the choir. "Wonderful. What music this is!" he said. "We can talk about little details another time, Ruth. Now, the rest of us need to go through the service for next Sunday, but thank you so much for coming tonight." He spoke kindly, but it was Aggie who came over from the other side of the choir, said nothing, but took Ruth's hand in both of hers, smiling warmly. A young bearded man, whose place had been in the row behind hers, also moved forward to whisper, "Could you possibly wait? We will only be half an hour now." Ruth thought it might be rude to hurry away, and there was something disarming in the toothy smile surrounded by the beard.

They had agreed to meet on Saturday afternoon at a small café in Poselska. Ruth was early but recognised Stefan's figure walking along the street ahead of her. When she entered the café, he was dithering about where to sit, and was glad to leave this decision to her. They began a conversation in which Ruth soon decided that Stefan was the most serious young man she had ever met. Coupled with this gravity was transparent sincerity. He spoke of singing in the choir and took some time to say that he could not explain why he loved doing so. He mentioned the atmosphere in the church during evening choir practise but felt the need to say that he had no religious convictions. Ruth was now unsure of her own faith, and in order to keep the subject on Stefan's opinions, she asked what he did believe in. He commenced a lecture about solidarity with all working men. Then, he broke off as if he realised that Ruth might be bored or disagree and changed the subject abruptly.

"I have a friend, Witold Lutoslawski, who is studying composition at the Warsaw Conservatoire," he said proudly. Ruth was impressed with this, because the Conservatoire was famous and she knew that the study of composition would only be granted to a promising musician.

Stefan told her that he was going to Warsaw to hear the Conservatoire perform Lutoslawski's choral work later in the year.

"I must go to this because it may be so unsuccessful that it is never performed again."

He made this comment without any trace of humour, and Ruth had to stop herself from laughing.

"If you would like to accompany me, you would be most welcome," he added.

Ruth demurred and Stefan did not try to persuade her. However, there were many factors at work in favour of acceptance. She had never been to Warsaw, and she wanted to visit the Conservatoire. To meet a young composer would be interesting. Perhaps there was also something attractive in the person of Stefan. She thanked him for the coffee.

"Yes, it was a success," he replied in his direct way, then continued boldly,

"So, I think we should have lunch together next Saturday. You can meet my real friends then, not the mad choristers of St Andrej."

The lunch provided a new insight for Ruth. All of Stefan's friends were male, under twenty-five, bearded and wanted to talk about politics. Ruth was aware that old Marshal Pilsudski had been criticised for behaving as a dictator and that younger people were disillusioned with him. Newspapers told of strikes and marches. It was 18 years since the Russian Revolution of 1917. The communist regime in Russia was proving itself to be strong, and it was well known that communists in Poland were associated with The International. Ruth had picked up the thinking of the Polish middle class, whose children attended St Xavier's. There was a general recognition that the business class and the landowners must be alert to the threat of Communism. The friends' discussion of politics was noisy and disordered. It was interrupted by jokes and the exchange of cheerful insults.

"You always say that, Tadeuzs, and it sounds more boring and pig-headed each time you trot it out!"

"No, I am telling you that what the workers need is education and support for their families. I have been to their homes. Many are filthy and the children neglected, but in others, the family takes care of the place, there is enough good food and less drink. So, it's obvious; some of them need help."

"Nonsense, the problem is the conditions of work imposed on the workers. If your mind broadened enough for you to think at all clearly, you would accept that poor living conditions are caused by rapacious employers, not idle workers or feeble-minded parents. Working conditions in factories are so bad that the man who comes home has been brutalised and cannot be expected to provide nurture and support for children. He needs a drink just to survive!"

"We all need a drink to survive the tedium of your arguments, based on ignorance and developed in prejudice," answered Stefan.

Ruth and Stefan left together. "Goodbye, Ruth," they called and, "Don't waste your time with him!"

"I think they like you," said Stefan. "Thank you for putting up with them and their politics."

"I am happy to hear what everyone says here. I don't know much about Polish politics, since Pilsudski was in power most of the time I have been in this country. But I am very concerned about the Nazis in Germany. Is it possible that their thinking would be accepted here?"

"We are every bit as Nationalistic as the Germans, and some people hate the Jews. But I can't see the Polish people following a leader like Hitler. We are more independent-minded. Even Pilsudski, who was a serious war hero, couldn't persuade us to worship him. And, as you can tell from my friends, the spirit of the Communist International is flourishing in Poland."

They went on to talk about the Nuremburg laws which, since 1935, had imposed disadvantages on Jews in Germany and exemplified the ideal of racial purity and Aryan supremacy. Stefan held strong feelings against such injustice.

He asked whether she had been taught the theory of evolution at school.

"Yes, I think I know about the survival of the fittest and the millions of years taken for humans to develop."

"Can you think of any reason why the finest specimens of the human race should develop amongst the Aryan race? I mean that in every tribe or race and in any country where humans exist, those who are bigger, or more beautiful or more intelligent will procreate more than those who are small, ugly and stupid. Or so it seems to me," said Stefan.

"The Nazi theories are based on the most childish version of Nationalism which most boys grow out of in adolescence. Nations are likely to be different, partly because the genes of one prehistoric tribe differ from another. But that could not suggest that one is superior to the others. I cannot understand why the Jewish race should be singled out. The difference between a Jew and another example of homo sapiens can only be his religion."

"I have often heard it said that the Polish people are romantic, courageous and good at agriculture, while Jewish people are good at music, family life and cooking," replied Ruth. Following her usual caution, she had not told Stefan that she was herself Jewish. A few hints from Viktor had reinforced her mother's advice that she might prefer to maintain silent about her Faith.

"But there, we are talking about things which are not the result of evolution, just differences between the way of life of different races, or tribes as you say."

Stefan took seriously her contribution to any discussion, so that Ruth enjoyed the stimulus of his argumentative attitude. She frequently left St Andrej rehearsals with him. It was natural for Agnieszka to ask about him. Ruth told her that there was nothing romantic in their relationship.

After the successful performance at St Andrej, there followed another invitation to sing with the choir in part of an ancient Mass. This would be performed not in St Andrej but in a greater church, The Mariacki in the market square. Ruth knew the outside of the building well. It was a massive red brick structure with a pair of tall towers, different in height. Ruth and Agnieszka went there for the final rehearsal one morning in early summer. The high Gothic interior was illuminated by bright shafts of light from tall windows. There was a magnificent fifteenth-century screen above the altar. Its bright blue background was set off by its gilt frames and magnificent gilded figures. It dominated the East end of the church, adding a sense of bright excitement within a building which was otherwise dark and mysterious. Agnieszka told her that it was the largest altar piece in the world, the work of a German, Veit Stoss, who had lived for twenty years in Krakow. This was a perfect setting for the choir to perform Polish music, composed by Marcin Leopolita soon after the screen was made.

Ruth found a new sense of belonging, almost of kinship with the ancient makers of the building, the screen and the music. She tried to explain this to Stefan, who responded that all this was a human response to the religious stimuli created for the precise purpose of controlling the minds of the people. She complained that if he really thought like this, he should leave the choir.

"Not before I have persuaded you to come to Warsaw and meet my friend Lutoslawski," he replied. By now, she was willing to accept the invitation.

Before going to Warsaw, Ruth asked Viktor Auerbach if she could bring a friend to supper. The evening was not a success, because Stefan seemed determined to interrogate Auerbach about his business interests. Viktor brushed off the first attempt with a joke about keeping his commercial secrets, but when Stefan persisted, he told him firmly that he would prefer to talk about something else, and asked about Stefan's views on the political situation. Viktor wanted to know whether Stefan believed that the non-aggression treaty between Germany and Poland was a reliable guarantee for the Poles. In his answer, Stefan was quick to criticise Germany for the occupation of the Rhineland contrary to the terms of the Treaty of Versailles.

"If Hitler is willing to break one treaty, I don't see why he should not break another if he chooses to do so." He went on to refer to the visit made by the Polish Foreign Minister, Jozeph Beck, to Moscow. "He was well received there and I believe that we would do better to rely on the Soviets than the Nazis." He spoke with considerable force about the merits of the Russian government under Stalin.

During Stefan's homily, Ruth looked at Viktor. He caught her eye and when Stefan paused, he winked. Ruth made a slight grimace and raised her eyebrows very rapidly to show her agreement. When Stefan paused again, Viktor asked Ruth whether she had the same opinions. Ruth said she was mainly interested in peace; peace in Poland, in France, in Germany and Russia too.

"And your friends, Stefan, do they have similar views, so strongly held?"

"Yes, certainly, and many of my friends are far more serious than I am. They are committed Communists and strongly support The International." Ruth thought that this his sounded provocative and perhaps rude, but Viktor made a calming hand gesture to show he would not argue and replied, "Well, now you have a Capitalist friend too." He sat back in his chair and looked at the heavy American clock on the mantelpiece. It was plainly time to leave, but Stefan was slow on the uptake and it was Ruth who broke in to thank Viktor for his hospitality, commenting that they both had work to prepare for the next day.

At the door, Viktor spoke to Stefan. "I think there are three layers in our lives, our family, our religion, our nation. For me, this is not complicated. I no longer have any close family. My belief is in the Jewish Faith in which I was brought up, and my nation is Poland where my family have lived for generations. You probably have much closer family than I do. You do not have a religious belief, but Communism may be an equivalent. So, may I ask you about your nation?" He emphasised the last two words.

Stefan looked back into the calm dark eyes. There was no animosity, just a straight enquiry.

"I have all sorts of different relationships with members of my family; I agree that Communism takes the place of religion for me. As for my nation, I am a patriotic Pole. It is in the blood of the Pole, this belonging here."

"You have said exactly what I feel," said Viktor warmly. Both men smiled because they had achieved this agreement. Viktor summoned the chauffeur to take his guests home.

Stefan and Ruth sat together in the back of the Adler car. Leaving the gate of the grand house, they had to cross the main road and head towards the centre of Krakow. Stefan wrongly assumed that the chauffeur could not hear their conversation, and began by asking, "Well, did I pass that test?"

"Whatever do you mean?"

"I think he was sizing me up as a suitor."

"No, he was not. He is just an old family friend who would be interested to meet you."

"I think I failed. Anyway, I want you to know that I am not a suitor, however much I admire you!"

"But Stefan, we have never been anywhere near that sort of relationship."

"You are quite right. But I would hate to think that when you see him again, you feel any need to stand up for me."

"Very well, I promise I won't!"

"Ruth, please understand that I am a man who will never want a girlfriend, a mistress or a wife. I would like to tell you this and then change the subject. Will you agree?"

Ruth could only agree. They talked about Stefan's work as a journalist instead. But in truth, Ruth was disappointed by Stefan's statement, although she now looked forward to the visit to Warsaw in the knowledge that their relationship was friendship and no more. Sometimes, when they were together, she had experienced a strange mixture of frustration and tenderness. She had wanted to take his hand, laugh and break into his monologues. He talked of politics, the poverty amongst factory workers in the cities, and of the injustice that peasants did not own the land they worked on.

In her mind, thoughts were beating their wings against her skull like angry birds in a cage. But also, she knew that he needed her silent listening, that his own thoughts were being refined even as he laid them out before her, and that he was doing his best to clarify and crystallise a firmly held point of view. It was as if within Stefan's mind, there was already a perfectly formed and complete view of the world, and he just needed to extract it. The idea was rather like the sculptor confronted by a huge block of marble. Within this, there must be a wonderful statue waiting to be released by removing the material which surrounds the perfect work. She found his company engaging and challenging; he made her think. But she also admired the way he looked, the rough beard and the eyes which stared with unbroken gaze.

When they reached the school, Josefz asked for directions. Stefan suddenly realised that their private conversation must have been heard by the chauffeur, but Ruth was untroubled.

"Thank you so much, Josefz, and if you could take Stefan back to his house on your way home, that would be perfect."

On the train journey to Warsaw, Stefan said something which astonished Ruth.

"This Communist friend of mine, Michal. I have known him since we were babies because our mothers are old school friends. His mother is like an aunt to me. They are a Jewish family, like my mother's. That made it awkward with my father who was determined to keep a distance between his family and my mother's."

Ruth looked away lest Stefan should see the shock she felt at this revelation. Stefan, her delightful friend, was half-Jewish, just as she was. But plainly, his mother had "married out" of the Faith with the consequent damage to family relationships. Stefan went on to discuss the Jewish Zionists who wished that all members of their race should return to Palestine, the Holy Land, which they had been promised by God.

"As for me, I think that Polish Jews are Poles, and the right place for them is Poland. What do you think?"

Ruth had little knowledge of Zionism and it would have been normal for her to explain the situation amongst the Jewish population in Northern France. She merely agreed with Stefan.

"If anyone moves to a country permanently, they adopt that country. If they choose to live, work and raise a family there, they naturally belong." She went on to refer to her Uncle who ran a printing business in Strasbourg. "Before the Great War, it was German. Suddenly, it became French. Now Uncle Melchior is printing newspapers in French."

"Can we be sure it will stay like that?" replied Stefan with a world-weary smile.

The visit to Warsaw was very different from Ruth's expectations. Stefan knew the city and did not seem interested in showing her the fine buildings or monuments. Instead, they went to the house of his friends, who enjoyed political discussion enhanced by vodka. Ruth was aware of the turbulence in Polish public life, but had not established any particular position. She still thought of herself as an outsider, and unable to participate in Polish politics. She was not able to vote and politics passed her by.

When Stefan went out to meet someone, she remained in the flat. A thin youth called Stanislaw asked her why she was not a communist. It was a surprisingly difficult question to answer. Ruth did not like to admit that she had never considered the issue. Instead, she replied, "I am no expert, but I am unsure that it would help if every country followed the example of the Soviet Union. Why should the same system suit all nations?"

"The growth of Communism is not only good but is inevitable. Within a short time all workers will take action against their capitalist employers. We are growing in Warsaw, and in Krakow, despite Stefan's failure to take the lead there.

Soon the employers will be on the run and the workers will be in charge." Stanislaw seemed excited as he said this, with fervour almost religious in tone. Ruth made the decision to be bold and to disagree.

"I don't belong to your Party because my life experience has been different. My father is not a capitalist. He does not own any factory. He is paid to work in one. But he is a manager who provides good working conditions for the labourers and designs a method of work which allows the business to sell what it produces. I should have said he works in the porcelain industry in France. He is a director of the company because he is an engineer who has specialised in this type of work."

"He is a capitalist. He has made use of an expensive education to exploit his workforce!"

"No, he works hard. He exploits no one by earning more than the labourers. His salary simply reflects his value to the business."

"Wrong. The workers are paid just as little as the employers can get away with. This is the exploitation which we will end. You and your father will see."

Ruth was hurt by this tone. "Leave my father out of it then. I know only one person who owns factories. He works in Krakow where he runs a number of businesses. As he builds up one profitable enterprise, he uses that success to start another. He is able to employ more workers, and they choose to work for him because he is a good employer."

In truth, Ruth only knew Auerbach's chauffeur and housekeeper. But she could not imagine that he would treat anyone unfairly.

"Do you know what he pays his labourers? Have you seen the conditions where they live? I will wager he pays no more than the factory next door. This is not the first time I have been told about a capitalist who is a perfect gentleman at home, in society or in the city council."

Stanislaw demanded to know how the factory owner lived. She could not persuade him that Auerbach's fine house was anything other than a wasteful indulgence. She fell back on the argument that it might encourage other people to work hard, set up a business and emulate his success. She felt she was on weak ground here.

"Self-indulgence, showing off and waste. That is the way of the capitalists until we pull them down." Stanislaw sniggered, confident that he had won the argument, and went to the kitchen with another lanky youth in order to make tea.

After a short time, Ruth went to join them, not realising that they were discussing her and Stefan.

On the threshold of the kitchen, she heard the unknown youth comment:

"He is a good guy, but incapable of organizing anything. He couldn't organise his way out of a paper bag. We don't want him trying to run the Krakow cell, however good he is on a platform or in a debate." Stanislaw replied with his usual mixture of derision and aggression, "All right, Stefan has a penetrating mind. But that's the only part of his anatomy that ever does any penetrating!"

Ruth stepped back from the kitchen. She had heard enough and decided to wait until they came back with the tea. She diverted further questions by saying that her subject was music, which was far more international than politics. The conversation, brittle and pointless, came to an end.

Ruth was relieved when Stefan returned and pleased when they set off to the Conservatoire to meet Lutoslawski. Directed to a rehearsal room, they soon heard the voices of Lutoslawski and his composition teacher, Maliszewski. These two musicians, one very senior with a handlebar moustache, the other, youthful but no less serious, were locked in an impenetrable debate about the use of the "Wagner tuba." Stefan was about to interrupt them, but Ruth tugged his sleeve, putting her finger to her lips. These two needed to complete their conversation. Perhaps she was also interested in the intensity of the dialogue and the commitment of Lutoslawski to his own opinion. He contrived to maintain a deferential attitude to the older man who had just said there was no point in writing parts for Wagner tubas because they were rarely used and might not be available.

"I accept your point, and realise it could cause problems. It will be my own fault if the work never finds an audience. But I want that deep fat sound, the power and sonority of these tubas. In the right place, they give exactly that profound tone I need. I know I am a perfectionist, but look at the way Richard Strauss uses them in 'The Price of a Shadow'. It would never be the same without them." Lutoslawski paused, thinking, and then adding to his argument. "And again, in the adagio in Bruckner's 9th symphony. There is no substitute for them..." The older man broke in.

"But Witold, that's really my point. Only two composers have used them since Wagner's day. Not even Mahler, who habitually threw the kitchen sink into his orchestration. It would be a mistake, when you need to get your work into the concert hall and heard by a discerning audience."

"I am sure you are right. But it will be my mistake!" replied Lutoslawski.

Neither Stefan nor Ruth interrupted this rarefied debate. Then Lutoslawski noticed them, broke off the discussion and apologised to his teacher. He cheerfully introduced everyone, explaining that Stefan had told him all about Ruth and her work in Krakow. Ruth immediately felt at home with these men, both deeply musical, and allowed the privilege of working in their chosen field. Lutoslawski had a distinguished appearance, almost as if he was a young actor in rehearsal for the part of an older man, a composer and conductor of international repute, which, in due course, he would become. Ruth was drawn to him. His gracious manners were appealing, and she admired his ability to allow others to talk until he needed to join in with an observation, either amusing or perceptive. Lutoslawski was the same age as Ruth, and pursuing the very career she would have wished to follow if she had not been born both female and Jewish.

The young composer was plainly interested in her. They all went to dinner together, and at the end of the evening, he asked what he might do to persuade her to come to Warsaw.

"I am lucky to have my position at St Xavier's, but I would love to be transferred to The Conservatoire," she answered honestly.

"I am not yet in charge of the institution. Just give me time."

"Don't forget me, and come to Krakow if you possibly can," she replied as the group dispersed.

On the journey home, Ruth reflected that Stefan was always generous in his friendship. Many people preferred to keep their friends to themselves, some collecting them like stamps never to be touched by anyone else. She tried to say this to Stefan, who answered that it gave him great pleasure to find Ruth enjoyed the company of his old friends.

"They all liked you, especially Witold Lutoslawski. I thought you took to him as well."

It was a question which Ruth chose not to answer. Instead, she replied, "I am quite sure that Stanislaw did not approve of me."

"Don't worry about him. No one can persuade him to take any interest in mere humans. We are all either workers of the world or filthy capitalists. But Lutoslawski is different. You can tell from his manner that he was born into the aristocracy. They left their estates here when the Germans invaded in the Great War. Then they were caught by the Russian revolution and his father was executed by the Soviets. He is not a very likely communist. I know that he had to visit his father for the last time when he was in prison awaiting his death sentence."

"That is tragic. He has had a traumatic childhood but has become a model of good manners."

"Careful, Ruth. I think you have just admitted that you were attracted to him!"

"You win, Stefan. He is an absolute delight, but I don't think he will find time for the school teacher from Krakow."

Chapter 18: Christmas 1938

Ruth's busy life at St Xavier's continued during these years of her friendship with Stefan. She made some new friends amongst parents of boys whom she taught. There were few changes at St Xavier's. The Headmaster remained inscrutable. New faces appeared in the staff room, but they were mundane figures by comparison with BB. When she saw Agnieszka at choir practise, she learned that Witold had joined the Air Force in 1936. She was not surprised that he was followed by his younger brother in the summer of 1937. As the political picture darkened, Agnieszka admitted that she was concerned for her beloved boys. She complained that they were far too brave for their own good. "They are both under twenty, and don't care a monkey, provided that they win some competition or other. Luckily, Bruno Berling is still their squadron leader and he has much more sense." Ruth sympathised. She was also glad to hear that Agnieszka thought highly of Bruno.

In Germany, Adolf Hitler had become Chancellor in 1936. He made warlike speeches in a voice which sounded like an enraged cockerel. He held rallies in which he complained about other nations' mistreatment of their German populations. News reels recording the Chancellor shouting at huge crowds attending a rally were shown in one of the cinemas in Krakow. He had no hesitation in displaying his hatred of the Jews and his anger with the post-war settlement with France. Although the Polish audience responded with jokes about the man, his manner and his moustache, the reporters expressed serious concern. Ruth saw one of these news reels and wrote of her anxiety to her parents. She wrote tactfully in support of their decision to encourage Vivien to go to England, but she also hinted that they should do the same. She knew that her mother agreed, but her father would be reluctant to abandon his work on which the family income depended. When the newspapers described the vicious attacks on Jewish businesses at Krysallnacht in November 1938, Ruth wrote again.

BB was granted leave in early December 1938 and Halina encouraged her husband to go back to St Xavier's for the carol concert on the first Friday of the month. She suggested that he should go on his own, making the point that if he was enjoying the company of old friends, she did not want to feel that he was leaving early just for her. BB was keen to go, and looked forward to seeing the school, his many friends in the Common Room and to enjoy the Christmas music in the place where he had heard it throughout his life. Ruth was also in his thoughts. He wanted to see her. In the front of his mind, he hoped that she would be glad to see him, and that their friendly letters would set the tone for their meeting. In the back of his mind, some other idea may have lurked scarcely detected by the man himself. He had not given to her any indication that he might join the congregation for the carol concert. BB drove to the school in the twilight of early evening. The little Lancia followed the same route which it had taken day after day in previous years. Its owner could not help reflecting on the happiness he had sometimes experienced in anticipation of joining his beloved.

At St Xavier's, BB went into the Common Room where his arrival drew a welcome from all his former colleagues. Ruth was in the church, busy with final preparations for the concert.

He walked across with other masters, and they took their seats along the side of the church, which was lit only by candles. The concert began and as the well-known carols proceeded, Bruno felt his emotions rising. He was in the building which he had loved as a boy. The hymns were his favourites. The slight changes to the service were the work of a woman he had loved with an intensity made the stronger by two years' absence. He had missed her more than he ever acknowledged.

Towards the end of the concert, there was a short organ introduction, the choir stood, and the organ stopped. Ruth's voice emerged from the darkness. Bruno drew an agonised breath. She sang simple words which he knew well, and with a purity which brought tears to his eyes. Then, the organ and choir came in, her solo finished. He had never heard her sing like this and, in truth, her voice had matured to a new depth of expression. The concert ended with its final hymn sung by the choir, the school, parents and masters. Afterwards, there was a glass of wine in the Common Room to celebrate the final week of the term. Ruth did not attend it. As the staff left, so did BB, with many a promise to keep in touch.

There was a silence in the darkness outside. His feet then moved onto the pathway which could lead to the school gate. But they moved in the opposite direction, towards her flat. The light was on in her little drawing room. He knocked. She came down to let him in. She had not known that he had been at the school, at the concert, and was longing for her. He caught her in his arms as soon as he saw her. She closed the door and locked her mouth onto his. They spoke no words, but kissed and embraced there in the little hallway at the foot of the stairs. She did not invite him up. They went together. They were soon naked in the bedroom.

"I love you," he said.

"And I," she replied.

She felt that she must ask him about his service in the Air Force. In return, she explained about her work in the school. "I have taken over some French classes where the boys had been so badly taught by some master who must have been sacked for incompetence".

"That useless teacher is now a pilot of immense skill and courage, my dear!"

"I think he was always just a show off, whatever he did."

"Does he have any skill at all, in any field of human endeavour?" he asked, leaning across to touch her. She kissed him, laughing as their mouths met in a happy explosion. Now she was on top of him. He tried to slow her movements lest it would be over too soon. Assenting, she desisted. Did both or only one of them know that this was their last time? Nothing was said. Together, they moved up the hill to the summit. They reached the very place, panting together in their passion. Here, there was no longer any delay nor holding back. No more could be found or achieved between lovers. When it was finished, he lay still but sobbing, while she remained calm, pensive and smiling. Ruth knew that she was loved. At this moment, the future was not in her mind. The present held the rapture. Tomorrow was best forgotten. They spoke little more. Later, he must go. She held him close but he said farewell and left the little flat.

Chapter 19: Easter 1939

Ruth returned to the choir at St Andrej in late January. She had been feeling unwell in the cold January mornings and wondered whether there might be a specific cause for these symptoms. Later, when she was sure that she was pregnant, Ruth reacted calmly. She needed to retain her position at the school and was determined to keep her baby. She had to decide whether and when to inform Bruno. She would not tell her mother, or at least not yet. Then, she would need medical help and someone to care for the infant when the autumn term began. In all of this, she found in Agnieszka a reserve of support and friendly advice. Agnieszka dd not mention the issue to her husband, but sought out her son's girlfriend, Maria. It was agreed that Maria, together with a midwife colleague, would look after Ruth in her pregnancy and they made appropriate plans for her confinement at the end of August. There were no complications and Ruth visited a gynaecologist only once. She saw Stefan at choir practises and Sunday services, and she sometimes invited him to her flat for supper. They remained firm friends.

Stefan was a disorderly mixture of social entrepreneur and careless intellectual. His friend Lutoslawski had written a choral piece including a soprano solo, and now nothing would suffice but that his other friend, Ruth, should sing this work, together with the choir from St Andrej. Lutoslawski was willing to conduct provided that he could obtain leave from the

Army Signals unit he had joined. The organist at St Andrej was reluctant. Agnieszka, who liked the idea of modern music and the chance to participate in a new work, supported Stefan and together, they persuaded the authorities at the Mariacki to allow a concert performance of the piece.

The original work had been composed for orchestra as well as choir and solo soprano. Lutoslawski sent a revised version for organ instead of the orchestra. Ruth and Stefan met Lutoslawski at the station the day before the performance. She had been captivated by him when they had met in Warsaw, but found it difficult to gauge his feelings for her, disguised, perhaps, behind his old-fashioned and courteous manner. The composer insisted on giving them lunch at a café where they ate outside in the cool April sunlight. Lutoslawski was delighted to have the chance to perform this work once more. They went into the Mariacki for the rehearsal, finding many members of the St Andrej choir already in their places. When he entered the church, the composer looked up at the blue and gold altar screen which dominated the chancel. He stepped back and took his time to appreciate it.

"I had heard of this but I have never seen it. We must make the music worthy of the setting."

The organist arrived and they played through the piece, Ruth practising singing in this space. Lutoslawski then asked where were the timpani. There had been a misunderstanding. He had sent the music for the organ together with the timpani part. Although he had received the timpani music, the organist had assumed that it had been included in error. Lutoslawski remained calm, but insisted that the drum beats were essential and a timpanist must be found. Someone remembered that Vlad Glast used to play drums in the school band. He was found and rapidly persuaded to help. The battered timpani were brought over from the school. Lutoslawski was now relieved that the work could be performed properly and was soon helping Vlad to tune the drums.

The decision had been made to perform the Lacrimosa at the end of the Good Friday service on 7th April 1939. Meanwhile, the Germans had invaded Bohemia, thus demonstrating that the Munich Agreement failed to satisfy Hitler's demands. Any Pole who studied the map would see that, on three sides, his country was surrounded by the German aggressors. On Good Friday, the atmosphere in Krakow was thick with mixed anxiety, patriotic determination and deep uncertainty. Some citizens were confident that the recent alliance with France and Great Britain meant that if the Germans invaded, they would surely be defeated because the enemy would be fighting on three fronts. Some feared gas attacks from the air or believed that Poland was so weak that the only course would be to cede whatever territory Hitler might demand. Others considered that the Polish army was strong enough to defend either the entire country or a reduced territory using rivers as fortified borders. It was against this troubled background that the choir prepared for the traditional service to be followed by the Lacrimosa.

On Good Friday, when the country was under threat, the great Church was packed. The nation's road ahead might be as hard as the path to Calvary. Piotr Zeleski, Lukas and Witold, both in blue Air Force uniform, attended to support Agnieszka in the choir. Witold had invited Maria. Halina Berling and her mother had come in from the country, but Bruno was absent. The choir of St Andrej, including Ruth, sang throughout the service, conducted by the assistant organist. A Good Friday sermon emphasised that in the last days of his life on earth,

Christ was a prisoner. He no longer had freedom to pursue his ministry, to preach and heal. He must submit to captivity, mockery, violence and death. For this, as for any aggression, the whole world must seek forgiveness. Ruth found it difficult to concentrate because she had soon to perform, but her mind was filled with distracted thoughts about the bitter cruelty inflicted by Romans on the Jewish population, the despair and the dreadful death. She understood the point of the sermon, that the world, society as a whole, as well as every individual human, must seek forgiveness.

At the end of the Mass, the priests took their seats and the congregation was still, anticipating the new music. An aroma of incense hung in the atmosphere. The great altar piece, splendid, blue and gold, rose above them all. Vlad Glast took his place behind the timpani. Ruth sat at the front of the choir and stood as Lutoslawski came forward to conduct his work. The spare figure, dressed in black, turned and bowed briefly to the congregation. He stepped onto the raised podium, his head cast down. Then he looked up toward the choir. Above the narrow lips and flared nostrils, his intense gaze turned upon the soloist. This look, staring but somehow sensitive, expressing his purpose and confidence, would be an inspiration to Ruth. She loved his face, she loved his music, she loved this man and she loved every man. She would be singing a prayer for us all. Ruth was now over three months pregnant, her mind teeming, every sense sharpened and her spirits high. The organ played slow plangent chords. Ruth's voice, high and ethereal, now floated upwards, increasing in power as she sang slowly the four syllables of the one word; Lacrimosa. She watched the face and expression of the conductor more than his baton. Lutoslawski retained the same pedantic pace, as Ruth went on to sing the lower tones more softly than in rehearsal. His right hand with the baton kept time, the left held out with palm upwards meant that the singer should now use her own skill, judgement power and control.

Now, Ruth must wait while the organ continued, rapidly building to a crescendo. Lutoslawski brought in the choir with a new surge of sound. Drum beats marked the moment for Ruth to join again. Together, all reached the last words, Pacem, peace. They came over powerful but piteous, sung by Ruth over the choir. The soprano, shimmering like pale moonlight, seemed to project all human anguish throughout the medieval space. Lutoslawski was now keeping time, holding the baton clenched in both fists, lost in his emotion, weeping as his work reached its conclusion. It was as if the barometric pressure within the church had changed. The entire congregation were involved in this performance, committed to it by witnessing the perfect singing of a masterpiece.

The Lacrimosa is a hymn seeking forgiveness and peace, which, in the Christian tradition, is not earned by good behaviour but given to the faithful by the grace of God. These thoughts had lived with Ruth; indeed, she had suffered them while she was preparing for this occasion. It became both her finest singing, and her personal prayer. It was also her last public performance. The sombre waves rose and fell, supported by organ and timpani. It was as if the sound waded through dark waters, then fell throughout the great church, sonorous, deeply sad and yet clearly expressing her prayer that God would forgive. Lutoslawski stepped towards Ruth as the performance was completed. He held out his arms to her, and she found herself locked with him in a sudden, shuddering embrace. The emotion was too deep to interpret or explain. This music meant everything to all mankind, triumph and despair. There was prolonged silence, a stillness, until at last, the priests stood, bowed to the altar and moved in procession from the nave.

Before the congregation left the church, Maria looked anxiously at Witold. When the soprano voice first sounded, she had heard his sharp of intake of breath, a gulp for air. His body seemed to judder alongside hers. He was looking upwards but she saw an unwanted tear move down his face. He used a cuff to wipe it away. He said nothing as they remained in the church waiting to follow after the others. When she said she thought that the music had been wonderful, he replied with a non-committal noise, probably because he could not trust himself to speak. Maria did not know Witold well enough to guess whether his reaction was religious, musical, or concerned with the beauty of the singing. Agnieszka joined them, delighted with the performance of her friend. The conversation became normal and, before long, Witold participated with apparent ease.

The Lacrimosa is still performed. It forms part of a lost work including Requiem in Aeturnam by Lutoslawski. When he escaped from Warsaw a few days before The Uprising in 1944, he brought with him only the Lacrimosa. The rest of the work has never been found. When Poland was yet again struggling for freedom from the Soviet Union in the 1980s, this hymn was frequently sung in Poland by the great soprano, Stefania Woytowicz, accompanied only by an organ. The beautiful voice and the deep sadness of the words were both a call for better times and a reflection on the bitter struggle.

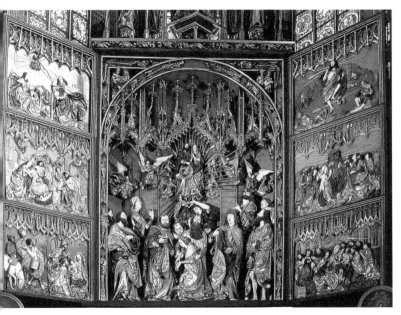

The Altarpiece which Veit Stoss created for the Mariacki Church Krakow between 1477 and 1489. This immense screen was removed during the German occupation but after the war it was recovered and is in its rightful position today.

PART TWO

Chapter 20: August–September 1939

Bruno, Witold and Lukas were allowed a weekend leave at the end of August 1939. BB spent time with Halina. They chose not to discuss the impending war. When they went to dinner with her parents, they followed the usual pattern by which Bruno spent the end of the evening discussing with his father-in-law the realities for Poland and its air force. They left the dining room and moved onto a terrace looking out over the flat agricultural landscape. Initially, they could see for miles, but the evening light gradually faded. Bruno knew that all of these fields belonged to his father-in-law. Two bats arrived, flickering in the twilight, twisting in the air and finding flies invisible to the two men. Jezioro lit a cigar and puffed out aromatic smoke. He began the discussion on a pessimistic note.

"Whatever happens, Poles need to fight with honour. We cannot submit now. I know the German forces are overwhelming, and I have less confidence than the journalists in the enthusiasm of the French to rescue us."

"Sir, you know far more than I about the international politics. In the air, our planes are fewer and slower but our training is based on the need to attack bombers. They won't get away with the tactics which they demonstrated in Spain. I am sure of that."

"That sounds good," replied Jezioro. "But I wish we had put the same money into fighter planes as maintenance of the splendid cavalry."

Bruno told him that the fighter squadrons had been moved from their established airfields and instructed to work in support of army units.

"It will work well, because we can make usable grass airfields on any flat field. It is so dry this summer."

His father-in-law agreed that the plan to move away from the known airfields was wise, because the Germans might invade at any time. "They will know where your existing airfields are, and will bomb them at daybreak on the first day. But the dry summer means low rivers, which are easier for the invaders to cross."

"Our real problem is to co-ordinate our defences. We know the Germans have good radios, but we are going to be out of contact with the ground forces from the minute we take off. If we can find the enemy, I am confident in our training. We have found that it is useless to fire from a distance. We know we must be close enough to bring down the enemy, and we have worked out how to do this."

At the end of their discussion, in a rare moment of frank emotion, Jezioro brought himself to express his feelings to his son-in-law:

"I would like you to know how much I admire your decision to join the Air Force. Whatever happens, be in no doubt that you are deeply respected here, by all of us."

"Sir, you have been supremely kind to both Halina and to me."

During his short leave, Witold said that he was taking the bus into Krakow.

"Are you going to say goodbye to Maria?" his mother asked.

"Probably."

Witold went to St Xavier's and knocked on the door of Ruth's flat. There was no response.

He went away. At an expensive ladies' outfitters, he bought a pair of fine grey leather gloves. They must be beautifully wrapped. The shop assistant smiled when Witold drew from his pocket a small silver trophy, asking her to put it in the box with the gloves. She raised her eyebrows, as she asked to read its inscription: "Aerobatics, Deblen Viktor Ludorum 1938." In the early afternoon, Witold returned to the flat, knocked again and heard slow and heavy footsteps descending the staircase. The door opened and there was the face he knew so well. But he also saw the swollen body of a woman in a late stage of pregnancy.

Witold had not really known what he would say to Ruth and was taken aback to see her condition. She spoke first.

"Zeleski! What can I do for you?"

"I am leaving for the air battle soon. I have come to say goodbye. I want to tell you what your singing has meant to me; what you have meant to me. I had not known…" He hesitated, unsure how to express his surprise to find her in this condition.

"Ah, this," said Ruth, pointing to her abdomen. Then to her mouth. "Shush. Tell no one at all. It's a secret; you promise?"

"Yes, Miss Neuman." He had never used any other name when he spoke to her, but months later, he perfected all that he should have said to Ruth, about going to fight for her, being content to die, but if he returned alive, he would do anything for her. It would have been the declaration worthy of a chivalric knight.

"I wish you the very best if it comes to war. I know you will be courageous and am confident in our success."

"I also wish you the very best," he said, lost for words and picking up on those she had just spoken.

"Good-bye then," said Ruth.

"Good-bye." Ruth wondered whether the tongue-tied young man had intended to make her a present of whatever might be inside the beautiful parcel he was carrying. She could never know, and dismissed the thought from her mind. The weather was warm and she was having difficulty in sleeping. The baby must be coming very soon.

Witold walked on through the humid city to the Hospital of the Daughters of Charity where Maria worked. He left a polite note for her, along with the pretty parcel. He had carefully removed from it the trophy, which he still wanted to give to Miss Neuman, if he could create an opportunity to do so. He had not said or done anything improper, but felt foolish about his visit. There was no danger that he would tell anyone about her condition.

When the mobilisation orders were broadcast on the radio, Witold's reaction was excitement and confidence. Lukas was more measured. He had been training for little more than a year. But the brothers had mastered all they had been taught. They were sure of their tactics, their own skill and their fellow airmen. They put on the uniforms they were proud to wear, and checked one another for correct appearance. They went downstairs, each with a small grip of luggage, and set off with their mother for the station. Agnieszka had dreaded this day, but was determined to be brave as she said goodbye. Witold and Lukas would not want to be embarrassed by tears as she gave each a last embrace. Lukas made a joke which was not very funny and all three laughed as if much amused. The sons boarded the train. The mothers, wives and girlfriends of several other airmen were on the platform, with handkerchiefs ready to first wave and then wipe their eyes.

Lukas asked Witold if Maria was coming to the station.

"No, we have already said all we can."

Another airman joined the conversation. "Much better not to have a wailing woman on the platform. I've done the same."

"It's not good for anyone's morale to see floods of tears," said Witold in agreement. Lukas was surprised by this remark. From what he had seen of Maria, she was entirely sensible and would never have made an emotional scene in public.

The steam engine was panting and emitting smutty smoke. Agnieszka grimaced towards it and took advantage of the excuse to say she would leave now. She wished them a good journey, said no more about its purpose, and turned away. The engine was making more noise as if the driver was struggling to restrain it. Soon they would be gone. Agnieszka went down the station steps and found her way to the Café de Paris. She dropped into a chair overlooking the market square. A waiter sought her order, which she gave briskly and turned away to look out into the vast open square. Krakow was cheerful, the horse-drawn carriages smartly turned out. They waited beside bars and cafés, bright with multi-coloured tablecloths and matching awnings against the mild sunshine. Agnieszka looked hard at the lively scene, concentrating on the details she knew so well.

When her tea came, and she turned from the square to look down, Agnieszka was horrified by two heavy tears dropping onto the tray of petit fours. She could not help recalling previous visits to this café as a young and proud mother of the two little boys. They attracted attention from other customers with their fair curly hair and admirably polite manners. She had brought them up to behave well whenever in public, and now she was making a little scene by herself. A flock of starlings swept in swooping circles around the buildings of the square, enjoying flight, companionship and offering to all the world a brilliant aerobatic display. Agnieszka kept her head up to watch the birds and distract her mind from its worry. But even the birds made her think of flying.

She suddenly finished her tea, left two coins on the table and set off for home. She had taken the pony and trap for this journey. The animal seemed to be sad and tired as it walked through the early evening. There were few sounds to accompany them. As she neared a barn, Agnieszka saw house martins lining up and chattering in preparation for their migration. The birds must be discussing the route South and expecting to make the journey Nature had prepared for them. Some might not survive, but all were getting ready to set off, to face whatever lay ahead. Agnieszka turned her mind away. The pony walked on, its head also down. There was no human presence. No one would see or hear her if she chose to sob now rather than keep her grief for her pillow. At last, Agnieszka gave way, crying and sobbing as she confronted the danger to her bright boys, her highest pride and her deepest joy. "Pray Jesus bring them home safe. I cannot bear a future without them."

She had borne them in her body, fed each at her breast far longer than most mothers and often kept the little child close in her bed, smelling of warm milky infancy. She nurtured them through childhood illnesses. She watched over them as they took first steps, then walked, ran and raced. Agnieszka patched up knees hurt when they came off bicycles ["Slow down a bit, Witold; you get there slower if you have to go to the hospital on the way."] She smoothed cream of camomile onto bruises when a sword fight played with sticks caused more harm than intended. ["Be more careful, Witold; if you kill your brother you will have no one to play with."] To her, they were the most handsome boys among dozens who took their first communion when Witold was eleven and Lukas nine. She stitched or knitted most of their clothes; she helped with homework. She watched with surprise and pleasure as they grew in size, in confidence and in understanding. They had responded with their own love for her. A goal at football, a prize for physics, each reported happily to his mother. She who had cherished these boys from their first breath could not bear to think of them in peril. But war meant dreadful danger to a fighter pilot. "Pray Jesus bring them home safe."

She turned the corner of the front drive and saw her husband sweeping the bricks of the yard. Had he heard her prayer? She was not sure if she had spoken these words out loud. But he saw her distress and came straight to her. Each held the other, words not needed now. She separated from his embrace. Piotr did not follow her. The old dog, Griff, looked at her, whined in sympathy and limped back to his kennel. Agnieszka turning away, disconsolate, went indoors, up to the bedroom and there, wept and wept. She experienced at its ultimate depth the truth that the child is the fulfilment of the mother's life: war is hardest for the mothers.

On the train, Witold found seats in a carriage already filling with cigarette smoke and light-hearted conversation. No one was discussing the German threat, the Polish government's response or the prospect of war. Witold appeared to be content to join a conversation about the cocktails and waitresses at Maxim's bar. To Lukas, this was a childish game. Everyone knew that there was serious danger, that war was highly likely, and to his mind, this should be the only topic of discussion. He withdrew into himself, avoided the eyes of others, and studied his reflection in the carriage window. What were the chances? How strong was the army? Would the German bombers be easy prey to the PZLs of the Polish air force, or would they be well-protected by the faster Messerschmitts which the Luftwaffe boasted about? Lukas fell into a shallow sleep, frequently waking and fitfully dreaming. In the next compartment, after much noisy banter and plenty of brandy, Witold and the group of airmen were running out of energy and optimism. They also began to sleep.

Witold was awakened by a vibration running through his body. It took a moment for him to realise that he was seated next to an airman who was shuddering and noiselessly weeping. Witold was embarrassed and said nothing. Then, he stretched and moved in the hope of waking his companion who should then realise where he was and control himself. The shuddering continued. The young man was awake. He looked at Witold.

"I know we are finished. I have no chance. I will never come home. This war brings death. I cannot bear it. I have not even finished my training and will be hopeless against the Luftwaffe."

He was now tearful and red in the face, breathing in gulps of air between his sobs and exhaling in great brandy-laden sighs of despair. His body leaned against Witold, as if he sought some physical comfort. Perhaps he wanted Witold to put an arm around his juddering shoulder. To Witold, this behaviour was unmanly and intolerable. He was also tired and had no time to offer sympathy.

"Who do you think you are?" he demanded. "Get away from me. We have to fight as we have been trained to do. If we have the right spirit, we will surely win." Such words were cheap and useless. Witold knew they carried no conviction and would give no comfort. He moved back to the first compartment, saw Lukas asleep and found a seat opposite him. Just before Witold closed his eyes, he looked at Lukas, and, seeing his eyes open, made a sign with his thumb to his mouth to show he had had too much to drink. Lukas offered in response a mild shake of the head in mock disapproval.

It was late morning when the train pulled into their final station. On arrival, Bruno was waiting with the transport and gave them the news that their squadron had been transferred from its established base to an airstrip close to the Headquarters of Army Group Krakow. Witold was concerned to find that his tearful companion was also assigned to this Army Group. However, the young pilot was looking more normal. Witold went up to him, now feeling able to offer a show of cheerful confidence, but it seemed that the man had no recollection of his conduct during the journey.

Chapter 21: The Invasion

Hitler's Directive No 1 for the Conduct of the War:

> *Since the situation on Germany's Eastern frontier has become intolerable, I have decided upon a solution by force. The attack on Poland will be undertaken ...Date of attack 1st September 1939.*

The fighter squadron had been ordered to move from its previous base because it was likely that the Germans knew its position. "Let them bomb an empty airfield," said Bruno.

They were to be under the control of army units, which Lukas and Witold thought might be a mistake. Military officers would have minimal knowledge of how to use the air force. Bruno's flight were committed to an army group well to the West of Krakow on the Obra river. Bruno met the colonel in charge of the soldiers who had no time to deal with the air force, and when asked about replenishing fuel supplies, had no suggestions to make. They could provide ammunition for the machine guns, and if they needed help in levelling the landing strip, he had plenty of manpower and spades. The strip was already good enough for the PZL planes, and the pilots had no further work to offer the soldiers. Alongside the airstrip, there was a small hut available to the airmen awaiting orders, but it had only a bench and a table, not even a telephone.

The colonel was a regular army officer, with abundant pale moustaches festooning his face like rope running from ear to ear. He was eager to repel the enemy with or without aeroplanes. His men were digging a trench beside the road and he gave out firm instructions about how to handle the anti-tank units. A fuel truck arrived, to the delight of the airmen, leaving half of its his load at the base. The driver had orders to move on to another squadron several miles away. Bruno checked the map reference so that his flight might refuel there once they had been in combat. He suggested to the colonel that any earthworks to protect the fuel would be worthwhile, because they might face bombing or strafing if the Luftwaffe were able to follow planes back to the base.

On 4th September, the colonel received orders to hold a bridge over the Obra river. Additional trenches were prepared. An anti-aircraft gun had already been set up, in anticipation that the defenders might be targeted by German bombers. They learned that the Germans had crossed the border in force. The colonel took the initiative to prepare demolition charges to destroy the bridge if he could not hold it. Before they finished for the day, Bruno had a last discussion with the colonel.

"I don't want to bring it down. This is a fine old bridge which has lasted a hundred years. But if it is also a route in for the German tanks, what can we do?" Bruno agreed that there was no other choice.

Early in the evening, Bruno and Witold searched for the colonel to clarify their instructions for the next day. They were told that he was with the Signals unit and directed to a nearby tent. The colonel was giving orders to a junior officer about a message to be sent to the general close to the Front. There was a rapid discussion about the news that the Polish army was under attack to the North and West. There was no suggestion that there might be an imminent assault on the river. Bruno proposed that at dawn, his flight should take off, both to support any units under attack and to bring back information for the colonel. This was immediately accepted. Witold had recognised the Signals officer and turned to him. "It's Lutoslawski, isn't it?"

"Yes, I am sorry. Have we met before?" asked Lutoslawski, gravely. He was concerned that he ought to recognise this officer who plainly knew him.

"I was just in the audience, I mean the congregation, when you conducted your music at The Mariacki a couple of months ago."

Lutoslawski smiled at the recollection.

"Feels like a different life, not a few months. I am glad that you remember it, although the piece is a bit gloomy for the present. She is a beautiful soprano, Ruth Neuman, who made the very best of what I had written. It was more than I dreamed possible."

The composer turned back to his Morse code equipment, the fingers accustomed to a piano keyboard ready to seek orders from a distant general.

The two airmen walked back, Witold feeling embarrassed to have brought Ruth's name into the conversation. The three friends never discussed Ruth although Bruno was constantly aware that the brothers knew what had happened between them three years ago. He had never mentioned his return in December 1938. To move the conversation away from Lutoslawski or Ruth,

---

The composer Lutoslawski was captured with other members of his signals unit in September. The musician escaped and reached Warsaw. He lived there, supporting himself by playing in cafés.

he opened a discussion about the tactics needed tomorrow, and this continued as all the members of the flight met for their evening meal.

At the end of a long day, Bruno sought out the brothers to make an unusual request. They shared a room so small that he must stand in the doorway.

"Heaven knows what will happen. But I have one thing I need to ask if I don't make it. I guess they are never going to get us all, so if the Germans kill me, I need to know that you will deliver two letters in Krakow for me." He gave to each of them an envelope which had instructions inside.

"Please just keep them safe for now, and when we have won the war, you can return them to me. But if not, please, one of you make sure they reach their destinations."

Although Witold had said nothing about Ruth being pregnant, he and Lukas guessed that these letters must be to Bruno's wife and to Ruth Neuman. Witold's mind returned to Ruth and he remained awake long into the night, somewhat annoyed by the deep breathing of his brother who seemed to have no qualms about the fighting required next day.

The following morning, they were ready to take off at dawn. There was a delay because there should have been eight PZLs in the flight, but Witold's machine had developed an engine fault when tested the previous evening. The fitters had failed to solve the problem and were still working on the engine. Having slept so badly, he was almost relieved that he must watch as the seven planes now started to move ahead over the rough airstrip, rocking and then bouncing as they neared take-off speed. Stray leaves, twigs and acorns were thrown up as they accelerated, engines booming. Witold felt that he was with his brother in spirit, left hand on the throttle to maintain speed, and right hand on the joystick to keep the nose well up. On take-off, the tail came up smoothly and the gull wings now cut the air more cleanly. Watching, Witold saw the squadron increasing speed and the planes receding into the distance. The noise faded to a mere rumble in the West and then to nothing. Witold turned back to the workshop where the mechanics had most of the Skoda engine on a make-shift work bench. He offered help and spent an hour learning how little he understood of the machinery he depended upon. Then, he returned to the hut where he sat still and brooding, his thoughts revolving around the circle of his friends.

He re-tied the silk scarf which he wore inside his shirt collar. As usual, he had brazenly copied Bruno's choice of clothing.

"Good idea these silk scarves. Much more comfortable if you are turning your head as much as you should. You will see the German in time to break away," Bruno had said, then he added to lighten the message:

"Wear a fine silk scarf for elegance and because it will also save your life!"

Witold continued to cudgel his brain about the two letters to be delivered if Bruno were killed. They were evidence that he could not rate their chances very highly. He also began to think what might happen if Poland were successfully invaded. Would the French really come to the assistance of their ally? Would the British? There were no answers to these huge questions.

His mind turned to consider his final meeting with Ruth. He pondered what he should have said, playing over the words which he should have spoken and working out how she might have replied. In truth, he had been so shocked to see that she was pregnant that his disconcerted brain offered nothing sensible for him to say. He must have looked foolish, and the beautifully wrapped present might have added to his ridiculous appearance. But pregnancy without marriage was scandalous in the eyes of proper Polish society. Such misconduct would never be mentioned. Witold assumed that Ruth's pregnancy and her decision to keep it secret meant that the father had not proposed marriage to her. One reason might be that he was not free to do so, a married man. Taken with the reference to two letters, Witold drew the conclusion that the father must be Bruno. If so, Ruth was in serious trouble. She badly needed a husband. Few men would marry a "fallen woman." But he, Witold, with his romantic notions and increasing devotion to a woman he scarcely knew, would offer himself to her. So he was thinking, as his eyes closed, and sleep overtook him.

Through the open doorway of the shed there ventured a weasel, either exceptionally hungry or foolishly inquisitive. The little animal eventually startled Witold when investigating the small stock of apples on a table. Looking up, his head movement frightened the weasel which jumped away and through the door into the sunshine. Witold picked up an apple and bit into it. He had not realised how tired he was. He took only two bites before his eyes closed again. The weasel returned, observed the motionless man and reached the apple bowl. Witold stirred, momentarily awake, and the animal fled.

Witold slept again, and was eventually disturbed by the sound of approaching aircraft engines. As he woke, he saw the weasel now had an apple in its jaws. They both leapt for the doorway, Witold only concerned to know if the aircraft were the enemy, or his flight returning. They were PZLs not Germans. How many? One arrived but the others appeared soon after Bruno had landed. There had been an easy victory over Stuka dive-bombers. Two had been shot down, and Bruno decided not to pursue the others in order to conserve fuel and lest they led the flight into awaiting Messerschmitts.

The squadron waited for orders, but when none came, Bruno decided that there should be another search at the end of the day. They set out and returned to tell Witold that they had seen no German planes but burning farms and roads full of refugees. They had also seen German trucks full of soldiers. Bruno was regretting his decision not to attack the invading troops from the air. The real reason behind this decision was that he was reluctant to machine gun German soldiers who would be unable to defend themselves. He told himself that he was following orders to shoot down enemy planes. Since they had not seen any German bombers or fighters, they began to speculate that the Luftwaffe might be frightened of the Polish airmen, but Bruno would not allow this line of thinking to develop. The Luftwaffe had gained experience in the Spanish Civil War; the Me109 was much faster than the PZL and would fire four machine guns instead of two. The German fliers had never tasted defeat and would not be fearful.

On the 5th September, Witold's plane was repaired and the first flight of four set off soon after dawn. Four bellowing engines disturbed the peaceful countryside as the planes lifted off, the judder of the racing undercarriage ceased and to the pilots it was as if a heavy weight had lifted from each plane as the PZLs became airborne. They had received no orders, and had no information about where they might find the Luftwaffe.

Bruno decided that they should find and attack the German army anywhere in the Warta region to the North West. It was a day of bright blue sky but dappled with occasional clouds. Flying away from the rising sun, they could see columns of smoke ahead, while below there were peaceful oak copses and a church spire. When Bruno saw the main road crossing their route, he turned to follow it, and now the Polish airmen saw the invading army for the first time. A long line of vehicles, some drawn by horses, was heading East. Having seen burning farms and refugees on the roads, Bruno decided to aim for the front of the column in order to attack commanders, better equipped units and then cause a blockage to the German progress. Did he think this out? Perhaps it was a more primitive instinct to aim for the head of any attack.

The Polish planes rapidly overtook the German column and saw, ahead of the leading tanks, crowds of Polish fleeing from the enemy. There were a few vehicles, moving slowly, some horse-drawn carts, and at least one carriage. Most of the moving rabble were carrying possessions in sacks or bundles, refugees in their own land. The Polish fighters would attack the tanks in the German vanguard. The Second Light Division had only one battalion of tanks, preceded by a motorcycle reconnaissance unit. The Polish planes swept down, now very close to the ground, where they encountered fitful firing from German troops in the column. They came in at less than two hundred miles an hour, following Bruno in line astern. Each pilot aimed for the individual Panzer he had selected and most recalled Bruno's advice to fire at the tank tracks, disable the enemy and leave him vulnerable. The tactics worked well, and two tanks came to a halt. Bruno led the flight in a tight turn and came back, flying close to the ground and hoping to attack enemy soldiers escaping from stationary tanks. They were unsuccessful because the Germans remained in the tanks, but Bruno himself saw the look of astonished despair on the face of the officer in the leading tank. The heavy vehicle was slowly describing a circle in the road propelled by only one track.

They dived ready to fire on the infantry lorries, but Bruno then saw ahead of them a mass of German bombers flying at low level. He turned towards them and the rest of the flight followed. They were flying in line abreast as they tore into the German bombers. In training, they had found the greatest difficulty in hitting a moving target from the side. From the rear, the attacker would be bucketing about in the bomber's slipstream so that accurate shooting was impossible. "Head on hits hardest" was a phrase they all learned. They had also found out that to expend ammunition at a distance was a useless waste. The four planes sped on, straight for the formation of Heinkels, and as the bombers dived to avoid them, they were plastered with short-range machine-gun fire. "Use only enough ammunition to take out one bomber, then find another target," Bruno had taught his team. Now he had to put his method into practise. Each had less than a minute of ammunition in the pair of machine guns, and when this was used up, Bruno turned back heading for the airfield to re-arm and refuel. Two Heinkels had been shot down and at least another two had been damaged. Lukas was sure that he had sent one down because he had seen the crew parachuting from the burning plane.

They retraced their outward journey, observing the same church spire and copse of oak trees before they saw the cloud of smoke over the base. The Bridge over the Obra had been destroyed, but they did not know whether this was done by the colonel's demolition charges or German bombing. The fine old bridge was lost for all time, whether destroyed by Poles or by the invaders. The Germans had bombed the defending soldiers, striking the few buildings around the landing strip, but had missed one of the fuel stores. Bruno led the flight down and the following pilots saw his plane swerve and bounce as he avoided or went into damaged parts of the strip. Lukas was less fortunate and his PZL suffered some damage to the undercarriage. The colonel and his infantry had withdrawn, taking with them the air force ground crew. Bruno could see the bodies of a few Polish soldiers, but there were no blue air force uniforms amongst them. The airmen carried out their own refuelling and Lukas and Bruno managed to lever the twisted undercarriage into its correct position. Then it was reinforced with a steel rod, wire and tape.

"Good enough to take off. But you had better miss the potholes when you land," said Bruno.

"Let's hope we will be landing on some smooth runway."

"Small chance of that."

Fuelling and rearming took time, spent anxiously looking skyward lest bombers should return. No one thought of finding food, let alone spending time on the ground consuming it.

When they took off again, the mood amongst all the Polish pilots was just as determined, but their elation at their early success was tempered by the progress made by the invaders. Before long, Bruno saw, on his right, a dozen German planes flying slowly towards the German border. His flight altered course to pursue them. He recognised the gull wing shape of a Stuka dive-bomber. The Germans flew on together. If they had seen the formation of PZLs, surely, they would have broken formation and scattered. As he closed, Bruno could see the black swastika on the tail of the last plane.

The Polish attack came out of the sun and caught the Stukas by surprise. Lukas watched the angular shapes of the German planes as the distance reduced. The pilots, heading for some airstrip on the German border, were unaware of any danger. Lukas heard the sound of Bruno's machine guns to his left.

The Stuka he was aiming for began to dive and the tail gunner started firing at Lukas. He dropped the nose for an instant and delayed firing until very close. He saw his bullets skipping along the hull from the cockpit to the tail where the gunner suddenly slumped in his seat. Then the Stuka exploded and fragments of metal caught the PZL, which Lukas now took in a short dive below the Germans. Lukas grinned, because he had done what he planned, to get close, fire a short burst and break away. As intended, he had used little of his ammunition. He saw Bruno's distinctive marking above him, following their established plan to attack first from above and then again from below. Lukas also moved upwards to fire on two planes in the German formation. The first of these Stukas was on fire and fell out of sight. Lukas used up his last ammunition on the second one, but as he did so, he suddenly saw above them all the distinctive shapes of the dreaded Messerschmitt 109s.

The two German planes had the advantage of height, speed and surprise. Bruno must have spotted them at the same time as Lukas for he abandoned his attack and headed towards some clouds. He had been seen by one of the Germans who dived after him. Lukas was now following both planes but flying much more slowly than the German. Bruno would never reach the cloud in time. The Messerschmitt fired two bursts. The second struck the engine. The nose of the PZL dipped, out of control. It twisted upside down. Lukas saw an arm emerge from the cockpit, then Bruno was out of the burning plane and falling. His parachute opened. Lukas was badly shaken by what had happened. Looking down, he lost height and remained fixated on Bruno's parachute. Then he saw the Messerschmitt ahead and below. It had gone past the burning plane but now turned back and went into a shallow dive. It was heading for the parachute.

Lukas watched, horrified and furious. He was witnessing the German pilot preparing to execute a man suspended in a parachute. The roar of the approaching aircraft must have alerted Bruno before the machine guns rattled again. He was staring directly at the enemy pilot. He had time for a last thought. Was it hatred, or fear or the loss of love? Lukas saw the body jerk as machine gun bullets ripped into the chest. Lukas was now acting on pure adrenalin and animal instinct. He was diving at maximum revs, the plane dropping like a hawk onto a partridge. The PZL would never have cut the air faster. Lukas concentrated on his single chance to strike at speed and from above. He had no ammunition left. He steadied the plane in its power dive and corrected his course to bring the undercarriage down on the tail of the Messerschmitt. There was a bang, a jolt then a grinding noise. A part of the Messerschmitt, visible to his right, tipped upwards as the machine fell out of the sky. One wing must have caught the propeller of the PZL. Lukas did not see this, but heard the roar of the engine increase as it was no longer turning the propeller. Automatically, Lukas reduced throttle so that the engine was idling. His plane was falling, but the rudder and flight controls still worked. Further reserves of adrenalin were pumping through him. This must be a crash landing. He was too low to bale out. The Air Force trainers at Deblen had taught Lukas that if he had lost power and had to bring his plane down, he must switch off the engine.

"Unless you want immediate cremation."

"Against my religion," Lukas had replied. The words came back to him. He cut the fuel and the engine noise stopped. He was in silence, gliding, looking for flat ground. He avoided a scrub of trees, and now saw ahead the hillside sheep pasture, rough and uneven. Into this terrain he must crash his plane, breaking his right leg and ankle, and swearing as he lost consciousness.

In the pasture, a shepherd and his son had arrived to move the sheep on to another field. They watched the air battle. They saw one plane on fire, the parachute opening and the figure of the descending pilot swinging in the sky like a pendulum. The victorious plane slowly dropped, turned and now came in to fire on the pilot. A third plane dived into view. It cut across the path of the German and dropped onto it. It was the turn of the victor to be vanquished, his plane diving into the hillside where it exploded. But the third plane was also coming down. Its engine had stopped and the fields regained their usual quiet. The plane was losing height. It came over a little wood to reach the open pasture. The sheep were not disturbed because it made no sound. The pilot was visible, working some controls and intent on keeping the wings above the ground. The plane struck the field, first with its landing wheels, but then with one wing. The plane began to rotate, held by the upper wing digging into the hillside. The lower wing flailed around, catching one sheep and flinging it high into the air before the machine came to a halt. Finally, the bloody body of the sheep landed and the shepherds ran to rescue the pilot.

Lukas was always in pain and only sometimes fully conscious as the shepherds extricated him from his plane, gave him fiery spirits to revive him, and eventually, shoved him onto a cart heading for Krakow.

At the Hospital of the Daughters of Charity Krakow, Lukas was embarrassed to see his brother's girlfriend, Maria. He was unable to leave the bed after the leg fracture had been re-set and he needed to use a bedpan. He felt foolishly anxious that she might be the nurse who would empty it for him. But she was coming to see him for another reason.

"Lukas, I heard that you were here, and want to explain something I have been told. When the Germans reach the hospital, they will take as prisoners of war any serviceman able to walk. Very soon, you will be mobile on crutches and if they see that you are listed as serving in the air force, you will become a prisoner of war. I don't know where they will take you, but you may not get the treatment you need. We must get the record changed so it shows that you are not in the forces. You might have been injured in a bombing raid."

Lukas absorbed her point rapidly. He was already thinking of getting away to Romania as other escaping airman were doing. A prisoner-of-war camp might be deep inside Germany. They agreed that Maria would take away his uniform. Further, she was able to set up the appearance of a traction device to make it look as if he needed long-term treatment on the ward. When the Germans inspected the hospital, they found Lukas in the fracture ward, his left leg elevated for traction, and his occupation recorded as office worker. They did not need to check that his personal effects included only civilian clothing.

Two days later, Maria returned to his bedside. She had heard about the German attitude to servicemen who were badly injured. There were rumours of shootings followed by the pretence that the injured man had been shot when trying to escape. Even a badly burnt officer with his eyes covered in bandages had been killed.

"Lukas, it was my idea to pretend that you are a civilian. If this is discovered, both of us are in dreadful trouble."

That evening, "Dr Lukas" limped out of a hospital lavatory wearing a white coat and with a stethoscope around his neck. His lower leg was in plaster and he had a surgical boot on the foot. A pair of spectacles, a hat and his walking stick made him look much older as he was accompanied by Maria in her nurse's uniform to the hospital entrance. He spent the afternoon in a café while Maria finished her shift.

Lukas had been thinking carefully. "There are two things I want to talk about, if you don't mind. First, I need to deliver two letters for our flight commander who was killed last week. I have opened the packet he gave me and I know where to go. Second, I am absolutely determined to get to Romania and then join the French and English in the fight against the Nazis. I would like your assessment of when I should be fit enough to make a long journey."

Maria talked it over with Lukas. Eventually, she said:

"I suggest that you stay in Podgorze tonight. It will be easy to find you a room. Tomorrow, you deliver these letters if you really must. Then, you need to get out of the city and into some country place where the Germans may leave people in peace. You won't be able to walk properly for at least three months and it would be foolish to attempt any sort of journey before December."

Lukas found it easy to agree to her suggestions and made his plans to take Bruno's letters to Ruth and Halina on the following morning.

Chapter 22: Ruth and Halina

"Only people who are capable of loving strongly can suffer great sorrow."

Leo Tolstoy

Lukas remembered the charming house in the country where Bruno and his wife had entertained the brothers while still at school. Leaning on a walking stick and with his ankle in plaster, he rang the doorbell. A maid answered and showed him into the small front room. He felt apprehensive and scarcely appreciated the sunlit tranquillity of the space with its scent of cut flowers and beeswax polish. The maid returned and told him that he would find Mrs Berling in the garden. He went out through French windows onto a lawn. Halina was on her knees working in a flower bed. He approached her, holding the envelope and now feeling embarrassed and anxious.

"I am not sure if you would remember me, Mrs Berling, but once, you and your husband invited me and my brother to have dinner here when he was teaching us at St Xavier's."

Before she could reply, Lukas went on. "He has been a wonderful example for both of us, but I have to give you very sad news." The meeting did not end well. Halina broke down, the maid came out of the house to assist, and Lukas had difficulty in persuading the maid to receive the envelope addressed to Halina.

Halina, like every wife in wartime, had thought about receiving news of her husband's death. Soon after Lukas had departed, she sent the maid back to her place and sat alone in her sitting room. There remained, on the little mantelpiece, the vase of flowers which she had picked the previous day. The room was bright in the morning sunshine. She drew a little strength and calm from the domestic comfort and sense of peace she habitually enjoyed here. She stood up and opened the envelope.

Dearest Halina.

I send you this letter knowing that you will have heard what has happened to me. As we have been preparing, our hopes have been high, but we also know that the numbers and the equipment of the Germans are in a different league from ours. We will do our best, hazard everything and trust that our country will not be defeated in the battle.

Above all, I need to assure you of my love and to say, as perhaps I have failed to express, that for me you have been the perfect wife. I have loved you sincerely and you have been a source of the deepest happiness and pride for me. When I am gone, I hope that you will only remember me with your loving kindness and not hold against me all my faults and failings, especially the main one which is the subject of the second letter enclosed within this one. You have been my true love, the love of my life. If God had granted it, I would have wanted to live out our lives with the same affection we have shared since we first met. These years may be taken from us by a vicious invader. If it comes to it, I must miss these years for which we both hoped, but must do all I can in defence of Poland. Remember me to your father whose generosity and kindness towards me has been a source of great satisfaction. I know how proud he is of his beautiful daughter and it has been an honour to have been so warmly treated by all of your family.

I have something very bad to confess to you, and this is written in the smaller envelope. Read it when you have strength, and please, also when you might find the power to forgive your ever-loving B.

Halina stood with her head bowed on her breast, like a rose broken at the stem. She knew that this second envelope must be opened. She grimaced and tore it open.

My own dearest Halina,

I have written only the truth thus far. I must continue now, because I have had to make an important disposition in my Will before going to war. The whole truth is that I made a mistake in allowing my heart to be captured for several months two years ago. I came to my senses after this time, and decided that the best course was to leave the school where the temptation resided, and join the Air Force. But then, at Christmas last year, when I returned for the carol service, I saw this lady again, and could not resist one last act. I most bitterly regret this, Halina. This is no reflection upon you, who I have always loved. There has never been any confusion about this. But I was sorely tempted. I alone am to blame. If I live on in some undeserved afterlife, I will watch over you, my dearest, and hope that you will find all the happiness and fulfilment you deserve.

I need to explain that after the school concert in December, she has written to me to say that she is expecting a child. I have therefore re-written my Will to provide for this child. I cannot keep this from you and feel it is better that you know everything about your loving husband, Bruno.

Lukas returned to the city to find Ruth in her flat at St Xavier's. When Lukas brought the envelope to Ruth, he said that it contained dreadful news, but he had been told just to hand it to her. Ruth nodded, scarcely taking in the words he spoke. Then she saw the handwriting on the envelope addressed to her.

"Pourquoi? Il e m ...." she could not say the final word.

"Oui, Mademoiselle," replied Lukas in the same language. "Je regrette infiniment."

Ruth understood.

Her figure seemed much fuller than he remembered. The baby made a sound from her bedroom. Lukas took no notice of this, concentrating on Ruth alone. She held herself together only long enough to usher the messenger to her door. Bruno had written of his deep respect for her, his gratitude for her kindness to him, and explained that if she contacted a certain lawyer, she would find the provision he had made for "our child." She collapsed then; she wept and remained incapable of any action until the next morning. Then, after very little sleep, she was awakened by the crying infant. She fed the baby. She slept again. Then she rose, needing to think. Her world contained only disasters. The failed love. The accidental pregnancy. The beautiful baby. No father. The Nazi invasion. Her Jewish race.

Two days after receiving the news, Ruth had made her decision and was determined to put it into action. Through her pregnancy, Ruth had lent on her friend Agnieszka for support and practical help. The fact that her sons had spoken so highly of Bruno made it easier for her to explain what had happened between them. It was Agnieszka who had found the medical help she needed. Agnieszka had given her the baby's cot and helped her to start feeding from the breast.

When Ruth needed her now, Agnieszka rose to the occasion. The two women, carefully dressed, set out in the little pony trap one September morning. Agnieszka watched over little Bruno in the travelling cot. Ruth did her utmost not to look at the little face. With the appearance of well-dressed visitors, they arrived outside the house of Halina Berling before mid-day. Ruth had told Agnieszka that she would first speak with Halina alone and asked her to wait. There was black crepe on the well-polished door knocker, and a modern bell-push beside the door. Ruth calmed her breathing just as she was accustomed to doing before a recital. She pressed firmly and a bell jangled within the neat house. A maid answered the door.

"May I speak with Madam Berling, if she is at home?"

The maid had no instructions to turn away any visitor.

"Please come in, and I will tell her you have come. May I ask what name to say?"

"Miss Neuman."

"May I ask you to wait in the morning room?" and she opened the door for Ruth.

It was this morning room that Halina entered, wondering who might have come to see her. She thought it must be someone from church who had come to offer condolences.

Looking at her visitor, she saw the cloud of dark hair, the delicate features and the deep eyes beneath the fine eyebrows. She gave the impression of intensity. Halina found all this intriguing and had a vague recollection that she had seen this face before.

"Good morning, Miss Neuman."

"Madam," said Ruth, who had decided to use the most formal language in this conversation. "I have come to offer to you my most sincere apology. What has happened has been the worst thing I have done in all my life, and I do not know if you could ever forgive it. Madam, I have been the music teacher at Saint Xavier's for four years, and have been guilty of a dreadful act involving your husband. I am very sorry to add to your distress at this time." She indicated the mourning gown which Halina wore.

As these words were spoken, Halina realised who this visitor was. Her reaction might have been to dismiss her at once, but an apology offered with such transparent sincerity was impossible to reject. Perhaps Ruth, who had much less training in social behaviour and manners, instinctively knew that deep contrition was a valuable opening.

"You ...", began Halina but stopped her exclamation as Ruth continued in her expression of remorse.

"Madam," Ruth went on, gathering some new strength, "your husband left the school which he loved because of this. He wrote to me to explain and I accepted that it was finished. Madam, I need to say that he has always loved you. He said this and I knew it. However, I need to confess more to you..."

"What?" responded Halina whether in exclamation or as a question.

"Madam, after the Christmas concert in December, he saw me. I was most distressed and he comforted me. Then another act. I cannot explain. I cannot excuse this. I take all the blame. He wrote again to say we must never meet again. He is, was, a good man. He was a great man. He loved you sincerely. Alas, as you see, I also loved him. I had never known anything about love before. And then I found that I was expecting his child. I had no experience or understanding. I thought I must write to him to tell him this, so he knew."

"You!" Halina said again. Perhaps she was going to say something offensive, but Ruth ploughed on, now using language which she had thought over and designed to achieve what she needed from Halina. "And so, I have this baby, now three weeks old. He is beautiful. I love him as much as any mother must do. I have not registered his birth, nor brought him for baptism yet. I have told no-one who is his father. What can I do for him? He has little chance with me. The school is closed. I have no profession to pursue here. I am trapped in Poland and cannot re-join my family in France. And Madam, although no one knows this, and I worship in Christian churches, my family is Jewish. The Nazis...." her voice broke and there was a pause.

Rallying again, she said, "I believe that those who have died and love us may continue to watch over us. I feel sure that the father would wish that you..," her voice broke and she could only whisper the words, "care for his son." There was a momentary silence between the women. Ruth added, "Not me."

A full minute now passed. Ruth was sobbing soundlessly. She had pleaded her case like a skilled advocate, but with such intensity that she was now exhausted and swaying on her feet. As she sank towards a couch, she said what she had come to ask.

"Madam, if you would take this baby as your own son, he will be perfectly cared for and you will be proud of him."

Halina said nothing. She sat down, astonished at the proposal put to her. Both women remained seated for a moment, but the position of Halina's chair made it unnecessary for either to look into the face of the other. It was Ruth who recovered the initiative and now that the speech was over, she became a stage director. "I will tell my friend to bring him to you." She walked towards the door, leaving Halina, still seated and in shock. Ruth went to the front door, beckoned to Agnieszka and, as she came across the road with the little crib, she whispered, "Tell her his name." She pointed to the little room and then left the house and crossed the road. Sitting in the trap, her mind trusted that Agnieszka would return alone but her heart hoped that she would come back with the child. She had done her best for Bruno.

Agnieszka glided into the morning room. She was of middle age, carefully and modestly dressed, with a tall figure and braided silver hair. She spoke perfect Polish with an accent which Halina must associate with a cultured position in society.

"This is Bruno," she said. "He is so beautiful."

Halina looked at the infant and, she later told herself, she knew she could not turn away this last link with her husband.

"Thank you for bringing him. If it is possible, I would like to avoid seeing Miss Neuman just now. It is difficult. I cannot find forgiveness for her." Halina was sure that she had seen this woman before, but could not recall the time or place.

Agnieszka replied, "I understand. And so will she. If I may say so, it seems to me that you have been most gracious. And by taking the child, you are most generous in your forgiveness." Halina heard these words from someone she did not know, but recognised the truth within them.

The following morning, when Halina's mind was clearer, she discussed with her mother how to present to the outside world the arrival of her son. It would not be too difficult, they decided. She suddenly remembered where she had seen Ruth Neuman before. She had sung that slow and haunting music in The Mariacki at Easter. Her mother, who had gone to the Good Friday service with her, also remembered the black hair and beautiful voice. "A remarkable woman," she said. Neither would see Ruth again.

Lukas had complied with the instructions of his former teacher, flight lieutenant and dear friend. It had taken most of a day, when he needed to get ready for an escape from Krakow and make whatever arrangements he could to move on when fit enough to do so. He never wavered in his determination to reach France and continue the fight there. His mother had also heard rumours about the Nazis' treatment of prisoners of war, and was keen to help him on his way. She could not tell whether the Germans would seek out their little patch of fertile ground, but if they were left alone, Piotr said that they could take care of themselves. She lent to her son and Maria the little trap and sturdy pony which would carry them on towards the Romanian border.

Maria left Lukas in no doubt that he required medical care or he would never fly again.

"You need me now, and if I can do my part for Poland by going abroad with you, I am ready to do so. I will come with you all the way to France if necessary."

They set off at first light, and although there were others on the roads leading East, their map showed them a route leading to tracks towards the Carpathian Mountains and eventually, to the town of Kuty on the Romanian border.

They travelled for two long days. Lukas had time to appreciate to the full the resourcefulness of his brother's girl-friend. At the end of each day when the pony was tiring, she walked alongside to encourage the animal and lighten its load. Similarly, with Lukas, she made him relax and even laugh. Her cheerful imagination and sense of humour entertained him. She invented the idea that the horse had the mind of an elderly maiden aunt.

"Young people today, no manners nor etiquette. Just fancy, two young people getting into a trap without any proper hats. Indeed, I am not sure the young man has combed his hair this morning…" In truth, Lukas was a serious young man, but he joined in with Maria's nonsense as best he could.

On the second day, they were in the foothills of the Carpathians, where there was a variety of scenery and wildlife. They saw deer, grazing watchfully, and some of the lower slopes contained cattle in bleak pastures. There were a few isolated homesteads. Storks flew purposefully in line overhead, aiming for the place their instinct and destiny had ordained for them. The humans moved on at a slower speed and in a different direction. Compared with the storks, they were unsure of their route and their destination. Lukas was glad to have the opportunity to think over the recent tumultuous days, or at least to allow his mind to come to terms with all that had happened.

In the late afternoon, Lukas had been silent and thoughtful for a long time, as the trap swayed and jolted on its journey. Maria left him with his own cares for a while and then said directly:

"Would you like to tell me what happened, about your last flight and the crash?"

"No. Really; not yet."

"So much has happened. You need time. No need to talk about it now."

Then, realising that it might be good for Lukas to think about something else, she asked him to tell her about his flying training. Lukas did his best to describe the atmosphere of the Air Force Flying School at Deblen, tense but enthusiastic, his training in bi-planes and the thrill of his first solo flights. At first, Maria responded with interest, but before long, she fell asleep, her body leaning against his and swaying gently as the pony pulled them along the path. Lukas knew how busy she had been and could feel no irritation that she had stopped listening to his monologue. Her mind and body were taking the chance to rest. Lukas looked up at the pale sky, where a buzzard had slowed and was now hovering high above some moving mammal. But the bird changed its mind, or the prey disappeared and the hunter flew on.

At the end of the day, they reached a high, wooded silent country, far from any village. They saw a shepherd, coming down the slope with a dog. When they asked if they might stay somewhere, he directed them to a cottage two miles away and hidden at the edge of the wood. It was not easy to find. The single-storey dwelling belonged to a peasant called Leon and his wife. Their sons were both in the army and they did not know whether they were alive nor where they might be. Maria's face showed her understanding as she offered her sympathy. The couple seemed surprised by such human warmth from a stranger. It was simple to reach an agreement to rent the sons' room until it was needed. The woman could not look at Maria as she told her she did not know when that might be. Limping slowly around the trap, Lukas unloaded their possessions, including the poultry and rabbits which his mother had provided. Leon brought in some additional furniture and Maria made up two beds. After supper, Maria was given an oil lamp and Lukas hobbled after her into the bedroom, where he now found himself alone with her.

Maria laughed. "You look confused, Lukas. I think it's easier than you think. You get your night clothes ready by your bed, I will do the same and then douse the lamp."

She giggled. "You should look disappointed, you know."

Lukas laughed with her. "You have all the answers," he said.

Maria's solution nearly worked well, but Lukas, hampered by his plaster cast, lost his balance, fell heavily and cursed loudly. Then he apologised. "I am sorry about that. No harm done really."

He lay in the darkness, thinking for a minute and then tried to express his thanks.

"Maria, it has been a miracle that we have reached this little place. You have done so much for me. I will be very lucky if we get through all this and then I find myself your brother-in-law."

She made no immediate response, because she was considering how to answer him. Lukas lay in silence for a minute and then, exhausted, he fell asleep. And so, he never heard Maria's straightforward reply to him. "You are mistaken about Witold and me. We have been friends but not close. Your brother has never said anything to me about a future for us both. I doubt that I would have given him a favourable answer if he had done!"

In the morning, Leon negotiated with a neighbour that a local boy would drive the pony and trap back to Agnieszka and return on foot. It took the lad six days, partly because he was carrying on his shoulders a leather bag which held half a dozen live rabbits. He was awarded two of them in payment for his efforts. He also had a note from Agnieszka. It told them that on the 17th September, the Russians had entered the war, invading the East of Poland. Although many Poles first assumed that they had come as liberators, Agnieszka wrote that their purpose was to take a share of the spoils of the German victory. She warned Lukas to avoid all soldiers, whether Russian or German.

The intellectual Witkiewicz [author of the Cuttlefish] had published a critique of European thought in 1935. He concluded that its sterility would be fatal. His prophesy of disaster was fulfilled in the fall of Poland, and he committed suicide on this date, the day of the Russian invasion.

Chapter 23: Witold in the Defeat of Poland.

"Your country is desolate, your cities are burned with fire. Your land, strangers devour it in your presence."
Isaiah 1:7

In the battle which claimed the life of Bruno Berling, Witold was about to join the attack on the Stukas, but veered away when he saw the Messerschmitts. He maintained height. His wingman, Topol, joined him and kept station as he headed for a space where he would be in the line of the sun. Looking back, Witold saw Bruno's plane on fire; he thought he saw a parachute but then he saw another plane crash and explode into flames. Presumably, that was his brother. He had no reason to think that the burning plane might be a Messerschmitt. They were flying to the West and around him, Witold had only empty sky.

Witold looked across to Topol flying beside him. They kept together heading North. There were no orders and Witold simply decided to return to the area where he had previously seen the German bombers flying East, on their course for Warsaw. Topol flew alongside. Usually, the pilots communicated with gestures, a grin or a thumbs up. Witold could not bring himself to make eye contact. The sense of hurt was settling in his mind. They flew on for a grim half hour. The planes approached the scene of a ground battle in which Polish soldiers were defending the road from a position on slight hill. They were dug in but there was no visible artillery support. Witold was now watching a classic part of the Blitzkrieg tactics. A column of German tanks seemed to be waiting on the road while a flight of twelve Stuka dive bombers came over their heads towards the Polish positions.

Seeing the German planes, Witold indicated to Topol that they would attack. Following their training, they drew apart in the hope that they would be less conspicuous. They then moved into a position which would allow them to attack from slightly ahead of the twelve Germans and with the patchy afternoon sun behind them. They were now coming in at an angle of about 60 degrees, trusting that the enemy pilots would fail to notice them if they remained outside the direct line of sight. It was not surprising that the Germans, expecting no opposition, never saw them until the attack began. The Stukas flew in their formation like sheep unaware of a pair of wolves. Witold delayed firing until he was close enough for every bullet to count. As he fired, he immediately heard another burst from his left where Topol had correctly waited for his leader before joining in. He hit one Stuka hard and then immediately transferred his attack to a second. As this plane dived away trailing black smoke, Witold allowed himself the satisfaction of counting "one probable and one definite."

Witold turned, intending to come back into the fight from below, but he made the mistake of flying into the sight line of the rear gunner of another plane. He saw the tracer, he pounded the rudder, but a stream of heavy machine-gun bullets poured into the engine, just ahead of the cockpit. There was a loud crash, the aeroplane rocked and Witold's view ahead no longer included a whirling propeller. The engine died and coolant gushed onto the windscreen. His plane dived, and he struggled to regain some control. In training, he had glided down in a PZL once before when his plane suffered a fuel blockage soon after take-off. The plane had come down fast and landed heavily on the airfield. Now he was looking for any level surface, and found only a rough pasture. He switched off the fuel and then concentrated on trying to land. He was able to come in at a good angle and to get the speed down, but it was impossible to judge his height above the uneven ground. The wings blocked his view sideways. Guessing and praying, he hauled back on the stick. The plane dropped heavily onto the field, both wheel struts breaking. It turned and slid down the slope. Witold was thrown sideways. His head struck something and he blacked out. One wing broke off, allowing the plane to remain upright as it finally came to rest.

There was a brief silence, but soon soldiers ran forwards. They wore brown Polish uniforms and some had the leather boots of the cavalry troopers. Witold had crashed into a field on the Polish side of the battle. The soldiers were young and excited. "You got two," they shouted at the unconscious pilot. Witold moved slightly and eager hands helped him out from the cockpit. Gradually recovering consciousness, Witold tried to ask about the other plane, but received no answer. The soldiers did not point out the distant smudge of smoke which represented Topol's funeral pyre. They took him to their senior officer, a well-spoken man, younger than Witold, who was studying the ground ahead through binoculars.

"What will they do next?" he asked vacantly. "Please, no more of those screaming Stukas." He went on scanning the hillside pastures while Witold explained who he was. He said that he was not injured.

"That's good. We have lost our medic." As he lowered the binoculars, Witold saw the face of an exhausted young man. Although he wore glasses, Witold could see the eye sockets darkened around the pale blue eyes. He had a fair moustache beneath his aquiline nose. Witold sensed that the officer, wholly preoccupied with the Germans' next move, had no idea what to do with this airman who had suddenly arrived in his unit. Witold offered to join the soldiers, and indeed there was no other option. "Would be delighted to have you," said the young officer with all the courtesy of a gentleman organising a tennis team. The reality was that these soldiers were the remains of a Polish cavalry regiment whose colonel had been killed two days earlier. The youthful lieutenant had taken over command and was doing his best to maintain an air of confident authority despite his inexperience and a demanding situation.

Witold stayed in the command post saying nothing. Sometimes, his mind returned to the air battles, the losses, and his own fortunate escape after the crash. He pushed such thoughts away and concentrated on his situation now. There was no further attack by Stukas. From the top of the hill, the young lieutenant could see German troop carriers heading around the lane to the North and he correctly anticipated a flanking attack. Before it came, he had organised two heavy machine gun positions to meet it. Witold saw the machine gun crews working to conceal themselves and set up their weapons. The officer turned to him, saying in his cultured, somewhat deferential voice, "Do you mind going over there and just repeat what I have already said, that they must hold their fire until the very last moment? No getting excited and blazing away too soon. You just cannot say it enough, even if we were not running short of ammunition."

So, now acting as an army runner, Witold set off down the slope and delivered this message to both teams. He had run downhill, and was still panting as he walked back to the command post. "Thank you so much, and good of you to make such good time. This attack is just beginning now."

The politeness appropriate in a drawing room was strangely welcome to Witold as he watched German infantry move up the hill. When very close to the Polish position and when the largest number of soldiers was available as the target, the heavy machine guns swept the hillside. Suddenly confronted by gunfire at close range, the Germans were decimated and this attack was beaten off.

As darkness came, the young commander decided to withdraw. He called the men together. However tired he was, somehow, he contrived to look confident and capable. Even his boots appeared to be polished and his uniform showed no sign of the recent skirmishing. His spectacles made him appear older, but he could not have been more than twenty-three. That afternoon, he had earned the respect of his men as their commander.

"If we are here in the morning, those Stukas will be all over our position. We will get some rations inside us immediately, take five hours' rest and then set off for Warsaw. The more ground we can cover in darkness, the nearer we must be when daylight arrives."

The soldiers assembled, yawning but not complaining, soon after midnight. The retreat began. They were heading for a forest where they should not be vulnerable to air attack, and where German tanks could not penetrate. It would take over six hours on foot, and they would be at risk as soon as the Germans realised that their hillside was now deserted and sent planes in pursuit. Witold was given a backpack and a rifle, taken from a casualty, and joined the soldiers' retreat. He was thinking clearly although his spirits remained troubled by the loss of his brother and BB. He had not fired a rifle for five years, but he was glad to have it. He worked out how to reload the weapon. Even this process reminded him of childhood with Lukas, playing soldiers in the garden. But in the grim darkness, sure that his brother was dead, he must concentrate on the man in front as they made their way across the rough terrain. The movement of the soldiers brought sounds of boots on the ground, the rustle of equipment and the occasional bout of swearing when one man tripped over an obstacle or two soldiers collided. Nature made no sound; no nocturnal animal, no bird nor wolf called after the retreating men. Witold walked with them in the disconsolate silence of the night.

After four hours, they paused and the officers held a brief discussion. They rested for a short time. Then, as the pale sun rose in the East, from Russia, bringing danger and renewed worry to the soldiers, they set out again. They reached the woodland, and found a path which they followed for two more weary miles. At last, they were permitted to stop and to sleep. There were no rations, and to drink they had only the water bottles they carried. Some of these were already empty. Occasionally, they heard the low rumble of distant aero engines but the invading air force could not be seen through the canopy of the trees.

After a short pause, they moved off again. At one stage, they heard the sound of another group of soldiers. They stopped, waited and listened. The voices they heard were Polish. These men were led by a wounded lieutenant. His pallid face and bandaged leg matched with his willingness for his men to join the retreat under the orders of the young cavalry officer. The injured lieutenant first tried to walk with a stick but as his pain increased, he could not keep up with the rest of the force. Witold spoke with him, encouraging him to come on if he could. He also gave him his water bottle. By this time, a few of the soldiers had deserted, hoping to find food or safety in smaller groups. There remained well over two hundred men, tramping through the forest. As the light faded, the group reached the level countryside outside Warsaw. They could see the lights of the silent city in the distance. In the woodland, men cursed, hungry and tired. Some sentries were posted around their makeshift camp and the men found spaces to sit and complain, or to lie down and sleep. Before long, a slender moon rose and the occasional call of a night bird broke the stillness. The men, famished and forlorn, waited for dark before moving out of the safety of the trees.

The young officer had organised the sentries and sent forward three soldiers, dressed to look like peasants, to scout the way ahead. The intention was that they would follow a compass bearing as far as they could and fire a signal light if this path was clear. One of them was to return to the camp if he could find anything to eat. The soldiers joked as they put on peasant smocks and old boots. One of them put a straw in his mouth. "Good luck to our peasants!" said the young officer, cheerfully. "Send up your flare only where you need to change from the compass bearing. Or if you have been going two hours and it's all clear."

"No light means it is dangerous," said a sergeant, sounding despondent. Witold recognized the man who was grizzled and grim, but normally taciturn. It was the young officer who replied, "Nothing much is safe now, but the idea is that we can move faster if we believe we are on the best route and have no special reason to be cautious."

Witold was impressed with the way the young officer had responded to the casual pessimism of the older soldier. When the soldier had left, he said, "You were very kind to him."

"Too kind probably."

"No, you are right. If he knows you are trying to keep him safe, he will try that bit harder."

"I hope so."

Witold changed the subject.

"Do you think the French will move? Perhaps they already have?"

"It is not promising. I know the defence plan was to hold the Germans back for up to a week while the French mobilised and attacked on their Eastern border. If they would do this, they would soon be at the rear of the invaders, and with some of their tanks, the Germans' communications would be in trouble. That is why we have tried to fight at all borders instead of defending on a much smaller front. The British liaison, Carton De Wiart, said we should defend a smaller perimeter. It makes you wonder if he knew the French were never going to move! Without any help from the allies, the Germans can attack where they please. They can bring reinforcements and supplies anywhere they choose."

The young officer went on to explain that some years before he joined the army, he had met the French liaison officer working with the Polish forces. "He was a strange man, tall, couldn't speak a word of Polish, but impressive. He was keen on mobility. If we had a mobile tank division in reserve, we would never let the Germans operate these long lines of communications. As it is, they drive to and from Frankfurt in perfect safety."

If the young officer had met a French liaison officer years before he joined the army, he must have important family connections. Witold had no chance to enquire further because, at this stage, one of the "peasants" returned pushing a wheelbarrow. As it drew nearer, the soldiers had been delighted to see that it was full of recently slaughtered poultry.

"Witold, do you mind dealing with the distribution of this stuff? I could do with a bit of a rest before we set out again." It was the first time that he had used his Christian name, but Witold still did not know the identity of the young officer, who was now utterly exhausted. Witold organised a make-shift oven to roast the hens, and the men were reasonably fed and rested before the night's advance towards Warsaw. Witold began to feel hopeful that they would reach the city, but as he considered his situation, he felt less confidence that he could do anything to defend Warsaw. His mind moved backwards. Warsaw was the city where Ruth had encountered Lutoslawski. Their meeting had led to her singing in the Mariacki at Easter. His memory included the emotion he experienced when he heard her voice, high above the choir. She was singing of sorrow and for peace. He had responded, as a young man often does, with desire and love. These confused thoughts and recollections moved around his tired mind, until Witold eventually slept.

The night operation proceeded well. The column followed two flares sent by the advance team. They moved rapidly over the fields and eventually found a track. In the very first glimmer of dawn, they saw some lights ahead which could well be the outskirts of Warsaw. Although tired by the night's march, they now went even more quickly, knowing that if the Luftwaffe found them in daylight, they would be an obvious target. The sun was well up when they heard the sound of approaching aero engines. This increased. It must be a huge number to be audible before the soldiers could see them. Some of the men ran back to a barn they had passed and crowded into it. Many others remained visible on the track.

Sure enough, the air fleet divided and a squadron of Stukas dropped upon them, falling almost vertically. The screaming sirens made an intolerable noise. No order could be heard, and men ran for cover or flung themselves on the ground in the chaos. Witold saw a stick of bombs dropped too late but the tail gunner then directed a stream of fire onto the Poles, running, taking cover, or motionless and maddened by the noise. Running men were chopped down like hay under the scythe. They fell groaning to the ground. Men lying prone were suddenly twisted by bullets. It seemed to Witold, cowering in the doorway of a stone barn that the noise of the plane had faded even while he could still hear the spattering sound of the machine-gun bullets chipping the walls of the barn. When the planes had disappeared, he emerged, his emotions a mixture of anger and fear. He tried to help one soldier in great distress, and, while attending to him, he saw amongst the dead bodies, the brown boots of the young lieutenant. His uniform was tattered and stained with blood, but the face with its fair moustache retained the composed expression which had so much impressed Witold. He would have liked to have known him in the world of order and good manners from which he came.

The wounded were left inside a building and the survivors of the group moved on towards the city, stopping to seek cover when aircraft approached, but they were not targeted again. They passed a line of zig-zag trenches manned by soldiers. They had rifles, one mounted machine gun but no anti-tank weapon. As they reached the centre of Warsaw, the atmosphere was a mixture of desperate panic amongst many civilians and disorganised determination amongst the military. The city mayor provided calm civic leadership and the army was determined to defend the city at all cost. Even as air attacks continued, teams were hauling anti-aircraft weapons into new positions. Civilians and soldiers rallied to extricate survivors from the rubble of buildings destroyed by the air raids.

Witold knew that his duty was to find a superior Air Force officer so that he could receive orders. He was given directions, but on his way to the Headquarters, he saw the uniforms of two airmen coming towards him, picking their way over the debris of a bombed-out building. They were going to meet others and he decided to join them. On the way, they told him that the Polish government had already departed Warsaw on the 4th September, retreating to Krzemieniec. The commander in chief had left for Brzesc. This was the well-known Marshal Smigly-Rydz, who Witold had seen during a military parade in Krakow earlier in the year. Although he would not be present, the Marshal had given orders that Warsaw should be defended to the last man. As they walked through the busy streets, the clamour of an air-raid siren added anxiety to the uncertainty. Then came the roar of approaching bombers. Anti-aircraft guns opened up. The road was now empty of humans. Witold and the airmen found a cellar from which they heard the noise and felt the vibration of bombs landing a short distance away. Crouching and fearful while the air raid continued, Witold's longest-lasting emotion was raw rage against the Germans.

When they reached the Headquarters, they were shown into a large basement room where more airmen were congregating in comparative safety. Two senior officers took their names and learnt how they had reached Warsaw. An urn of milky tea was produced together with incongruous cups and saucers. Then, the Commander looked at his watch, stated that he was making this announcement at exactly 1600 hours, and proceeded to address the airmen. He congratulated them for what they had done. It was believed that the Germans had lost a quarter of their warplanes, and the Polish Air Force had fought with immense courage. But this phase was over, and trained airmen would be of minimal value in the defence of Warsaw. They should evacuate Poland, and head for Romania, which was a neutral country. They should then join the allies who would need their services in France.

As they left, a junior officer sought out Witold.

"You came in with the Krakow cavalry unit?"

"Yes."

"Do you know what happened to the officers? I understand you found yourself in charge some of the time."

"Not really. The unit was led by a lieutenant and I helped out as best I could until he was killed in a Stuka attack."

"Do you know the name of the lieutenant?"

"I am afraid I don't. He had no real need to give his name. But he did extremely well in very difficult circumstances. He saved many of us."

"Fair hair, glasses, moustache?"

"Yes, sir."

"Just as we feared. That is Ludwik Smigly-Rydz, nephew of the Commander in Chief. I will have to tell the family."

He checked the name of Witold Zeleski and wished him good luck. Witold re-joined the other airmen. They decided to leave at first light, because some of the airmen had family in the city and were determined to say goodbye to them before they left.

The journey to Romania was made partly in a lorry and then on foot. They joined a large group of Polish soldiers and airmen following the same road.

Chapter 24: Occupation of Krakow: Feuer Einstellen: Cease Fire.

Stanislaw Klimecki was the civic leader of a defence-less city. Courageously, he positioned himself in front of the advancing German forces. "Cease Fire!" He offered himself as a hostage and was taken into custody.

The Germans entered Krakow on the 6th September 1939. There was no immediate resistance.

Polish citizens did not know how to behave. A curfew was imposed, new regulations came into force and announcements were made from loudspeakers in the streets. Bedraggled refugees arrived from surrounding areas and towns where the Germans had destroyed homes and businesses as they took possession of Poland by right of conquest. In Krakow, which was little damaged, commercial life continued. The refugees made sure that they blended into the local population. There was a minority of ethnic Germans within Krakow. They seemed to be delighted at the success of their compatriots. Many were entrusted with minor positions of power in the growing bureaucracy of the conquerors. It took time for the new authorities to establish themselves, allocate offices and

---

Klimecki attempted to organise education for Polish students, but was arrested and taken captive. Eventually, after release and further imprisonment, he was executed on 11th December 1942.

issue the decrees which would reorganise every part of the life of the conquered city. There was a parade of triumphant German soldiers. Officers enjoyed sunshine and coffee in the cafés in the spacious squares. Some were polite and a few were arrogant. The Polish population adopted an attitude of unsmiling obedience. The Nazis paid their restaurant bills. Their flags flew from public buildings. Libraries and Museums closed. Some schools were requisitioned.

St Xavier's did not open for the autumn term. The Headmaster disappeared. Ruth continued to live in her little flat, from which she removed every trace of the baby. She saw no one except the caretaker, Jan, and his wife, who also retained their accommodation in the gatehouse. They had recently met at the Wobnungsamt, the new German housing administration office. To their surprise, they were issued with cards which seemed to permit them to stay where they were. Ruth had heard that all Jewish schools had not merely been closed, but their buildings turned over to other uses. She feared the same would apply to St Xavier's. Soon after this first encounter with German bureaucracy, Ruth had to navigate an interview at Arbeitsamt, the Labour Office. Financially, Ruth did not need immediate employment. She had been living very simply, had savings from her salary at St Xavier's and, for the time being, she had free accommodation there. She received a few requests that she continue teaching children. She was willing to do this, but did not offer lessons in her flat, because she did not want to draw attention to it. At the Arbeitsamt, she expressed willingness to work in any shop or office, explaining that her skills included speaking German, French and Polish. These answers seemed to satisfy the Polish office worker who was struggling to speak to her in German.

In any official matter, Ruth stated that she had come from France but no longer had any connection with that country. She was wary of any investigation into her family background, and hoped that she would be perceived as French rather than Jewish. Her concern was increased when a few days after the meeting at the Arbeitsamt, she encountered her former landlord, Hainski, outside the school. He could only have been waiting for her. He asked whether she was still living in her flat, but said nothing else. He responded curtly to Ruth's polite enquiry about his wife, and then departed. He had said nothing unpleasant let alone threatening, but Ruth knew that he felt aggrieved about her departure from their home. She also suspected that there had been something perverted in his interest in her. Remembering his anti-Semitic views, his behaviour seemed even more suspicious now that she considered it again.

Towards the end of the year, Ruth heard the announcement that all Jews must wear a white armband with a blue star. Jews had already been required to register, and had their own council, the Judenrat, which negotiated with the German authorities. Ruth did not register. When the streets filled with the first heavy snow of December, it was cleared by teams of men wearing the armband and star, overseen by German soldiers. Ruth sympathised with these sorry snow-shovellers, but did not feel that she was in any way related to them. It was like a penance for belonging to the race they had been born into. But so had she. Once, on the road into the town centre, she saw a cruel trick practised on an elderly orthodox Jew who was forced to cut his own beard and locks with a pair of scissors brandished by a group of young Polish men. The Jew was left sobbing pathetically, his hair in the snow beside him. Shocked,

Ruth did nothing to comfort the old man but passed by on the other side of the road.

In late November 1939, Ruth set out early to the Sunday Mass at St Andrej. It was a windy morning threatening snow or rain, so Ruth wore a head scarf and heavy overcoat. She told herself that she wanted to go to the church to meet Agnieszka. Was there another reason in the back of her mind? If she attended a Christian church, she was less likely to be perceived as Jewish. She expected to see Agnieszka walking in with the choir, but it now appeared that the choir had been disbanded. She was searching for her friend through clouds of incense. She saw two German soldiers in uniform. They were seated at the back of the church and it was difficult to guess whether they were there to worship or to check on the large congregation. Ruth identified Agnieszka with another woman. When closer to the two women, Ruth could see that Agnieszka was distressed and her friend was trying to console her. Ruth asked what was wrong. In a sudden tumult of tears and words, Agnieszka told her. "They have taken Piotr."

She explained that he had been required to attend a lecture for university staff on plans for higher education, but then he and all his colleagues were kidnapped. "They have been taken away. They will not tell us where they are. The weather is getting colder and he has no winter coat," she added pathetically. "I pray. I pray but I fear the worst."

Agnieszka was able to tell Ruth that she had seen Lukas, who had been brought back to Krakow wounded, and she hoped that Witold had survived. The news was that his plane had been shot down but he must have been alive because he had been able

---

This kidnap of professors was called Sonderaktion Krakow

to land it. Agnieszka invited Ruth to go home with her after church on Christmas morning.

"I would so love to have your company. Mine is a family house and I feel alone and lost in it now." Well-wrapped against the cold, the two women used the little trap to go to Agnieszka's house. Ruth learned from her that Auerbach's factory had been taken over by a German Treuhander, or supervisor, and was producing military equipment. When Ruth asked what had happened to Auerbach, Agnieszka would not answer. "I cannot say," were her words. Ruth was unsure whether her friend meant that she did not know, or that she could not bring herself to pass on bad news. Agnieszka was plainly very troubled and Ruth knew that her company was a comfort to her. Ruth thought it best to make no enquiry about Piotr, knowing that if there had been any information, Agnieszka would have told her. There was an oblique reference to her husband when Agnieszka admitted that her rabbit pens became so overcrowded with young that she had to learn how to despatch them.

For Ruth, Agnieszka had cooked a stew using a rabbit, parsnips and a turnip from her garden. "Living here, I can manage for ever. I doubt if the Germans will bother to come so far in order to take it away from me," she said. Then she added, "Ruth, if your situation changes for the worse, come to me, won't you?"

"Not if you make me kill small animals. I just could not!"

She explained that the occupying forces seemed to take no interest in the school. She found this surprising because the empty buildings and courtyards were spacious and eminently useful. It was on the Eastern edge of the city which was now the capital of the "General Government," controlled by the Germans, and not far from the Russian sector to the East.

Ruth tried to visit Viktor Auerbach. She could only go there in daytime, because of the curfew. When outside the house, she saw immediately that it had a new owner. There was a swastika hanging from the parapet and a German military staff car outside. She walked on to the factory. Thick smoke was billowing from the two chimneys and as she went nearer, she could hear the heavy machinery at work. It was mid-morning. No one was going in or out. She did not dare to enter the office. On the following day, she returned to the factory in the early evening when she expected to find workers finishing their shift. The factory was operating and, after waiting for half an hour, she decided that the shift times must have changed. Eventually, she joined the stream of factory workers as they left, and asked one of the women about Auerbach.

"Nobody knows. There must have been some sort of dispute. He was summoned to meet one of the German officers. When he came back, his secretary arranged a train ticket and hotel room somewhere in Silesia. We have not seen him since."

"You don't think they have arrested him?" said Ruth.

"If they have found him, he will be in dreadful trouble. They say they are making examples of anyone who tries to resist them. They have not made any announcement." Ruth walked home worrying, but hoping that Auerbach had got away.

The days were long and dreary. They were dominated by German propaganda and regulations. Polish life was restricted. Theatres were closed and the cinema only open for Germans. There was no attempt to hinder Christian church services. For Jews, it was very different. Ruth continued to go to St Andrej, where the choir was now reforming. She accepted that one motive was to provide confirmation that she was a Christian. She was now singing regularly with the choir. There was none of the anxiety which accompanied a solo performance but she had to concentrate sufficiently to take her mind off other subjects.

Every Sunday, the choir sang the words of the Nunc Dimittis. "Lord, now lettest thou thy servant depart in peace, according to thy word. For mine eyes have seen thy salvation, which thou hast prepared for thy people Israel. To be a light to lighten the Gentiles and to be the Glory of thy people Israel." They were sung in the Polish language, and Ruth had never concentrated on their meaning. Then, in one of the Sunday services, the same words appeared in the Bible reading for the day. The priest ascended the elaborate Baroque boat-shaped pulpit of St Andrej where he gave a simple explanation. When Jesus was a child, a wise and devout Jew called Simeon had been told by the Holy Spirit that he would not die until he had seen The Messiah. When Jesus was presented in the Temple, after circumcision in accordance with Jewish law, Simeon was guided by the Holy Spirit to go to the temple. There he saw Jesus and recognised him to be "A light that will be a revelation to the Gentiles and glory of thy people Israel."

The Polish priest emphasised that Jesus was Jewish, that the Jewish Faith was the foundation of Christianity and that God's Will must have been that the Jewish people would "glory" in recognising him. Ruth considered the Bible story and the thought-provoking sermon. They suggested that her own Jewish, fast-fading Faith might be fulfilled by the religion of the Christians. Ruth had never admitted her Jewish background to anyone apart from BB. Hearing this sermon, she concluded that the two religions need not oppose one another. She remembered Auerbach explaining to her that he would always go to a Christian wedding or funeral if invited. He had stated, "If you study the prayer used at every Christian service, which they call The Lord's Prayer, there is absolutely no part of it which conflicts with any Jewish belief."

Ruth accepted, as she had done since childhood, that God had chosen the Israelites to be His people, but she was now convinced that He had sent his Son for the Christians. This conclusion also involved belief in the ultimate forgiveness offered to all men. Her journey towards this simple conclusion had begun when she first sang The Messiah in Toul and had advanced further when she had prepared to sing The Lacrimosa in Krakow. She had become a Christian.

One morning, Ruth, walking into the city through icy streets, was overtaken by the green Adler car. For a split second, she thought she would see Viktor Auerbach leaning back in the comfortable rear seat. But there was, in his place, a German officer, smoking a cigar. Perhaps he has stolen the cigar as well as the car, she thought in her disappointment. She wondered whether the young chauffeur, Josefz, might still be the driver, remembering that he spoke good German and had been maintaining the car for several years. It was a useful job which he did very well. But when she saw other private cars containing German officers, she noticed that they were always driven by a uniformed soldier.

In the spring, Ruth heard of the battles in Northern France. News, or more accurately, propaganda was broadcast from loudspeakers in public places. The Germans were brave and victorious. The French were ready to surrender and the British were running away. She had no way of knowing what was happening in Toul, but when she bought a German newspaper, she learned that there had been no battle for the city. She was worried about her brother Jakob who had enlisted two years before. She knew that he and his friend Marcel had been junior officers in a tank regiment, but had no recent information about which division they belonged to or where they might be serving.

Earlier in 1940, Ruth had been instructed to work in a shop selling clothing and fabrics in the city centre. It had belonged to a Jewish family called Blumenthal, but was now taken over by an ignorant Pole. The new owner needed the help of Dan Blumenthal but he was struggling to serve customers, order stock and keep the books. Ruth's ability to speak good German was a benefit to the trade, so she took over the sales work from Dan and soon proved to be a competent shop assistant. She continued to live undisturbed in her flat at St Xavier's and, as the days lengthened, so her apprehension reduced. She taught two more of her former pupils privately when their parents contacted her through the St Andrej church. She even found some moments of enjoyment, strolling alone through the undamaged city or playing records on a wind-up gramophone which she had acquired in happier times.

One afternoon, having returned from work, Ruth was listening to a record of Bach's St Matthew's Passion. She did not have the sheet music, but having listened to it many times, she knew the soprano part [Pilate's wife] well enough. She joined in, enjoying again her own voice, singing for the joy of singing and delighting in the beauty of Bach's music.

There was a knock at the door. No one had visited her for months. Ruth thought that it might be Jan the caretaker. But the figure she could see through the tiny window looked much taller. She opened the door and saw a German officer in full uniform. He was smiling. He spoke in Polish with a strong German accent.

"That was delightful. I came to look at some dull buildings and I receive a concert of Bach's music! If I may, Miss, I would like to reassure you about the plans for this part of Krakow. I believe that there is nothing which will trouble you." His words must have been a kind response to Ruth's fearful reaction when she opened the door. She stammered a polite reply, first in Polish and then put the same words into better German. The officer stood there and then replied in German.

"I think you would like to know what we are expecting to do here. May I explain now, or should I come back on another day?"

"Not today, thank you." She spoke as if dealing with a door-to-door salesman, then realised her mistake and was beginning to offer some explanation. He smiled.

"May I ask your name?"

"I am sorry. I should have said, my name is Ruth Neuman. I have lived here since I was teaching at the school."

"I might guess that your subjects included music, perhaps. I have no need to inconvenience you today. Perhaps if I were to return on Thursday at the same time?"

She could only agree to the appointment he suggested but she ignored his question about the subject she taught.

Chapter 25: Colonel Emil Mendler

Ruth continued to see Agnieszka at St Andrej on most Sundays. She also joined her at another city church, St Anne's, where the wives of the Jagiellonian University staff met for a Mass every Thursday. In front of a painting of St Jan of Kenty, they prayed for the welfare and safe return of their husbands. It was a helpful gesture of solidarity amongst these women. Their prayers were rewarded in that some of the oldest professors returned to Krakow in the early part of the year. Agnieszka learned that Piotr was alive in a camp at Dachau. Her thoughts were focussed on her husband, and when she heard the news of decisive German victories in France, she hoped that the conquerors might no longer need hostages and would soon release Piotr. The city was draped with red flags and swastikas, as the Fall of France was celebrated by the Germans. Poles realised that their last hope rested with the only nation still at war, Britain. Some feared that the little country was too far away to rescue Poland. Others heard, on their illegal radios, the voice of the new British Prime Minister, claiming, "We will do our best to defend our island and we will fight until the curse of Hitler is lifted from the brows of men." If these phrases reached Poland, they contained the grim truth that even if Britain held out, the war and German occupation would continue indefinitely.

The German officer who had said that he would return did not come on the agreed day. But he appeared the following week, apologising as if he had missed a social event. He respectfully enquired if they might fix another time. Ruth decided to invite him in. He took off his cap revealing pale blonde hair fading to grey, and a beaky nose beneath calm grey eyes. There were deep lines around the mouth. He must have been over fifty. The face would have suited a far-sighted and successful business leader, which indeed was what Emil Mendler had aspired to be. He gave his name, Colonel Mendler, and then explained in some detail about the Germans' wish to use this part of the city as a marshalling point. The train line would be extended from the station and the courtyards would be used to store and maintain equipment and vehicles, while the school buildings would become rooms for officer's training or planning. This was the military project he was to oversee. It would take at least a year because the authorities had given all this a low priority.

"You have lived here for some time?"

"Yes. I used to teach music at the school. It is closed now, of course."

"Yes. I am sorry for this." There was a pause as if he would have liked to add more to this unexpected apology. "I will decide that you should stay on at this flat and I will make sure that the Wobnungsamt give you appropriate housing if we need to requisition it later on. I will put this down as the same accommodation as the caretakers which we obviously prefer to keep occupied." He asked for her full names, recorded them and made a brief note in a file.

The officer's explanation and careful approach was in contrast with the reputation of the German occupation authorities. Ruth had heard stories of families evicted from their homes without warning and the building then standing empty for months. Now, Colonel Mendler was giving an explanation to her as if he needed to gain her support for his plans. He did not stay much longer. He told her that he would come back, if it suited her, at the end of the week when he should be able to confirm everything and bring her the plans for the buildings on the far side of the courtyard. Ruth's mind was working hard. The colonel seemed straightforward and even pleasant. But she retained a vestige of suspicion. Why would this officer wish to show her his plans? Why should he pretend that her flat was part of the caretaker's accommodation? He could snap his fingers and put out her out on the street if he chose. Yet those grey eyes seemed sincere, and his manner that of a concerned and professional gentleman. Why would anyone with sinister intent behave with such sensitivity?

"Before I go, may I ask if I am I right in thinking that you attend St Andrej church?"

When she confirmed this, he made another comment about the quality of the choir and said that in his own town, Koblenz, the choral music was not nearly so good. He made a light-hearted comment. "And now, I am making better progress in understanding the Polish sermon too."

She laughed and so did he. She noticed his teeth were white and well-preserved.

Early one evening, when walking home from the shop in the city centre, Ruth saw a woman with a perambulator leaving a building on the other side of the busy street. She recognised Halina. She stopped in surprise, uncertain whether she should call out to her. She desperately wanted to see inside, but the hood of the perambulator was up. It was moving away from her. Ruth felt a jolt when a pedestrian bumped into her. "You can't stop here. We all need to get home!" Ruth had to return to reality and follow her usual route back to her flat. As the immediate emotion faded, she recognised that she had been right to say and do nothing. The child belonged to Halina. She tried not to think of little Bruno but she frequently dreamed of him as her baby who must now be growing into her little boy. When she awoke from such a dream, she thought that there must be some residual maternal instinct working in her subconscious mind. She must get on with her life as best she can. There was no point in dwelling on the past.

Colonel Mendler returned on the Friday of the same week. There was more conversation about the school buildings, their potential and the need to retain them for the future. Summoning a reserve of courage, Ruth dared to ask a provocative question. "Can you tell me what is this future for the school, I mean for the education of all Polish children?"

He sighed. "I wish I could give any answer, Miss Neuman. We are speaking privately now. Surely, we both know that this blot on the story of a great country such as Poland will not become a permanent stain. Your institutions will reopen. The Reich will change its ways. My people are too civilised and so are yours. The schools must continue at some time and I hope it will be soon."

"So, you would not have wanted the statue of Mickiewcz to be demolished?"

"This is just the sort of thing done in the heat of a sudden victory. But nothing can eradicate the history that he and Goethe met and shared a mutual respect. If Goethe appreciated the poet in his lifetime, it is difficult for the Germans to claim he is irrelevant today."

"There is even a plaque commemorating the house in Slawkowska Street where Goethe lived when he was in Krakow," said Ruth.

"We are all part of history, and the present is one link in a long chain. Anyone who steps back to look, must see that we cannot continue like this forever."

To Ruth, this was a fascinating line of thought. Living through the defeat of her adopted country, to be followed by the fall of her native country in the next year, she had no positive views about the future. She had hoped Germany might be defeated by France and Great Britain. Now it seemed that Germany had prevailed over these allies and it was beyond her imagination to think that Poland or France could recover their national identities and live alongside the German nation. She realised that she was learning from someone who had thought much more deeply than she had.

She told the colonel that she had only noticed the Goethe plaque because her sister hated having to study his work in school. The colonel laughed.

"I think in Germany also we study him when we are too young to enjoy his work. Is your sister still in Toul with your parents?"

"No, she has been studying at a university in England for a few years now."

She gave no explanation for the need to leave France in order to go to university.

The conversation returned to music and then back to the present, the colonel's plans. Ruth found it easy to ask why he was taking so much trouble to explain everything to her.

"I thought you would like to know. It has been my way in commercial work, and I find it just the same now I am in the forces."

This seemed almost convincing. Ruth had enjoyed his conversation and now told him about her position at the school, and that she also taught violin.

On the following Friday, the colonel visited her again, bringing a gramophone record of a Bach violin partita. "Miss Neuman, I hope my guess is right, but I thought you might like to have the sheet music as well." He opened his attaché case and brought out his present. Ruth was delighted. When they played the record, both listened in silence. "I hope you would not think me too forward if I ask you to consider playing the Bach partita some time." Ruth could only assent. He stayed with her for most of the afternoon. He complained that the conversation in the officers' mess was boring at best and disagreeable at worst. He asked about her background. She told him that she had come from Toul to Poland because her family had visited Krakow. She admired the city and applied for the post as Head of Music in order to live independently. She avoided any mention of the Jewish school, Viktor Auerbach or the reason why it had been difficult to advance her career in France. Conversation came easily to them both. He was a sensitive listener, and asked the right questions, neither personal nor difficult for her to answer, but showing a genuine interest. Like Ruth herself, he seemed to be kind-hearted, intelligent and wanting the other person to enjoy his company.

During this evening, Ruth asked the colonel to tell her more about his childhood. He explained that when his father had succeeded in business, he could afford to send him to an expensive school controlled by Roman Catholic monks.

"It sometimes happens that an intelligent father who lacks a good education makes a huge effort to get this benefit for his children. As you might expect, the school instilled high standards in all of the boys. The problem was then that my education and my moral standards were more advanced than my father's."

"This is an interesting thought, and I assume it applies in your case. Please go on."

"As a schoolboy, I absorbed all that I was taught. I had an accepting mind, like a sponge soaking up whatever these impressive teachers told me. This Faith has stayed with me. I concede that it was no help when I had trouble at home. I am not sure that it will help me now, but I am stuck with it!"

He said that when he was a young man, his mother had died in the flu epidemic of 1918, which badly affected his father. He did not say more about his differences with his father, only that he had decided to leave the firm. Emil had been recruited by a military acquaintance to work as a specialist in logistics for the Reichswehr. They were talking very frankly. Since he had already admitted that Germany could not pursue a military course indefinitely, Ruth felt able to ask a direct question about why he should join the forces and give up a business career.

"Surely there would have been other business opportunities open to you in your home city?"

"That is a fair question. There is an answer to it, and I promise I will give it to you. But I wonder if you might allow me to respond to it some other time." He left soon after this.

"You must call me Emil. It is such a pleasure to talk about music with you."

Ruth had also enjoyed their conversation, but in truth, their conversation and their enjoyment of these hours had not been concerned with music. After he had left, Ruth had a vague recollection of something which Viktor Auerbach had told her family, concerning a German businessman and his son who left the business and joined the Reichswehr.

Returning to her flat a few days later, she found a note from the colonel. It suggested that if it would suit her, he could come to see her again on Friday evening of the same week. There was no address to which she could reply. He arrived, bringing a bottle of Moselle, saying that he hoped they would both appreciate the wine since it came from between her homeland and his. She played some of the Bach partita. The colonel mentioned to her that the well-known musician Dr Hans Rohr would be coming from Munich [in the early summer of 1940] with the objective of forming a Krakow symphony orchestra. He asked her if she might be interested. Subsequently, Ruth discussed the project with members of the choir at St Andrej. They told her that members of the orchestra would have to register with the Propaganda department. No one liked the idea. When Emil raised the subject with her again, he spoke tentatively. "If you consider joining the Krakow Symphony Orchestra, I have no doubt that they would be pleased to have you, but I am not sure that you would care for the music to be performed."

"I wondered about that. Our audiences are used to hearing Chopin, but under the General Government, we must pretend that there is no serious Polish culture."

The colonel did not dispute what she said and added, "I fear that the Governor may want waltzes and marches. And the orchestra may be playing more for the Germans in Wawel Castle than for the public. I would try to find out more if you were interested."

"I am feeling my way here, Emil. I have arrived in Poland from France, and I am loyal to Poland now. I am trying to do the best I can. I want to do what is right at this time and in this place. I think most Poles would decide not to join an orchestra organised by the occupying government."

"I am not surprised that you see it like this. But if the Krakow orchestra demonstrates that Polish people are as cultured as we both know them to be, and if the public enjoys their music, then you might decide that you would be doing good. It is a situation which calls for an answer like Christ's response to the clever question about whether Jews should pay Roman taxes. Render to Caesar that which is Caesar's and render to God that which is God's."

Emil paused, perhaps because he saw that she had not understood the New Testament reference.

"I mean, we might say here render to Hans Frank the power to create an orchestra but perform in it for the love of music and the joy of the Polish public."

"I doubt if I would ever do this, Emil. I believe that I should stand in solidarity with the Poles who have welcomed me here, and do nothing to collaborate with Governor Frank."

Emil nodded and changed the subject.

"Do you know the artist Meissonier?"

"No, I don't think so."

"He is not so famous as many of your great French classical painters. I keep bringing to mind one picture, which I think you might have seen somewhere. It keeps appearing in my head like a tune you don't really like but which continues to annoy the mind. It will help me if I describe it as best I can. There is a group of horsemen following, at a respectful distance, a man on a white horse. He wears a black hat and a heavy grey coat. His bearing is serious. He carries his head somewhat downcast, but his gaze is fixed ahead. He is a man deep in thought and bearing on his shoulders the weight of his own defeat and disappointment. The artist has spent less time and energy on his depiction of the men following on their brown horses; they are plainly much less important. In the foreground, there is deep rutted snow as if heavy wagons have been dragged ahead of this group. The background shows an army grimly proceeding through a desolate white landscape."

His description brought back a memory of a picture in a history book. "Is it The Retreat from Moscow?"

"So it is, Ruth."

They had been drawn together by this conversation, although she was not yet sure why he had mentioned this painting to her.

"I promised that I would answer your question about joining the Wehrmacht. I must tell you about my personal life. I have a wife. Her name is Renata. She has become impossible to live with and one reason I joined the army was to escape an unbearable situation at home. I am the sort of human who needs contact with other people, and I used to have many good friends in Koblenz. But Renata has made trouble with most of them. You cannot imagine the way of life in a provincial town such as Koblenz, so small-minded and petty. I seldom went out alone. If I ever did so, perhaps for business reasons, Renata would make all kinds of accusations against me. I found it impossible to live with Renata in my own home. I believe that I had no choice but to leave. Perhaps I should not have told you all this. It was suggested that my experience of organising transport would be valuable to the Wehrmacht and I was easily persuaded to join."

The searching grey eyes studied her face for her reaction. Ruth was at a loss as to how to respond to this surprising and very personal explanation about Emil's private life. She tried to say something to the effect that she was sorry. He was plainly embarrassed and reluctant to continue the conversation. When he left the flat, he made no suggestion that they might meet again and for many weeks, she did not see him. She began to miss his company and conversation, which she had found to be always respectful and also interesting. She realised how little she had told him about herself, her family life or Bruno. He had never pried for such information from her but he had shared his own private sadness. She wondered what he would say if she told him about BB and Little Bruno, who still recurred in her conscious mind and, even more frequently, in her dreams.

Chapter 26: Lukas and Maria: Romantic Love and Nonsense

When they had travelled out of Krakow into the Carpathians, Lukas had found that he enjoyed every conversation with Maria. Initially, he was keen to learn about his prospects of recovery from his fractured ankle. She gave a clear explanation, praising the surgeon who had treated Lukas. The bones needed to re-set in the correct position, which she believed they would. Then, he would need to exercise gradually before he would walk normally. There was little chance of his being able to walk far or fly a plane for six months.

As they drove on in his mother's trap, he had asked her about her family.

"May I ask you about your home life, Maria? Witold did not tell me much about you, whereas you know all about me."

"That I don't, Lukas. And I fear that Witold hardly mentioned you to me!"

"You came to see us all, met my parents, and could see exactly how we all lived."

"Only joking, Lukas. Our house is far less interesting. We have lived all my life at Podgorze. I had a brother, much younger and a sister, much older. My mother seems to have conceived like an elephant, every seven years."

"Is that true? Do elephants really conceive every seven years?"

"Of course. Nurses know everything about stuff like this. Perhaps I should not expect a footballing airman to know too much biology."

"All right, Maria, carry on and I promise I won't interrupt again."

"I don't mind the interruptions, especially if they give me the chance to teach you something. The sad part of this story is that when my brother was born, my mother died. It was one of those cases when the doctors had to decide who to save. It meant that my sister became responsible for me and the household, and I brought up my little brother, while my father just got on with his job at the big sawmill. My sister was a marvel. She was fourteen and I was seven when this happened. It was as if she could not wait to have a house and family to look after. She made it such fun for us both. She let me do all sorts of things my mother would never have allowed. I helped her with the housework. She taught me to cook all of our meals by the time I was ten. But sometimes food was a bit scarce. Father's wages were low. And then, when my brother died, my sister was such a comfort to me. We have come through all this gaining strength and confidence in one another."

"You make it sound like an adventure. I cannot imagine our family without our mother. She provided all the stimulus, most of the fun and much of the encouragement."

"When it happens, the human adapts and survives. Children sometimes cope with a disaster better than adults. I suppose I experienced grief. I know my father did. But I have forgotten mine. I have a stronger memory of the arrival of my little brother than the loss of my mother. Is your memory like that? Leaving out the bad bits and keeping what you enjoyed most?"

Lukas thought carefully and then, gave a long answer.

"I remember summers of constant sunshine and family life with never an argument too. But it is different this time. Even if we recover our country, we will never forget what has happened. The memory of defeat by the Germans, this injured ankle, and the need to escape to other countries are unforgettable. But the troubles of today may be overtaken by events. Now, I worry about my parents and whether I will see my brother again. When I know what has happened to my family, the present anxiety might fade away."

He had already explained that he had heard that his brother's plane had crash-landed, but no one knew whether he had survived or evaded capture by the Germans.

After their first night in the peasant's cottage, Maria was determined to make herself useful, whether working with Leon in the vegetable plot, or helping his wife who suffered from arthritis. Lukas, sitting alone in the bedroom, often heard the sound of merry laughter between the two women. They would eat their evening meal together, but they then retreated to their bedroom. On their second night, Maria returned to the subject of the plane crash. She asked if he was still troubled by what had happened, saying that it might be good for him to talk about it.

Lukas explained that the crash was not the problem. He told her about BB, describing him as an inspiring teacher who had become a wonderful friend. He said that he was the motivation behind his own decision to join the Polish Air Force and how he had led the team preparing to defend their homeland. When he reached the part of the story in which he must tell of BB hanging in his parachute, his voice gave way and he was unable to complete the account. Maria helped him out.

"Stop there, Lukas. That is enough for today and we can finish this another time." She put an affectionate arm around his shoulder.

Maria was herself moved by Lukas' loss of his friend and mentor, but tactfully put off talking about it for several days. When she asked if he was ready to complete the account, Lukas explained about the attack on BB by the German pilot, and his reaction, to ram the plane.

"He was a murderer. Am I not right to say that he deserved to die? I think about this too often. Did I take a foolish risk just because it was my friend who he killed?"

"If you want my opinion, I say it was your duty to your country to destroy the invaders. No one could ever blame you for what you did, and I think your friend must be proud of you. He will also approve of your efforts to get back into the fight."

It was typical of Maria to imply that BB was aware of what Lukas did within seconds of his death and might be watching his progress now. Lukas responded by explaining BB's charismatic teaching at school and the words beside the blackboard emphasising that everyone has only one life and a responsibility to make the most of it.

"This must be just the sort of instruction a boy of sixteen needs," said Maria thoughtfully.

"Yes, but only if the instructor is himself a role model. Boys are very quick to see through the teacher specialising in bluster and hypocrisy."

When they were together in the evenings, Maria was often tired by a day of physical work. Lukas decided to tell her the stories of some of the books he had enjoyed. He prepared for this by making notes which he consulted as he explained the story of the great epic With Fire and Sword. Maria lay on her bed, eyes closed. Lukas thought she might be asleep. He pruned out some of his memory of the fulsome description of the countryside in spring, and kept to the narrative. He looked at her again. Her eyes remained closed.

"Am I boring you, droning on?"

"Not one word is boring. I am concentrating on everything you tell me. It's what I need just now, sleepy after a long day. I am making up for my poor education by using all the work you did at school."

"Not really. This was not school work, it's just a story, but it's still a good one to know, especially if you are Polish."

Lukas had reached the part where the dashing lieutenant met the beautiful Helen. She sang for the company and he fell in love with her. They had an opportunity for a short conversation and now she was in love with him. Maria interrupted.

"This is nonsense! It is like a fairy story. The sleeping beauty is in love with the Prince she has never seen before! Surely your famous author did not pretend it happened like that?"

"He did. He is writing a book, not describing the humdrum life the reader may experience. And this is the work of Providence. They are destined to meet. For every fine hero there is a romantic heroine awaiting him. They have only to meet, to find one another and you have a happy ending, or in this book, a happy beginning."

"Do you believe in any of this?"

"I do, Maria. But perhaps I am wrong and foolish here. If you read enough of this, it seeps into your mind. Sienkiewicz is writing about romantic love, when one human being finds the one other who is right for that person. Is it all nonsense? What do you think?"

"As I have told you, I am a simple Christian. I believe that God is watching over us all the time. He knows when a sparrow falls dead to the ground, as Jesus said. It is sad for the sparrow, but part of His purpose. So, when my mother died, I was told that it was His will. Some even said that she was so good that God had need of her. So, He took her on purpose and she is with Him now. My older sister said this. She believed it, and was not just comforting me. It is part of me to have this belief in God's purpose, but I still have trouble with your Sienkiewicz making a man and a woman fall in love in half an hour's conversation."

"I seem to remember my father saying that he thought you had a very sharp mind, Maria. In fact, his words were that you were one of the many nurses who were better than most of the doctors. Now it's my turn to make a judgement, I think you would make an excellent professor of Polish literature!"

"Did your father really say that? What a lovely man he is. Did he truly have such a low opinion of doctors?"

"He should know. His work was teaching medical students, whether they were drunk or just hungover."

Lukas asked Maria about her childhood. She explained, "My brother had a medical condition, causing lots of tummy trouble and needing a special diet. I was looking after him, and because he was such a lovely little boy, I did all I could for him. He died six years ago. My sister said I had learnt much about nursing already, and she thought I would be good at it. She encouraged me to go in for training as a nurse. It was a big help to me to do that, after Jan died."

"That is so sad, Maria. How tragic to lose a little brother." He touched her hand.

"So it was for me at the time, very sad. But it did set me on this path to nursing, which is work I love to do. Also, he is keeping my mother company in heaven."

Maria said this so simply, but there was something in her tone of voice which sounded as if she was challenging Lukas. He responded, "Is there a difference between what a person truly believes and what they choose to believe?"

"I can see how you are thinking, Lukas. But what you do not truly believe makes no difference to your life, how you act or what you do. It is only what you truly believe that can have any effect. Anyway, if I am wrong about Heaven and whether recognisable people can be found there, it is still true that if Jan had not died, I would not be nursing. And I am completely sure that this is the work I am meant to do."

There was a pause while Lukas thought over what she had told him.

"Maria, I am saying nothing to dispute what you have told me. As one of your patients, I completely agree that nursing is your calling. I wish I knew what mine might be! But I am thinking that if your work is intended by Providence, meaning that you have been called to it by God, that is not so different from my favourite author's view of romantic love. The human is called by Providence to meet the one other person he is destined to love. But you are looking tired. I will pester you with these thoughts tomorrow night."

"Good night, Lukas. I have enjoyed listening to the story. Sleep well. We will continue with my literary education tomorrow."

Lukas thought over what Maria had said. She was unfailingly kind to him. This was to be expected of a good nurse, caring for her patient, but he sensed far more than professional concern, and at this stage, he still believed that she was his brother's girlfriend. If she was learning about Polish novelists, she was teaching him about the real world. He also thought more deeply about his religion. He came from a church-going Catholic family, and had never questioned what he was taught at home, school and church. But his participation had been superficial. Religious belief and Christian conduct were essential to her character, whereas it was mere background in his. But friends always accused Lukas of being serious, and Maria was invariably light-hearted.

The autumn days passed slowly. Lukas moved about on crutches, sometimes helping inside the cottage, while Maria was outside doing farm work. She had no experience, but was willing to learn. There was a vegetable patch close to the cottage, where root vegetables and some cabbages were growing. The stony soil was enriched with the dung of all animals including the humans. Following instructions, Maria was working on this patch of ground one morning when she heard angry voices from the track leading to the cottage. Instinctively, she kept out of view and watched as two ragged men in dark green uniform walked behind Leon. One had a rifle pointing at Leon, the other had his weapon still slung on his shoulder. The rough green uniform was not German, and was presumably Russian. Ruth was very alarmed, but remained still. The peasant's wife and Lukas would be inside the cottage and could do nothing against these armed men. The door closed behind them, but there were no gunshots.

After a very anxious half an hour, Maria decided to get into the cottage using the low window of the bedroom. She wanted to hear what was happening in the living room. She reached the bedroom, from which she could hear the intruders' voices and occasional laughter. The language must be Russian. From this relaxed tone, she guessed that they were seated next to the stove. Then she heard Leon's voice speaking in Polish, and offering something. She realised that the men were being given drink and food. She did not know where Lukas was until she heard his voice speaking in Polish.

"This is very good brandy. We call it 'I take rifle you use axe'."

"That's right, but not yet. More drink good." Leon replied.

Maria decided to stay inside, but to conceal herself under the bed. As she tried to do this, she made something drop noisily to the floor. In a moment, the door opened and the Russian with the rifle was there, pointing it at her. He had a black beard, unkempt hair and now a sudden lascivious expression. He said something but as he did so, a blow landed on his arm and he dropped the rifle. Leon had picked up the little axe kept by the stove and struck out at the Russian. When he moved quickly to recover the rifle, Maria pushed it away as she scrambled to her feet. She took hold of it, and so did the Russian. There followed a tussle between them. His breath was foul in her face. His body was rank. But she had a good grip of the stock of the rifle while he had difficulty holding onto the barrel. He could not wrestle the rifle from her. Suddenly, Maria stopped pulling and pushed the rifle hard into the stomach of the Russian. He gasped and doubled up, but maintained a hold on the weapon. Leon joined the struggle holding the man from behind. Lukas had taken the rifle from the other man and came into the bedroom to end the confrontation.

"Hvatit," said Leon, who knew a few words of Russian. He now took possession of the other rifle.

There followed a short exchange in which the intruders were ejected. They were deserters from the Russian army.

"You go now. If you come back, we kill you. We keep guns."

This was the end of the incident. Leon made sure that they had taken all their ammunition before the Russians departed. Maria was shaken by the violence. In the late afternoon, she had recovered enough to work with Leon to conceal the entrance to the track. Two small trees were cut down and pulled into place. From the mountain road, no one would see the turning towards the cottage behind the wood. They also devised a trip wire which would cause something to fall from a windowsill in the cottage if anyone stepped through a gap between the trees. In the evening, Leon found more brandy and they drank to their victory. Maria thanked him for helping her, but Leon took a different view. "What would have happened to us if you had not been here?" he said.

When they were alone in their bedroom and Maria blew out the lamp, Lukas decided to ask her a question he had been preparing for some time. "You remember telling me that you have been called to work as a nurse? I needed your help when the Germans were coming. You saved my life then. Did you just decide to help me out of a sense of duty? I am asking because I now think you were sent to help me and I was sent to you. Today, you helped to rescue us all in the battle for the rifle too. Is this just an accident or does it mean something for us both?"

He had said it now. He waited in the darkness for the answer from the bed alongside his.

"Lukas, you are such a delight. So sincere and so serious. The answer is yes now. Come here."

She reached for him, and held him close to her. "You are meant for me, Lukas, if you think so too."

In the darkness, his fingers fumbled for her face and his mouth closed on hers.

Chapter 27: Carpathian Journeys

They passed the winter in the cottage high in the Carpathian Mountains. The dwelling had thick walls but the only heating came from the stove in the main room. Their bedroom was bitterly cold and they frequently lay together, fully clothed, beneath its covers to keep warm. Lukas grew a beard. They did their best to converse with their hosts, asking about the way of life, the growing of a few crops and the sheep. But generally, they were alone in their own room. They began a programme of telling one another of their first memories, then their childhood and adolescence. Although intended to help pass the time, the outcome was that Lukas found that he was learning far more about Maria than he knew about any other human. She included in her account exactly what had passed between herself and Witold. She had enjoyed his company, but they were little more than friends. She said that they never established any understanding that she was to be "his" girlfriend or that she would "wait" for him. She had been surprised that when he left Krakow for the war, he had given her a pair of leather gloves. He had left them at the hospital while she was working there. They had been too small for her, but the shop had been willing to change them. She told Lukas that the shop-assistant asked her about a silver cup awarded in a flying competition. She had been told to put it in the box, but it was not there when Maria opened it.

"All I can say is that my brother did win the prize and was very proud of it," said Lukas.

When describing his home life, Lukas did his best to be scrupulously factual. As he did so, he realised how fortunate he had been; his parents' solid affection for one another and for their boys, the cheerful rivalry with Witold and the excellent education. He told Maria more about the brothers' devotion to BB and his continuing influence when they were training at Deblen. The last instruction of the government to the Polish armed forces was to go to Romania. From there, they should join the allies of their country and pursue the war against their common enemy. Having relatives in Romania should give them an advantage. He found it difficult to explain his confidence in Henri, this characterful uncle who he had last seen at the age of thirteen. He concluded by saying that there had been some close bond forged between them. Whenever his uncle and aunt sent a letter or a card at Christmas, they included a reference to Witold and Lukas. He sensed that he would have revelled in having Henri as a father and he had heard his uncle express his own longing to have "sons like these". He tried to express this point of view without criticising Piotr, a thoroughly good parent but lacking the charisma of Henri. Maria realised that the visit to his Uncle Henri was important to Lukas and so she asked for a full account. Lukas did his best to remember it.

The Zeleskis' visit to Romania July 1932

In the summer of 1932, the Zeleski family went by train to Bistrita, where they were met by a horse-drawn trap. Its driver carried a large card bearing the name "Zeleski". He spoke no German but smiled broadly as he pointed to his own chest saying his name Tudor. Lukas and Witold sat alongside the coachman. The trap rattled over the cobbles outside the station. Before long, the road was unpaved and dusty. Tudor showed the boys where to hold on, and offered them two neck cloths which he wore against the dust. Looking like bandits, the boys turned back to see their parents in the closed part of the little carriage.

After an hour, Tudor halted in a village and spoke in his own language to a couple of elderly men who led the family into a farmhouse. Soup and thick bread were provided by the two daughters of a pregnant woman. She refused payment, and, by much sign language, wished them a good journey to the estate where Tudor was employed. The coachman seemed much more communicative after his meal. He had been drinking from a jug which was not proffered to the Polish visitors. Mounting the trap, he pulled out from under his seat a huge blunderbuss and encouraged Lukas and Witold to put on their face masks. Witold tried to find out about the weapon. Was it loaded? What with? What happened if you pulled the trigger? Tudor explained more by signs than words, that it was not loaded now, but in the past, he had fired it at a fox, which got into his hen house. The fox had been killed and only three out of his thirty hens survived. "Kill all foxes. They destroy every hen because they like killing. Some people are the same. We need to destroy all of these!" Having understood this, the boys nodded vigorously.

The family reached the stone farmhouse towards the end of the day. Behind it were extensive stables and outbuildings into which Tudor disappeared. Only Valeria was at home to greet them, explaining that Henri was at a meeting of a political movement called The Iron Guard. Lukas and Witold met their young cousin who was named Agnieszka after their own mother. They had been told that she was frail. She was also very quiet, and held Valeria's hand at all times. She was of little interest to her older cousins.

Henri returned from his meeting in time for a late dinner, explaining that he had been with The Guardists. "Tell us about them," said Piotr. "But not too fast, please." Henri launched into an explanation of this political movement, which attracted him because its principles valued country life, the unspoiled peasants' way of life and aspired to a spiritual reconstruction of Romania. As he talked on, Lukas noticed Valeria make a sign to their mother who then left the room with her. Henri said that the Legion of the Archangel Michael had been founded by Cornelie Codranu, following the thinking of Professor Cuza. This professor was concerned to uphold the Christian church and educate young people in a nationalist spirit. He argued that the arrival of Jewish people in important occupations and positions was damaging to society. He referred to the fear that Jewish people had an international attitude.

"They operate to benefit other Jews outside our country, and could never be truly patriotic. We need to be together, all Romanians."

Piotr made a mild challenge, half-joking about the part played by Saxons, a minority German population within Romania.

"Point taken, Piotr," said Henri. "And like the Jews, we do not marry outside our own tribe, with the famous exception of myself!"

Lukas and Witold were good listeners. Henri was enjoying the sound of his own voice, talking almost continuously, now, about the need to achieve a united Romanian nation and then, about the merits of the separate schools for the Hungarian and Saxon minorities in Transylvania. He spoke of the Peasant's party and the view that the family unit was a distinct and valuable method of production. He referred to the ideas of Virgil. To begin with, the boys assumed that he was talking about the Roman poet, and winked at one another as they both realised they were mistaken when Henri described meeting him in Bucharest. This was Virgil Madgearu, who proposed that Romania should find a third path in between the Capitalism of the west and the Socialist collectivism of the East. Piotr again joined in the discussion, expressing the view that a large farm would always be more efficient than a small one. Henri conceded that this might be true, but thought that the benefit of a family working together was inherently good.

When they were seated at the dining table, Henri said he had been enjoying a good discussion with the menfolk from Poland, as he called Piotr, Witold and Lukas. Valeria ironically asked whether his listeners had any questions. Lukas completely failed to see that this was a gentle joke about Henri's idea of a good discussion and so he took the opportunity to ask a question. "Uncle Henri, you mentioned the Jewish people in Romania, and said that the Iron Guard is against them. In Krakow, we also have many Jewish people, but to us they seem no different except in their religion, and run many businesses very well. I think you have told me this, Mama."

Agnieszka blushed. She had indeed spoken about the success of many Jewish people in Krakow, and how some Poles admired this, while others tended to be jealous. She was well aware of a current of anti-Semitism in her own country and was uncertain about the views of her brother-in-law. "Don't be too much of a know-all, Lukas. It's a big and complicated question. Just because we have a fine Jewish doctor does not make all Jews welcome everywhere."

"But Mama, you have said that our Jews in Poland are good; they run most of the new factories in Krakow and are at the top of other professions, not just doctors." Agnieszka intervened.

"Lukas, we should listen to your uncle. He is telling us about the situation here." Henri turned to Lukas. "No, my boy, I was not. I was talking about the international conspiracy of all Jews. I need to know more about what happens in Poland. You tell me, Agnieszka."

Lukas blushed as he realised that he had exposed his mother's disagreement with her brother-in-law. However, Agnieszka and Piotr were able to continue the discussion without embarrassment. They explained that the established Jewish community in Krakow added prosperity to the city, and referred to Viktor Auerbach as an example of one who employed a considerable workforce, only some of whom were Jewish. They conceded that it might be different in Romania, but said that there was no evidence of an international Jewish conspiracy in Krakow. Piotr concluded, "And so, we do not have an Iron Guard movement in Poland. If people talk of International Conspiracy, they will be referring to the Communists."

In the morning, the boys were allowed to ride two docile ponies into the fields, accompanied by the dog, Greig. He led them to a snare where a game bird had been caught. They returned to offer this contribution to the kitchen, but kept some of the feathers. Over lunch, they told Henri that they wanted to use the feathers for arrows. He took them down to a little courtyard where they found a workshop equipped with both carpentry and metalworking tools. There was an overwhelming smell of glue which was warming on the stove. A workman, who was repairing furniture, was willing to help them. Henri left the three of them and returned to his guests. By sign language, Witold explained what they wanted. Two straight lengths of wood were soon produced. A copper tube was adapted to form an arrow head, and pieces of the feathers glued into a slot. In the evening, they showed the finished work to the adults. Their mother did not need to remind them to thank Henri for organising this.

After dinner, the families strolled out into the garden. It was a beautiful still evening, with a clear crescent moon riding above vague milky clouds. Valeria suggested that they walk to the summer house beside the lake where they could sit outside. She would take her daughter back to bed and send out coffee. Lukas knew that his mother would reply that he and Witold should go indoors. She would say they needed plenty of sleep because they had a long day ahead. He decided to risk a request.

"Mama, if I promise not to interrupt tonight, could we stay out with you?"

It was Henri who took his side.

"All interruptions are welcome, young man. If we can't answer intelligent questions, it shows we are talking nonsense, which, as everyone knows, is my speciality."

"Great nonsense at greater length!" replied Valeria.

"Could you ask them to bring me a cigar with the coffee?"

There was no need for Agnieszka to say anything. Witold and Lukas took up inconspicuous positions on a rug behind the deckchairs. The sky held a pale residual light after the sunset. Some was blocked out by the black outlines of trees beyond the lake. As the moon rose higher and brighter, the dark surface of the lake glistened, showing a shining track of moonlight. While no one spoke, the animal kingdom provided intermittent sounds, the call of an owl, the splash of a fish entangled in the water lilies. Greig, the dog, silent and motionless seemed to have melted like chocolate around Henri's feet. There was no need for speech to express the feelings of each member of the group sharing in the enchantment of the evening.

The spell was broken by the arrival of the maid with a coffee tray, brandy and the cigar box. Naturally, it was Henri who spoke:

"There are few mosquitoes here because the carp in the lake eat most of the larvae, but it is necessary that at least one of us smokes just to be sure. Piotr can I tempt you to help here?"

"I never do, Henri, especially after such a fine dinner. We will rely on you to protect us all."

After lighting his cigar, Henri began as if the conversation of the previous evening had been broken off momentarily.

"Now, where were we? I have been thinking it over. I would suggest that if a family holding is large enough to maintain itself, it represents an ideal way of life. Children may join the farm when they grow up and the farm will support the old members of the family when they can do less themselves. In Soviet collective farms, I am not so sure about this."

Piotr maintained his argument that the big unit would be more productive because it could be more specialised. The family would grow root crops because it needs food in the winter, but if the land is better for grain, the farm should concentrate on wheat. Further, we have the chance to mechanise farming. If a nation fails to do so, its produce will become uncompetitive. How could a small family size unit afford modern machinery?

Henri had two answers: The market may supply the machinery or a bank could lend the capital required to buy it. He maintained that a family unit was the best way to care for the land from one generation to the next.

Lukas knew his uncle would not mind an interruption, whatever his mother might think.

"May I ask, Uncle Henri, what happens if a young person does not want to be a farmer like his father? Suppose he wants to go to university to study or to the army to defend his country?"

"An excellent point, struck in favour of your father's argument. The collective farm can easily release the intellectual for university or the warlike for the army. But don't you think that a loving father would always want his son to go where he chooses, follow his calling or his need to work in any profession? The family will probably have other relatives able to keep the farm going. For me, the family is the most important unit that God or man has created."

The conversation continued. More stars appeared in the night sky. Sleepy adolescents listened, dozed, enjoyed the fragrance of the cigar smoke and the warm sense of belonging which Henri engendered. When they left the lake together, Lukas said what he thought.

"I will not forget this evening. Thank you for letting us stay up, Uncle Henri."

"You should thank your mother for that."

Lukas answered cheerfully, "She would have sent us to bed, and we would have missed all of this."

Agnieszka laughed, and told them to go to sleep immediately to make up for the late night.

On the following morning, the Zeleski family were to depart, and Tudor brought the old carriage into the courtyard. The boys helped to load on the luggage and again borrowed Tudor's masks.

"You look terrifying," said Agnieszka. "If we meet another carriage on the road, we can easily stage a robbery!" Henri laughed and made Tudor produce the old blunderbuss again. "Don't tell anyone it's not loaded." Before his wife and daughter came out to the courtyard, Henri said to his sister-in-law. "These boys, Aggie. I would so love to have sons like these!"

Lukas had heard the comment. It justified his belief that when he needed it, his uncle would do all he could to help him.

Chapter 28: Romania and Freedom

"We must be free not because we claim freedom but because we practise it."

William Faulkner

Having done his best to describe the visit to Henri's home, Lukas explained why he placed such confidence in his uncle Henri. "He knows how much I admire him. He will never let me down."

He also talked over with Maria what he knew of the Fascist Iron Guard in Romania. The movement included an anti-Semitic element which Maria was quick to condemn. In the Podgorze area of Krakow, where she lived, the Jewish population was about a quarter of the total. She knew many Jewish families and had good friends amongst them. But Lukas understood that the Iron Guard also stood for a simple way of life, more spiritual and in tune with the Romanian countryside. Lukas believed that it was this aspect which had appealed to his uncle. Because of his interest in his Romanian relatives, Lukas had followed the news of their country. In 1937, the Iron Guard won seats in the Parliament, but in the following year, King Carol II began a period of autocratic rule. He turned against the Guardist movement which he feared might include agents of Germany. Many Guardists were interned in concentration camps. Lukas was worried that his Uncle, as an ethnic German, might be caught up in such reprisals, and the Zeleskis were relieved when Valeria wrote to tell them that they were all safe and well.

When Lukas gave his explanation of the Romanian Peasants' party, he was drawing on his uncle's description of its principles. The idea that the family unit was a valuable alternative to larger collective operations, especially in agriculture, appealed to both of them. Ruth asked a basic question. "If there is democracy in Romania and a majority of the population are poor tenant farmers, why do they not vote to dispossess their landlords, and take over all property themselves?"

"I am not sure. It may be that the leaders of their party are more middle-class intellectuals and they have only allowed the ideas to go so far. Perhaps they realise that you need to start with better education before you share out everything equally."

"Lukas, you are making this up as you go along."

He laughed. "You are right. I am just guessing. My uncle seemed to know everything. I should have pestered him even more than I did!"

"Perhaps the peasants have the right instinct here. They may have realised that to take over every large estate would never work. Just consider what would happen if our Leon were required to manage a big farm. He is efficient here, on his own land, but could never organise a complicated business. I tried to talk to him about what he would do with a larger holding. "But this is what we have," was his response. He could not imagine a change."

Although neither Maria nor Lukas had a true understanding of the way Communism was operating in Russia, Lukas had sometimes joked with his father about his enthusiasm for vegetables which were destined only for his family. Piotr would laugh and say, "No need for wages or clever communist theory. If I can raise a good crop of beans, they are the only reward I need to justify weeks of work."

Lukas and Maria were witnessing how the peasants survived on what they cultivated in their small plot. Leon's wife did all she could to share the hard work but she was limited by her arthritis. They were now hibernating like squirrels during the freezing winter months. Maria concluded that a larger farm managed by experts would never be as successful and productive as the small-holding worked by the owner and his family.

"Where I come from in lowly Podgorze, we often say that the intellectuals and middle-class managers are not nearly as clever as they imagine." Lukas agreed with her.

Maria was not accustomed to long discussions about politics or government. Initially, she listened to Lukas without real interest. He had admitted that his school nickname had been "The Professor," and she took to calling him "My Professor." She would sometimes interrupt his lecture and change the subject. But gradually, she found he was a good teacher, just as BB had been, and he took her opinions and suggestions seriously. Maria developed an interest in these subjects and grew to enjoy their conversations, and to talk nearly as much as she listened.

On another long evening, Lukas told her more about BB, both as his history teacher and his flight commander. When he reached the account of BB's relationship with Ruth, he was surprised that Maria's attitude was as understanding towards the married man. He had expected her to condemn him outright. His mother had never told him about Ruth's pregnancy, nor had she spoken of the help which she and Maria had given to Ruth. Lukas was surprised by Maria's response.

"Do you not blame him, Maria? For me, who became his friend, it is hard to forgive, but surely a good Christian like you could never excuse him?"

"Blame by others and guilt in ourselves, these are entirely useless emotions. What we all need is understanding and sympathy."

"But Maria, he is responsible here. He should never have begun this affair."

"Let he who is without sin cast the first stone," she replied, quoting the words of Jesus when asked if the woman "taken in adultery" should be stoned to death.

When Lukas described his confrontation with BB and his decision to leave St Xavier's, Maria said that she could understand that the person who holds himself out as a good example has greater responsibility. "He could not let you down, knowing how much you respected him."

"I had not seen it like that, but you are probably right."

Their own romantic life was frozen like the weather. However, Maria made Lukas happy. She said she loved him more each day. But she was also determined that she should not become pregnant and sexual intercourse was denied. They learned other ways to satisfy one another.

"If we had stayed apart, we would have frozen to death," said Maria.

"And I would have been completely miserable," he replied.

Maria devised a programme of exercise for each of them. When they guessed it might be mid-January, with the days growing slightly longer, she removed the ankle plaster and Lukas began to recover first movement and then strength in the joint. The exercise regime took much time, but was rewarded with an ankle which worked well and became almost pain-free.

They planned to leave in March, but as the snow lay thick on the ground, they awaited a thaw. When they thought they could walk through the remaining snow, they decided to set out just before dawn. They gave jewellery to their hosts in an attempt to repay them and set off with smiles, good wishes and promises of secrecy. The couple looked bereft as they departed. When they reached the edge of the wood, and before they turned out of sight, Lukas called back to them, "We must meet again, all of us, and your sons."

There were more smiles, but, in reality, there was very little hope that this wish would be realised.

It was a cool morning, but became brittle and bright as the sun rose higher. They were sweating as they pushed ahead with an arduous climb over the hills and then down to the long valley leading to the Romanian border. They did not know what to expect at this stage, and decided to keep walking through the hills so as to avoid any border control on the road. The kingdom of Romania was a neutral country and they hoped that they could travel freely once they had crossed the border. They achieved this by following the Dniester valley until they left Poland. After a cold night spent in a barn, they awoke, still fully dressed and set off into a dim landscape at first light. By mid-morning they knew they must be in Romania. They celebrated their achievement by standing together, looking out down a long green valley following the course of a river. Lukas held Maria in his arms, kissing her cheeks and saying, as he often did, that without her he would never have reached this stage in the journey.

Chapter 29: Border Crossing

"He shall defend thee under his wings, and thou shalt be safe under his feathers."

Psalm 91.

The day remained overcast, but clear and windy. They were on high ground in remote country. All around was heathland punctured by rocky outcrops. Lower down, they could see straggling fir trees and then thick forest. Above them, an eagle flew at great height. It was impossible to judge the size of the bird against the cloudy sky, but they guessed its wingspan must be enormous. They watched as the wings tensed and flexed. The bird seemed to stop in the sky, holding its position against the wind and then abruptly dropped. The eagle fell and suddenly checked its descent, as if caught at the end of a rope. The great beak and head were thrust forward, twisting as it searched the ground below. The humans had stopped walking to concentrate on the spectacle in the sky.

"I hope he is looking for something smaller than us!"

But the eagle lost interest in the ground and set off upward, the great wings taking hold of the air, striving for height until the bird reached its chosen ceiling and went soaring ahead in the wind.

"He must have decided to leave us alone."

Lukas intended to follow the same route as his family had taken to find his Uncle Henri and his family. When relatively close to the Polish border, it was natural that some of the locals could speak Polish and so Maria went in search of help, while Lukas remained out of sight. She was able to secure information about a bus which would take them on to Clug Napoca and to buy bread and cheese which they ate with enthusiasm. Later, she was able to persuade someone else to change a few Polish zlotys for Romanian crowns. They made reasonable progress but had to walk for another long day before they reached their destination. They left the bus outside the town. When it began to rain, they were fortunate to find a barn in which they sheltered during the afternoon. After yet another day, they were close to Biertan. Lukas remembered the town for its fortified churches which Henri had insisted on showing to the Polish visitors. They were now much nearer their destination, and in mid-afternoon, they were looking down from high ground onto a grey lake below. A first, Lukas did not recognise it. Sun emerged from a cloud, the lake glittered and Lukas could now see, illuminated beside the lake, the summerhouse where Henri had enthralled his listeners many years ago. The extensive stone farmhouse and outbuildings were sheltered behind the hillside, and came into view as they descended.

It was his aunt who opened the front door. She had aged, and was thinner than Lukas remembered her. She looked more like his mother.

"Aunt Valeria, do you remember me? Your nephew, Lukas. This is Maria who has helped me to escape from Poland."

"I can't believe it's you! Come in, both of you. Lukas, I would never have recognised you with that beard. It's not even the same colour as your hair. Will you come and sit with me in the kitchen now, and I will get a bath organised for you while you explain?"

She took them into the farmhouse kitchen. Valeria now seemed completely at home, bustling about at the kitchen range and making tea for the three of them. It was clear to Lukas that his uncle and aunt were no longer enjoying their pre-war style of life. Lukas explained about his injury, Maria's role in his escape and the recovery with the peasants in the Russian sector of Poland. After telling Valeria about the disappearance of his father and the uncertain fate of his brother, he asked about their life.

"Much has changed. We are more self-contained now. Indeed, we seldom leave our own land. Henri still supports the Iron Guard, but avoids any leading role. He also wants our country to maintain its alliances with France and England. It will be the best for us all if Germany is defeated whenever war breaks out again. But these great countries are far away. Germany and Russia are on our doorstep. The King is trying to preserve our neutral position, but is under pressure from both of these neighbours. Hitler wants our oil supplies and the Soviets want Bessarabia." Valeria paused.

"I have been so hopeful about this country which was making such good progress. Now, I am not so sure, and nor is Henri. He will be back from the fields at the end of the day and he can tell you more."

Lukas asked her about changes in their farm.

"It is partly because we are not sure where Romania is going that we have been concentrating on our life here. We have invested in more agricultural equipment, modernised the house so we can run it without any servants, and we now have only one farm hand. You will remember him; the amusing coachman. We have kept him partly because he is devoted to Henri and partly because he can drive the new tractor. He will bring Aggie back from school in an hour or so."

In the evening, when Henri and Aggie had joined them, Lukas repeated his determination to join the allies. His idea was that he would get to Constanta on the Black Sea and then find a ship heading for the Mediterranean. Henri seemed somehow subdued. He was no longer the erupting volcano which had been his character when entertaining the Zeleskis years ago. He admitted that his life now had more problems and fewer opportunities. At first, Henri was non-committal in his response to Lukas' proposal, but when the meal was over, he said that he would work something out.

It took all of the following day for Henri to produce his solution. The main element was a 1000 cc motorbike, and two cans of petrol. The machine was reliable, and the fuel sufficient. It roared into the farmyard and slithered to a halt on the cobbles. Henri dismounted, grinning as he used to do when Lukas had first known him. He had recovered his charisma and his joie de vivre. Valeria and Maria had heard the sound of the machine as it bellowed through the archway. Now, they met him in the yard.

"First this machine: it is Polish; a Sokol 1000. I know you can fly any aeroplane in the Polish Air Force. This machine was designed for your police service, so I am sure a pilot can handle it."

Indeed, when training at the Polish Air Force centre at Deblen, Lukas had once borrowed a motor bike, and had brought it back in one piece. Henri went on to explain what he had learnt in the town. The problem was that the police might stop them, and, if their true identity was discovered, they could be taken into custody. The authorities were under pressure from the Germans. Many Polish soldiers and airmen had been treated like this.

"But with Maria on the pillion, why should they stop you? It will look like a young couple going about their normal business.

Now, I have been told that there is an English liaison officer at Constanta. Officially, he is there to make sure that British goods get through customs or that the ambassador's children are sent off to school in England. But really..." Henri tapped the side of his nose. "Really, he is there to make sure that any good Polish soldiers get away to join the allies. I know where he is based and have a description here." He fished in his trouser pocket for a crumpled paper. "The name of the place you can find him at mid-day is The Old Wine Pot. He is very short, wears tortoiseshell glasses and has the shiniest shoes in Romania. What do you think of that?"

Henri did not speak Polish and was talking in slow German, which Lukas could understand. His face alight with excitement, he translated for Maria, who ran to Henri, put her arms round his neck and kissed him. "What a family!" she said.

"Valeria and I know what you have done for Lukas," said Henri, touched by her affection.

It did not take long to work out the best route to Constanta, avoiding Bucharest. The only major city was Ploiesti, which they might drive through in the early evening when they would be relatively inconspicuous. Maria had no experience of motorcycles. She suggested that she should learn with Henri before she entrusted herself to Lukas.

"You only have to hold on tight."

"What am I going to hold onto?"

"Only the rider."

"Perhaps I had better practise with Lukas then."

On the following morning, they set off in slight drizzle, which gradually cleared. Their route wound through the Central Carpathians. There were tight bends where Maria learned to hold on and move with Lukas as he slowed and leaned the machine into the turn.

"Is flying as good as this?"

"This is beginning to compete, and with me learning how to do it, must be nearly as dangerous."

Lukas was enjoying the machine, the countryside, the sense of progress and the happiness of his passenger. As the weather improved, they had a fine prospect from the mountain road looking down over the flatter countryside before the small town of Pitesti. They drove through the place, attracting no attention. Their spirits were high. Lukas suggested that they take a chance on getting through Ploiesti in the early afternoon but Maria disagreed.

"No, Lukas. Let's stick to the plan Henri proposed. We can stop and wait for a while. At the end of the day, we raise no more suspicion and will be harder to see, or to pursue. Busy policeman will be thinking of going home to their families."

They were travelling in a wooded countryside, and Lukas found a place where they could push the machine off the road and conceal it behind some bushes. They ate cheese, bread and onions which Valeria had provided for them. Lukas lay back, looking up at the pale sky visible in gaps between the tree tops. Above them, a raucous crow began a noisy fight with two magpies who were defending their territory against this annoying invader. Maria moved to look into his face.

"Well done, the motorcyclist, the man who can do anything. I have enjoyed holding on."

Their mouths tasted of onions but they did not mind.

In the afternoon, they went on towards Ploiesti and again drove serenely through the town. It was with a sense of relief and satisfaction that they stopped for the night at a village beside the river Ialomita. On the following morning, they reached Constanta and went in search of the short Englishman in The Old Pot.

"Come outside for a moment." He gestured to the rear courtyard. Lukas followed the short steps of the shiny brogues. The conversation was in the appalling and mangled French of the British diplomat and the better version of the language which Ruth had taught to Lukas.

"Yes. I can get you a berth on a Greek tramp steamer which normally goes to Malta. He may go further, but I don't recommend allowing him to take you anywhere in Italy. What do you have to show you flew in the Polish Air Force?"

Lukas had anticipated this request and produced his payslip and a certificate.

"Good. That's fine. But I can't take the girl. She is no use to the war effort in France or England, so that is out of the question."

"I suggest that we complete this conversation inside." In the bar of The Old Pot, with Maria beside him, Lukas struggled through the language barrier. "Maria is a nurse. She is qualified and worked in the main hospital in Krakow. She rescued me and mended my leg. The Germans would have taken me as a prisoner of war. My fracture would never have been treated properly. She helped me to escape from the hospital before the Germans took over. In the mountains, she has already fought the Russians. We have defeated them. She has saved my life twice and we have come here together, seeking freedom. If you think you can tell me to leave her here so that I can go and die for your country, you need to think again. Sir, I do not believe that we Poles would treat an ally like that!"

There was something about the resolve of the Polish airman and the sensible expression of his companion which made it impossible for the British officer to argue with them.

e Polish PZL fighters shown here came into service in 1934, when they were
anced machines. Aircraft development progressed rapidly and by 1939 they
re no match for the Luftwaffe's aircraft.

PART THREE

Chapter 30: Ruth and Emil

There was an interval of months before Ruth saw Emil Mendler again, and during this period, she received a visit from Stefan. She was delighted to see him, but surprised to find him so thin, the beard unkempt and flecks of grey in the chestnut hair. The man badly needed a bath. He was plainly pleased to find her in the same flat, and checked that it was safe to visit before the curfew. He would need to leave soon in order to get back to his lodgings in time. Then, as if he desperately needed to get something off his chest, he said with his usual flow of language, "Ruth everything I have ever thought and said to you about Communism is a lie. The Soviets are the new empire-builders. We need to talk a lot more. I have been so deceived, I can hardly bear it. We have all been victims of Stalin."

She smiled and ruffled his hair as she used to do when he was carried away by his own eloquence.

"Come next week, but at an earlier time, if you can. I will lend you my bathroom, hot water, a towel and give you a proper meal. You need all these material things, you filthy Communist!"

"Bourgeois values, as always!" he replied.

Stefan agreed to come on the following Saturday afternoon. He ate prodigiously and they talked for hours. He was deeply distressed by the mendacity of the Soviets as well as the aggression of the Red Army.

"They have taken our country. They have been killing anyone at random, abusing women and targeting Jews, stealing farm animals, plundering the few possessions of the local people throughout the part of Poland they have taken."

Plainly, he had revised his more extreme opinions and recognised that Poles were entitled to Poland and Polish peasants should be allowed to keep their own property. The International Communist had merged into the Polish patriot. Ruth remembered the penetrating question put to him by Auerbach so long ago, leading to Stefan's admission that he, like Auerbach, was a patriot at heart. Sometimes, Stefan referred to "we" and "us". Without saying it in so many words, it was clear that he had joined the Polish Resistance, called The Home Army.

Ruth told Stefan what she knew about Agnieszka and she did her best to explain that she was confident of retaining her flat because she trusted the colonel in charge of the premises. She was relieved to find that he accepted that, amongst the invaders, there might be some decent and honourable Germans.

"I understand, Ruth. The Germans are not all Nazis. It will be the same with the Russians we knew in Warsaw. They had principles. They must be as aggrieved as I am about this attack on the poor in Poland. Like me, they are probably more angry because they are also ashamed to have been so misled."

Ruth was not so sure that the Warsaw enthusiasts for Communism would lose their faith in the Party which they had continued to follow through every twist in its message.

Ruth missed the company of Emil. She was reminded of him when she played the music he had given her, which she did with increasing frequency. One Sunday, Ruth saw him in the congregation at St Andrej, seated at the back with another officer. He did not linger to meet her after the service, which, she confessed to herself, was a disappointment. She spoke to Agnieszka who was looking tired, her face more lined. These two women were pleased to see one another. One of them had lost her husband, the other her baby. Each tried to support the other. Ruth walked unhappily home to spend a lonely afternoon in the flat. She found her book and made an effort to concentrate on reading. As twilight fell, the silence was broken by the sound of the school gate opening. Ruth got up from her chair to look out. It was Emil coming along the pathway. Her heart lifted and she went down the stairs to open her door before he reached it.

"I thought you had forgotten where I live," she said. They enjoyed a pleasant evening.

As the colonel's visits continued, they agreed that they should not be seen in public together, but he brought food and ingredients which were no longer available to Polish residents in Krakow. She would cook for them both. Sometimes, he suggested a slightly different method, apologising for imposing German traditions on a French chef. He had a dry sense of humour and a gentle sensitivity which she had experienced with no other person. He was, she reflected, much older than Bruno, who she had loved so completely. But he made time to listen to her, to adapt to her mood in a way which Bruno had never done. His thinking was subtler too. Was it maturity, or more simply an exceptional example of human conduct and kindness? He made no demands on her. But when he was leaving the flat, he would say that his times spent with her were his one solace in days of difficult and demanding work. She would say the same to him, thanking him for coming and asking when she might see him again. Ruth had no means of knowing whether he wanted more than a close friendship with her, and she was too inexperienced and too delicate to initiate a romantic conversation or even a loving gesture.

"May I come again on Wednesday?" he asked her.

"Of course, please come any time."

"I am not sure you really mean that."

"Emil, you know me. Why ever would I say that if it is not true?"

After another quiet evening together, he asked if he could see her on Friday.

"I would be so pleased if you could. I often think of my family on Fridays. I miss them, you see. Your company would be a great comfort."

"Perhaps there is someone you used to see on Friday evenings in Toul?" he said with an enquiring smile. She looked at him quizzically, shaking her head.

"Nothing like that, I am afraid," she replied.

But on the Friday evening, she had readied herself to tell much more of her private life. She confessed to her relationship with "one of the teachers at St Xavier's." She told him he had joined the Polish Air Force and been killed in action.

"Are you sure that he is not a prisoner of war?"

"No, he is dead. A friend of his came to tell me the news just before the occupation here."

"Ruth, I am so sorry to hear this. It must have been heart-breaking for you."

The following passage of time seemed to move very slowly between them. She believed that he was resisting the wish to embrace her, to fold her in his arms, to show that he cared for her, that he shared her sense of loss. But she was unsure. This long moment passed.

"May I change the subject by asking you why you told me about the picture of The Retreat from Moscow?"

"I know you will not discuss this with anyone, Ruth. I should not have referred to this. Between us, I tell you that it is possible the Fuhrer will decide to attack Russia. Only a possibility. Plans are being made. Yet plans are always made, and for all eventualities. It is the job of the Ministry to do this, and my work as a logistics officer is to work out how to supply whatever army is deployed to whatever place. But Ruth, I feel that if the work by Meissonier might somehow be spirited out of The Louvre, where I have seen it, and hung above the dressing table of the Fuhrer so he confronts it every morning, well then, much grief and suffering might be saved."

"I understand that your country has a treaty with Russia, much to the disadvantage of Poland. I am not good at politics."

"You are right about that non-aggression pact. It was needed last year before the invasion of this country. But now that it is no longer required, we shall see."

In March 1941, Ruth was working in the shop when Daniel Blumenthal arrived late and deeply upset. He was reluctant to say anything while the owner was present, but later he explained that his parents, his wife and his two children had been forced out of their home in Kazimierz. They had been made to live in the Jewish Ghetto across the river. Their four-bedroom apartment would be expropriated by the General Government. The space allocated to his family in the ghetto comprised two rooms forming part of a dilapidated flat and they must share the kitchen and bathroom with two other families. His wife had tried to argue with the Judenrat, the Jewish council in charge of the Ghetto, but received a firm refusal. His mother was suffering a breakdown.

"It cannot go on," said Daniel, close to tears.

"It must get better," Ruth agreed.

"Or worse!" Daniel replied.

Ruth expressed sympathy, but could offer no other support to Daniel. Walking home and thinking over this trouble, she experienced a sense of guilt that she was masquerading as a Christian. Another voice in her mind responded, "But I am a Christian." In truth, she was unsure.

Ruth decided to raise with Emil the question of the German treatment of her work colleague and his family. He did not try to justify it, but agreed that it was wrong.

"It never used to be so. There were many cities in Germany with Jewish populations as numerous as yours here. But when things go wrong for a country, it is tempting for its people to look for someone to blame. If they find those who are separate from their own population, the temptation to allocate blame is all the stronger. This led to the Nazi wish to blame Jews for the defeat in the Great War and their view of the world. I hope it will burn itself out."

Emil seemed to become busier. He was seldom able to see her, and when he arrived, he was often distracted. He told her only that there was some sort of dispute between the Wehrmacht High Command and the Governor who controlled Krakow from Wawel Castle.

"The Governor wants my compound. The whole school. He must not get it. You could not keep the flat if he did." Then, he seemed to regret causing her this anxiety.

"I will go to Berlin myself if I have to. I need to get this settled."

He explained that he had a poor relationship with the Governor, Otto Wachter, and he would need to invoke higher authority in order to get his way.

"Emil, is this to do with The Retreat from Moscow?"

"Ruth, you know too much already. Please forget about that. It was a mere flight of fancy."

For once, his reply seemed insincere. Ruth was not convinced. She had struck something hollow, but she decided against asking any more.

A week after the discussion, Emil left her a note explaining that he was leaving for Berlin and if he did not return within a fortnight, it would only mean bad news "for us both." This last phrase was important to Ruth. It implied that they had a closer relationship than they had acknowledged. She did not know why he needed to go to Berlin or what was the purpose of the compound or the new railway line he had been working on. She did know that she missed his companionship. She went to St Andrej on Sunday. She had time for a long conversation with Agnieszka, who had heard that her husband was still alive and held in a German labour camp. She did her best to sound positive, but Agnieszka was deeply anxious about the food, working conditions and her husband's prospects of survival. Ruth did not choose to mention her visits from the German colonel.

When he had been away for ten days, Ruth began to worry about Emil. She recognised to herself that she depended on him. Then, he arrived late one evening. He was exhausted and unkempt. His uniform, usually perfect, was creased from days on a train and he had two days' growth of grey beard.

"I needed to tell you; the flat is ours for as long as I can stay in Krakow. I came to tell you at once."

He was so tired that she did not question ask him further. He asked to use her bathroom. He meant to ask if he might have a bath in it. He turned on the taps and immediately sank into a chair, closing his eyes. When the bath was ready, she woke him, gave him her best towel and ushered him in. He was in the bathroom for half an hour, and then emerged saying he had fallen asleep again. She encouraged him to lie down. He lay on her bed and immediately closed his eyes.

Sometime after midnight, Ruth put on her nightdress, lay down and tried to sleep alongside the heavy form of Emil. His breathing was slow but calming. Troubled as she had been when he was away, not sure of her own wishes, now that he had returned to her, it all seemed clear. She admired this man and she needed him.

In the morning, when they were both awake, he asked her the time and made as if to get up. She put her arm over his body. "Don't go yet."

He was looking at her, unspeaking. "I have missed you," she said.

She put her head on his shoulder. He would surely respond with a similar gesture of affection. Instead, he moved away so that his grey eyes now looked directly into hers.

"Thank you, Ruth, for all of your kindness. I have been thinking so much about you. I have never told you what you mean to me. The company of a lovely woman, always interesting, thoughtful and considerate, this has been a new and wonderful experience. It has changed me. I used to tell myself that many Germans will die in the East. I might as well be one of them. My home life has been hopeless. I have no dependants, only a few true friends. But meeting you, and spending this precious time together, has allowed me to think there could be a happy future, somehow."

It was very close to a declaration of love.

"Emil, I feel the same. You have treated me with such kindness. I am so fond of you, and I wish we could be together…". She was, probably, about to add the word "always" at the end of this statement, when Emil cut her off.

"Ruth, I have often thought of that, and been sorely tempted. Any man enjoying so much the company of a beautiful single woman will think of this. But Ruth, I am well over fifty and you are thirty years younger than me. I am old enough to be your father. Just think of your parents…"

Ruth tried to interrupt. She was unconcerned about his age or her family. She said that she loved to be with him. She could not now imagine being with anyone else. Emil would brook none of this.

"I have lived in this world twice as long as you. I just know about these things. I have seen such relationships. They are lop-sided and simply wrong. We would both know in our hearts that it is so. Your father would tell you the same. For all I know, he is the same age as me. He would never allow such a thing, nor should he. It would be absolutely wrong for me to take advantage of a woman who is on her own and so much younger than I am.

I know what you have told me about the past, and I sympathise with you. You would like someone to care only for you. In many ways I have offered you that and always will. But if we were together, how would it end? If I am killed in the fighting, you would have lost another lover, which does not bear thinking about. If I survive the war, I would surely love you into my old age. And you would feel bound to this old man, you would feel obliged to stay with me and you would suffer all the grim consequences of being tied to someone a generation older than you. It is not possible and I must not do this. Indeed, I am not even officially separated from my wife. If we are seen together, people will assume that you are my daughter. If we were together, you would end your life as a nursemaid for an old man. Do you think I could let you do that? I tell you, I could not allow this to happen, that you should face such a future. Even if you could put up with it, I could never bear it."

His urgent manner and explanation demonstrated serious thought and a firm decision. Ruth felt an unhappy mixture of emotions, including both disappointment and renewed respect for Emil. They sat in silence while she came to terms with all that he had said.

"Emil, if you are right, then I must somehow accept this. But to me, it feels a sad loss."

"You must, and so will I. Because, if the whole world recovers itself, you will meet someone of your own generation, and you can then enjoy loving that person. You will have a love freely given and not driven by events and troubles."

Ruth could not find the words to express to Emil what she now recognised. Here was a truly loving man, denying himself because he loved her. She was too emotional to speak and left the room. When alone in the bathroom, she struggled to control herself. She took deep breaths. She dried her eyes. She blew her nose. She returned to him, summoning new reserves of calm and courage.

Speaking steadily, she asked him about his visit to Berlin. Emil made it clear that what he was telling her was secret. Hitler was about to launch the invasion of the Soviet Union, Operation Barbarossa. The decision had been made in the middle of 1940 and Emil's task had been to organise the logistics for this huge military project. Although every effort must be made to preserve secrecy, the site would begin to fill up immediately and the operation would start in June. Emil had been able to retain control over the two flats used by the caretaker and by Ruth. He had told his superiors in Berlin that if the present occupiers were ordered to leave, this might lead to further enquiries about the use of the school.

"And so, although I am going to be extremely busy, we can hold on here indefinitely. I feel a good deal more optimistic about keeping the flat than the military operation. It is far too risky. The Nazis imagine that their destiny is to take on the whole world. They think they can conquer any opposing force anywhere. I have explained that bad weather could slow down the invasion, and they should prepare for fighting in the Russian winter. But the Wehrmacht is packed with optimistic officers, telling their Fuhrer what he wants to hear. They are sure they will have defeated Stalin before Christmas."

Ruth asked whether he would be allowed to stay in Krakow when the invading armies set out.

"Yes; that is exactly my job, to control everything, the reinforcements and the material we are sending out from here. I would be useless in this role if I joined the forces in Russia. I believe also that you, Ruth, will be safe here too."

Emil paused. He looked into her face as if searching for an answer from her.

"Although I am a loyal soldier, I am deeply troubled now. My own view is that the Fuhrer's plans are reckless. It is entirely possible that the advance will be stopped, or that the Russians will repeat the tactics which prevailed against Napoleon. I might find myself trying to keep supplies flowing across thousands of miles in a Russian winter. I am distressed by these plans. I also know about the role of the SS units who go with the army. They will execute all Communists and all Jews. What can I do about this? I cannot desert the army. I wonder, if the information which I have were known to the whole German population, then if the Russian campaign goes badly, whether there might be a political change. Ruth, I find it very difficult to know where my duty lies. What is the right....?"

Emil could not find a word. Ruth looked at him in wonder. The grey eyes, always calm, were bright as if close to tears. He recovered his usual self-possession and made it clear that he must return to his office. He had to deliver the orders from Berlin. He said he should be able to come to see her in the evening. They parted as friends, understanding one another much better. When he returned, his mood seemed lighter as if determined to please her, to make the most of the time together.

Chapter 31: Peril.

"It breaks my heart. Better than words, your eye tells me all your peril."
Friedrich Nietzsche, Thus Spoke Zarathustra

When Ruth came back to her flat after work, she found, waiting outside, a young man whose face seemed familiar. He spoke German and asked to come inside the front door of the flat. They spoke, standing together in the tiny hallway.

"Miss Neuman, you may not remember me. My name is Glast and you used to teach me music at this school. I was a friend of Witold Zeleski. My family is German and I have been employed to work in an enforcement department of the administration. Miss Neuman, I have come from my office this evening because I have just seen a report claiming that you are of Jewish race."

Ruth swayed on her feet. Pale and worried, she did not know how to answer the young man. His hair was cut so short that she had not immediately recognised him as the friend of the Zeleski boys who had helped out when Lutoslawski insisted on timpani for the performance in The Mariacki.

"I think I can just lose the report and we can hope it goes no further. I have read through it. Someone says he provided you with accommodation, that you left owing rent and that he has recently discovered a Jewish prayer book with your name inside it. It may be easy for you to disprove this, if you have family or records to support a denial. Anyone could write your name in a prayer book. He has given no explanation for making this allegation so long after you left his house. He has not even shown a tenancy agreement to prove you lived there. He might be hoping for a reward for such information. This sort of false allegation happens every day."

His attempt to discredit the report was unsuccessful, for Ruth knew it was true. Hainski had stolen her prayer book. She remained speechless and troubled.

"Miss Neuman, forgive me. You don't look well now, and I wonder if I could come back tomorrow evening after work so that we can talk it over then."

"No need to delay. We can talk it over now. You are very kind. You should not take a risk for me."

"You also were kind, kind to us all, Miss Neuman. Risks are unavoidable in these times."

Ruth understood. Vlad, the star footballer who she had often seen with Lukas and his brother, did not know whether Hainski's report was true or false. But she did.

After further discussion, she asked him to destroy the report.

"Did he hand in the prayer book?" she asked.

"No. He just claims he has found it. If he had brought it in, I would have taken it myself."

"Will anyone know that you have removed this record?"

"Documents get lost in offices all the time."

Ruth trusted Vlad Glast to get rid of the report. But the fact that Hainski had kept her prayer book meant that he had retained the evidence against her.

Ruth had absolute confidence in Emil and she would have welcomed his advice and comfort. But their relationship was now pleasantly simple, she thought, and it would become complicated if he knew her secret. Perhaps she had been denying her race for so long, she had not felt any need to confess it to Emil as their friendship had progressed. When he next came to see her, they enjoyed an evening of conversation and music.

Ruth realised that the German attack on Russia was underway. The railway station, the roads and the pattern of life in Krakow all gave evidence of the huge scale of Operation Barbarossa. The military advance involved millions of men flooding across the demarcation line between the General Government of Poland and the Russian sector. Motorised columns of men, tanks and equipment had been prepared, assembled, poised and were now thrust at extraordinary speed towards objectives stretching from Novgorod to Odessa. The news was everywhere and the evidence all around her.

When she came home and recognised Vlad Glast, awaiting her return, she knew her situation had changed for the worse.

"Miss Neuman, the informant has come back. He has repeated his assertion and wants to know why you are still living here and not in the Jewish Ghetto. Miss Neuman, I am sorry but the allegation must soon be dealt with. If they find you, they will arrest you and you will need an immediate answer to the charge." Ruth decided to stall.

"I may need records from my home town. How long have I got to obtain them?"

"Miss Neuman, everything is in a rush these days. This sort of information is often false and so it does not take priority. I guess it will be weeks before anyone authorises an investigation. But Miss Neuman, it will surely happen one day. I can't stop it. I am sorry." Glast looked sad and anxious as he was saying this.

The messenger, bringing bad news or announcing an injustice, hates his task just as much as if he had caused the harm himself.

Ruth now felt sorry for Glast. She thanked him for all his help and said that she hoped they would meet again when things were different. Neither had any confidence that this would happen, but it made it easy for him to leave her. She thought about Vlad Glast as she let him go, back into occupied Krakow, his home city, controlled by his German countrymen. She considered what he had done. As a Pole of German origin, he had an advantage in this harsh new world. Had some innate sense of fairness led him to risk disobedience to the orders of the victorious regime? As a citizen of Poland, seeing the cruelty to both Poles and Jews, he wished to distance himself from the invaders. Even more important was his sense of personal loyalty to a woman he knew from his schooldays, and had respected and appreciated since then. Vlad Glast had been affected by her singing when they both participated in Lutoslawski's performance in The Mariacki. It was from Bruno Berling that Glast had learnt to be a team player. He knew which side he was on. If he had an opportunity to save this woman, he would surely seize it. Ruth reached this understanding of the man, and would not have been surprised to learn that in the following month, Vlad Glast joined the Home Army to struggle against the occupiers.

Emil did not come for a few days. Ruth needed to explain to him about Vlad Glast. This would require a full account of her background and her race. She was anxious about his response.

When Emil arrived one afternoon, he was keen to talk about his plans which were going well. He tried to explain to her how the logistics would work out as if proud of his own competence. Although he was doing exactly what the High

Command required, he had also provided a fair explanation of the problems which could occur in winter. There would be extreme cold, huge distances and the danger that the Russians would behave as they did in 1814. It was for the High Command to follow his suggestions or to disregard them. Emil finished by saying that after working furiously for days on end, he now had an opportunity to recover. Ruth had to break the bad news.

"Emil, I have things I must say to you now. There is so much which I should have told you before."

She moved to sit on the arm of the sofa, looking into his face, tired but calm.

"You said to me that you might die in this war. But you should be working on army supplies, perhaps staying out of danger as I hope you can. I believe that I am more likely to perish than you. If am lucky and survive this war, I would feel grateful to be a nurse if the patient is as kind and clever as you are." He stood, and she put her arms around his neck, her head again on his shoulder.

"Emil, I must tell you something really serious myself. I must tell you now. I don't want to. I know we trust each other. You have just told me secrets, which I must keep. I have to tell you something about my birth, about my parents. We are Jewish."

Emil waited and sighed.

"I know this. Ruth, I should have told you a long time ago, that when I was working in my father's firm, I knew Viktor Auerbach as a good customer and honest businessman. He encouraged me to leave the family firm when I had a dispute with my father about his commercial practises. I have a great respect for Viktor. So, knowing what would happen to Jewish business leaders here, as soon as I arrived in Krakow, I went to see him at his house.

explained that he could never retain ownership of his business, because my people would appropriate it. The best he could hope for would be to continue as a manager of his factory. He replied that there was already a manager who ran the factory perfectly well. He pretended to leave Krakow for Silesia. Everyone thought he had done that, but in fact, his chauffeur collected him from the first station on his journey and brought him back to Krakow. He has a new name and identity and works in a bar. He now wears spectacles and has a beard. I guess he owns the bar. When he told me that he was going to pretend to leave Krakow, he also asked about your position at the school. This was one reason why I have been careful to protect you from the start."

Ruth looked at him in wordless astonishment for a full minute. He was watching her face as she understood the truth.

"You have been looking after me even from the first day we met!"

"Not really, Ruth. You have done far more for me. It is I who am in your debt. You have kept me sane while I have been working, against my wishes, to wage an endless war against an enormous enemy."

"It is a relief to me that you know my race, and have continued our friendship regardless. But I have to explain why I am in danger now."

She told Emil about Vlad Glast, the first report to him and the latest news that Hainski had returned to repeat his claim. She explained about the prayer book. It was written in Hebrew but with notes in French. It would be difficult to suggest that Hainski had concocted such evidence against her. Against this, could she maintain a denial that she was Jewish?

"Ruth, that is serious, more worrying than anything I have thought about. I don't know what might be the chances of fending off this evil man. That is completely outside my experience. But I know more than I have ever told you about the Nazis' attitude to the Jewish people, whether here in Europe, or in Russia if Barbarossa succeeds."

"I will not ask you to take any risk for me. You have helped me so much already."

"For you, any risk. Anything at all. Everything."

"We may have no more time together. Let us not waste it."

She moved into his arms and they embraced with a tenderness appropriate to a long-established and loving relationship. This evening, they had all the time they needed. To Ruth, it was is if they had been lovers for a long time.

Later that night, he moved away to the bathroom. She was awake when he returned to her bedside and she had drawn back a curtain to let in the moonlight. She lay back as he approached her bed.

He was on top of her and kissing her mouth. She reached down his back as far as she could to touch between his buttocks. She had found that Bruno had enjoyed such touching and sometimes reacted to it with a sudden pumping rush. Emil raised his head to look into her eyes.

"This is a surprise."

The touch continued to excite. With the inevitability of a tide coming in, Emil satisfied them both and lay catching his breath as he held her beside him.

They slept. Before dawn, the woman awoke with the unaccustomed warmth of the human form beside her. Her body felt different, more alive. She knew why. A slight light filtered into the bedroom and awakened the man. His mind stirred and he was aware of her breast against his back. When fully conscious, remorse returned to him, in a new form. He had denied what they had both wanted. They now faced a loss of the happiness so suddenly realised. He said something indistinct, words to express his regret. Her body stirred too and she leaned over his face.

"Do not be troubled. You have done your utmost. We are together at last."

"Ruth, Ruth, we should have done this before; all these months of love between us. I have wanted this and denied us both." Ruth murmured something soothing, but he persisted:

"This dreadful German Catholic conscience. It has damaged me, I know. And it has hurt you too."

"Emil, we cannot be perfect humans, neither the Jew nor the Christian. We are thrown one way and another, afloat on the sea of Fate." Her hand moved over him. It was a loving touch. Her mouth kissed him and she forgave.

"Never have you hurt me. It is just that we have both been waiting a long time." She was right, but so was he. If his deep conscience was to be clear, he had to be sure that he was not taking advantage of the woman he loved. All was resolved between them and he responded with a gentle smile. He pushed back her black hair, bending towards her. Ruth put her arms around his body, pulling him close to her. They were together for the last time, Ruth holding tightly to him. Here, in the pale light of her bleak bedroom, she experienced a new sense of calm, knowing that she belonged to Emil. They had their victory alongside their defeat. He, more exhausted, slept beside her.

In the morning, action was required.

"They know you are here. This is your address. They will come back. It follows that you must go, if you can. Do you know anywhere that would be safe for you?"

"Yes, I have a dear friend, a Polish woman. She sings in the St Andrej choir. She lives alone outside the city. I know she would like me to stay with her. She says she is going mad living alone. She even has a little farm."

Emil trusted his driver to keep a secret about the journey with Ruth and her bags towards Agnieszka's home. They concealed the bags and a mirror behind some trees, while Ruth walked on alone to the house. Out of sight of the driver, she embraced Emil. She was holding the one human she wanted and she must leave him now. It was difficult to guess when or whether they might meet again.

"Thank you, Emil. You are the finest man I have ever known."

"Thank you," he replied.

Agnieszka did not answer the door. Walking round to the little stable, Ruth saw that the trap was in its usual place. She went on into an orchard and found her there attacking the weeds growing around her apple trees.

Chapter 32: Christmas 1941.

Piotr had been released from the concentration camp and returned to Krakow. He was reluctant to talk about his experiences at Dachau, and his wife concentrated on building up his strength. He had lost all his teeth, and the women made soup or ground his food using a pestle and mortar. In the winter cold, he was troubled by arthritis. He knew he must take exercise and did his best to move all his limbs. In the doorway of a cloakroom, he invented a device which used string and a leather strap to raise his arms above shoulder height. "The torture chamber," he said, grinning with his empty mouth. Wincing, he raised and lowered his enfeebled body from a stool, and insisted upon walking around the house several times each day.

After many months of careful diet and regular exercise, Piotr was able to move about more freely. He wanted to attend Mass on Christmas morning. Ruth had never been into Krakow through all the months since her decision to take refuge in Agnieszka's home. Christmas Mass was an important event for Agnieszka, who had loved this season since childhood. If Ruth would come, they would be able to bring Piotr too. She suggested to Ruth that they go to The Mariacki instead of St Andrej, in order to avoid the numbers of people who knew her there. There was also a chance that Prince Sapieha, who was the Metropolitan Archbishop, would be preaching. Well wrapped against the cold, the three of them set out early and made good progress through the forest tracks. The snow lay thick and heavy on the branches above. As the sun moved higher in the sky, their spirits were raised with the temperature. Piotr took over the reins and the women sat together singing carols. Piotr considered the miraculous change in his circumstances since his previous Christmas in captivity.

"If I had then known that I would be with you two this year, it would have been such a blessing. I can endure pain and discomfort so much better in the knowledge that it will come to an end. It was the uncertainty, the anxiety which made it so hard to bear."

They were in good time for the 11.30 service. Ruth and Agnieszka helped Piotr across the square and through the entrance doors. Ruth looked up. The great altar piece had gone. The blue and gold splendour of the East end of the church was reduced to the bare stone. Ruth gasped. Through her mind poured a series of angry questions. "Who would do such a thing? What kind of human would take the altar screen from the very church for which it had been crafted as its greatest adornment? What other religious or cultural institution could be so depraved as to accept and retain a vital art work stolen from a living church?"

She walked slowly behind her friends and took her place in the same pew. She followed the service, but was constantly thinking of the outrage which had been perpetrated by the conquerors.

The Christmas sermon spoke of the generosity of God, in giving his own Son to all humanity. The preacher had his back to the blank stone left bare by the theft of the altar piece. He did not say it but his audience must all have thought that the opposite of generosity is rapacity, theft.

She walked ahead of Piotr and Agnieszka as they left the church. Into her path stepped the only person who Ruth detested, Hainski. He presented a smiling face and extended his hand as if he were a friend.

"Ruth Neuman, I am glad that I have found you here."

Before Ruth had decided not to shake his hand, she saw two black-uniformed soldiers just behind him. They stepped in front of her.

"Your papers, please."

"You are Ruth Neuman. You are reported as Jewish. You are not living at the address given. You must come with us."

Ruth heard the gasp from Agnieszka behind her, but the Germans were focussing only upon their prey. They led her out of the square. She saw Hainski watching as, with sinking heart, she followed the Germans to their car.

Another person also witnessed Hainki's role in the arrest of Ruth. Vlad Glast went to the church because it was Christmas morning and his mother wanted to attend. He recognised Hainski before the service began. He saw him slip out soon after Ruth had followed Piotr and Agnieszka into the church. He watched as Ruth was arrested. Although Glast could do nothing to help her, he would tell his Home Army contact about Hainski's role as an informer.

Ruth was put into a cell and was held overnight without food. From the Gestapo offices above, she heard male voices singing German Christmas carols, and an hour later, the sound of men talking loudly between gusts of laughter. She did not sleep. On the following morning, she was brought before a young officer, who looked at her with contempt. There was, however, something about his jerky manner which suggested that he was neither as confident nor as experienced as he tried to appear.

On the marble mantelpiece, an ornate German clock ticked while the officer studied the document in front of him. It was as if he did not know where to start, but suddenly alighted on the fact that the alleged Jew had been arrested at a Christian church service.

"I am not impressed by your visit to The Mariacki. To me, that is meaningless. You are a Jew, born and bred into that foul race. You have failed to register as a Jew, which is a crime, punishable with the death penalty."

"Why do you believe this? You must know that I am a citizen of France working here when the war began. What you say is based on the word of one Polish person, a landlord who had a dispute with me when I left his house. You should ask my employers at the school."

Ruth was not sure why she was playing for time. Why stay alive for any longer if the outcome will be an execution sooner or later? Perhaps the young officer was waiting until his superior returned after the Christmas break. Perhaps some scruple of religion or conscience made him decide against applying his pistol to the back of the neck of this slender woman who he had arrested in a church on Christmas morning. Perhaps the cells in the prison were full of men and prostitutes and he did not choose to lock her in with them.

"You will be taken to the Ghetto immediately. That is where you belong. As for the offence of failing to register, the decision as to that matter..."

He paused and the elaborate clock ticked while Ruth waited. It was as if the uncertain officer was tossing a coin and waiting while it was spinning on the floor before he saw which way it landed.

"The decision as to that matter will be made later."

In case she looked relieved, he repeated, "You know the penalty is death."

In the early afternoon of the same day, Ruth was taken to the Jewish Ghetto in a closed van. It stopped and she waited in the darkness while the driver spoke to an official. The rear doors opened. In came light and stench. The strong smell of human waste repelled her, and she nearly choked, but she had to concentrate on climbing down into the road where two Jewish men were waiting for her. The van pulled away, leaving her outside the offices of the Judenrat. She was struggling to avoid being physically sick, while also taking in her new surroundings and uncertain whether she was in danger. One of the men asked her to confirm her name and said that he would take her to her place now. She asked what was going to happen to her. He looked away, saying that he did not know and the Judenrat would merely allocate her a place now. They were going to a flat where a family had a space, and she must join them.

"Choice is a luxury very hard to find in the Ghetto. Accept whatever you are given, whether it's a bed, a job, a meal or nothing."

He took her up four flights of stairs and knocked on a door. A woman's voice answered. She wore a headscarf and exchanged rapid words with the man from the Judenrat. Ruth was taken in, shown a room containing three beds and told that one would be hers. It was a bare bed. Ruth looked at the woman and then broke down and wept. Her knees gave way and she sank to the floor as if in prayer.

It was obvious that she had almost nothing, neither clothes nor food. She had a little money which she had put into the inside pocket of her overcoat, together with the ruby necklace which Bruno had given her at Christmas 1935. She had discretely removed these items when being taken to the Gestapo office.

She had decided to wear it this morning in honour of Christmas Day in what now seemed a different lifetime. The woman knelt with her, putting a thin arm around her shoulders. She was speaking consoling words and offering such human solace as she could. Ruth pulled herself together.

"Thank you. It is all too much. It has come upon me so suddenly."

They sat down together, and the woman explained that she had lost her son, taken prisoner by the Germans. There had been no word from him, but all had heard rumours of ill-treatment in slave camps for Jewish prisoners of war in Germany. She brought in her daughter, Mina, a shy and sickly girl of about twelve, Ruth thought, although it transpired that she was really fourteen. Her husband was working in a factory outside the ghetto and would return at the end of the day. Then, they would work out what to do for the best. The woman said a Jewish prayer, to which Ruth did not respond. Her husband, Sigmund, walked back late in the evening. He needed food and sleep, rather than a new problem to solve. Ruth remained in the background, grateful to his wife, Marta, who gave her soup and bread, and offered her a single blanket against the mid-winter cold. She slept in her overcoat.

Two days later, Ruth's situation seemed to have settled. Having told the Judenrat official that she was a schoolteacher, he allocated her work in an orphanage. Children over eleven years old were required to work, and so there were only younger children in the orphanage. Ruth did her best for them. The staff of the Judenrat stated that she must comply with the curfew and reside at the same address with Sigmund and Marta Levi. She must remain within the ghetto and no pass could be given to allow her to leave it. However, no one seemed to be looking or her. The Sabbath came after three days in the Ghetto. Marta aid an embroidered cloth on the table and set out an old challah plate. Sigmund brought some challah bread and candles were it in accordance with the tradition. The head of the household sprinkled salt over the challah, cut it and passed it among them. The familiar words were spoken, Ruth being treated as if she belonged to the family.

Ruth tried to help the timid child, Mina. Her parents were grateful for her gentle approach to conversation with her. She had become introverted and unwilling to speak since March 1941. The SS had arrived at their flat in Kazimierz, telling them they must get out that day. Sigmund had pushed a hand cart on which some of the furnishings of their well-established home were loaded. He and Marta carried bags holding clothing and kitchen utensils. Mina had followed, crying silently. She had remained very timid and quiet when Ruth first befriended her. Ruth persisted, taking her hand and helping her with any task. Above all, Ruth spoke to her whenever they were together. Very gradually, and over several months, Mina's mental state improved. She had a chest condition which worried her parents. Ruth was grateful to these Orthodox Jews who accepted her into their family and way of life but she missed her former happiness with those who she had chosen as friends. She thought deeply about Emil and was concerned for Agnieszka. She knew that they would worry about her, but it would be impossible for her to contact them, and indeed, dangerous for both of them if she tried to do so.

After months in the Ghetto, Ruth received a scrawled message from Stefan. She was astonished to learn that he was also in the Ghetto. He asked her to look out for him in two days' time, when he expected to be among a body of men and women

about to set off for Oscar Schindler's factory, Emalia. Thi
workforce was given its own name - Schindlerjuden, Schindler'
Jews. Even at a distance, she was able to recognise his distinctiv
gait, and the shape of his head, now shorn of its beard and lon;
hair. She saw his look of astonishment as he recognised her. Sh
knew that her present appearance was as much changed as his
Knowing they were both in the Ghetto was only the beginning
It was a very different matter to find out where each lived whil
complying with the curfew and instructions to work. Stefar
discovered her address eventually and they were able to shar
experiences. His mother had been identified as Jewish by ar
informer, and Stefan had been forced into the Ghetto with her
His father had tried to resist. Stefan had seen him knocked to
the ground and hoped that he had given up his protest rathe
than risk further injury.

Emil went to St Andrej church on most Sundays. As h
hoped, he saw Ruth's friend, Agnieszka. They did not speak, bu
exchanged a glance of recognition. But one January morning
before the service began, Agnieszka walked past him, looked into
his face very directly and then took off her glove. Ordinarily, h
would leave the church before her, but on this occasion, he waite
outside. Agnieszka walked past and dropped her glove. Emil wa
unsure whether she intended him to keep it or return it to her.

"Madame, you have dropped this."

"Ruth has been taken. I do not know where she is. Or
Christmas Day."

Emil's face registered the shocking news, but only for a
moment. He replied rapidly;

"I will find out. Do my best."

Emil went to the Wobnungsamt where he asked about th
flat allocated to Ruth. He learned that she had been taken to the

Ghetto and would not return. Eventually, he was able to pass his news to Agnieszka. Meanwhile, he went to find Auerbach. In the years since the occupation, Emil had avoided the bar where Auerbach worked under the name of Franciszek. When he went to the bar at the back of the building, Auerbach directed him to the lavatory. There was a door at the far end. He heard the sound of a bolt being drawn. Beyond it, a staircase led to a little store room where Auerbach awaited him. They spent a long evening considering Ruth's predicament. Viktor Auerbach knew many members of the Home Army and others who were in different parts of the diffuse Polish Resistance.

Auerbach also had detailed knowledge of the Ghetto, where his former chauffeur, Josefz, now lived.

"He works at Oskar Schindler's factory, so leaves the Ghetto every day for work and we can then exchange messages left inside the duct of a fan. Josefz may be able to find out more about Ruth. He would recognise her well enough."

"Is there any chance to get her out of the Ghetto? There must be some way."

"I have not heard of it in recent times. The Germans would take reprisals against any family who lived with her. Since she has no family with her, this may not apply in her case. I will try to find out more. But Emil, if we could get her out, where could she live in safety? Any contact between you and Ruth would be highly dangerous."

"I am only concerned for her welfare."

"In truth, Emil, if she escaped from the Ghetto, she would be in much greater danger trying to survive outside. She may be safer among the Jews." Emil had to accept this as sound advice.

Their discussion ranged widely over the present situation in Poland, including the part formerly controlled by the Russians,

and the prospects of any good outcome to the war. They wer
able to continue late into the evening, because Auerbach woul
spend the night in rooms above the bar. Emil was intrigue
by how much Auerbach knew about his home city unde
occupation, and how he had adapted to the role of organiser c
those who attempted to improve the conditions for the Polis
population and undermine the oppression of the Nazis. In hi
warmth and sincerity, Auerbach exercised all his charm an
personality to persuade Emil to support his activities. When h
left, Emil acknowledged that he had not enjoyed an evening s
much since he had last been with Ruth. The two men checke
from different rear windows to make sure that the back lane wa
deserted before Emil stepped out.

"Come again any time!"

As he walked back to his sleeping quarters, Emil knew tha
he had crossed a line in this meeting. Until today, he had bee
a conscientious member of the Wehrmacht. He had taken th
oath of loyalty to The Fuhrer. He had worked keenly, using al
his skill and experience in planning for Operation Barbarossa
From the outset, he had grave doubts about it, and had naturall
considered what might be the political consequences if th
German Army, hitherto victorious, were defeated. But now h
was working with the Polish Resistance. There was somethin,
about Viktor Auerbach, his straightforward conduct and hi
personal charm, which had led Emil to make this step withou
either of them referring to it. He was now working against th
Nazi regime, and he felt much better for it. He even slept well.

The meeting between Ruth and Stefan was a source o
consolation to Ruth. Apart from the pleasure of seeing her ol
friend, she was impressed by his determination to prove tha
he was a man of action, willing to plan steps to support thos

in the Ghetto and to take any risk to strike back against the oppressors. Stefan was able to give her another surprise; the news that Auerbach's chauffeur was also working as one of the Schindlerjuden and living in the Ghetto. Although Juliusz was an acquaintance, she had known him for several years as a member of Auerbach's staff. He was an intriguing young man and Ruth wanted to see him. When they met, he maintained his normal respect and deference, although they were now equal in their status as Jews subjugated in the Ghetto. His loyalty to Auerbach was undimmed and Juliusz sometimes saw him at Schindler's factory.

Over the coming months, Emil went to see Auerbach several times. He learnt that Ruth was surviving and that Josefz and her old friend, Stefan, had made contact with her. He could not think of any further step which might help her, and he knew that if he tried to communicate with her, they would both be in greater danger.

In the spring, Auerbach raised something very troubling with Emil.

"At the Auschwitz camp, they have bricked in the windows of a building, and the rumour is that Russian prisoners of war have been murdered by gassing them inside this place. Now I am told they have prepared another huge sealed space. Some of us fear that there could be a plan to murder Jews in large numbers Do you know what is really going on at that camp? I have had these reports from different people, and it is difficult to know what may be the purpose of this new construction. The rumours are very worrying." Emil replied that he knew nothing about Auschwitz nor what might happen to the workers held there. He understood only that there were munitions factories in the camp and these required a substantial labour force. He said he would try to find out more. They agreed to meet the following week.

In the course of his working day, it was easy for Emil to enter into conversation about rail transport. He now learnt about new railway lines and plans for long trains of cattle trucks travelling, fully loaded, to the East and then returning empty to the West. When Emil next returned to the store room at the bar, Auerbach told him more about the gas chamber at Auschwitz. The guards would pretend it was a shower room. Victims would be herded in naked and cannisters of Zyklon B then thrown in at the top. There was no suggestion that these Jews had committed any offence. This was a system for murder. Taken with Emil's recent information about the transport system, it was becoming clear that the regime were about to exterminate all Jews in occupied countries. Emil was astonished to reach this conclusion.

"I cannot believe that my people would allow this. The German people are not all like Himmler. Many may not love the Jewish race, but my people would not support a programme of mass murder. We are a proud nation. We could only be ashamed of this if it is really happening."

When he left, Emil was deeply concerned about what he should do. He knew something which was being hidden from the vast majority of German officers. The fact that it was kept secret implied that the regime realized that the population would react against it. Emil and Auerbach began to work on a plan to expose the extermination programme, to stop it and, if possible, to deal a blow against the Nazi regime.

Emil wondered whether the famous German author, Bergengruen, who lived in Munich, might be persuaded to help. He was known to hold firm views against The Nazis. Emil suggested that he might be willing to write an open letter like the famous "J'accuse", published by Zola in 1898, against the anti-Semitic French government. Auerbach thought that this was unlikely to work.

"It was a brave act and a vital step in the vindication of Dreyfus, but Zola was able to flee to England rather than face imprisonment. If Bergengruen would support us, there would be no escape route for him. It would be unbelievably courageous. Secondly, how could we convince him that the allegations were true? Thirdly, even with a famous author behind the letter, it is difficult to imagine any newspaper publisher agreeing to put his head in the noose by printing it."

Auerbach did, however, have a good friend, Melchior Neuman, who owned a printing press in Strasbourg. He had heard that the business had been taken over by a German corporation but Melchior was still working there. Newspapers were printed at night. Would it be possible to add a new version of "J'accuse" to the pages authorised for publication in one of the major newspapers printed in Strasbourg?

After discussion, they decided not to try to contact Bergengruen. Instead, Stefan would write a straightforward account of the system for exterminating Jews. It would describe the pretence that the families were to be resettled in Eastern Europe, the use of the cattle truck trains concentrating on Auschwitz-Birkenau, the system for separating the men from other members of their families, the pretence of the showers and the use of Zyklon B gas. Auerbach had now heard that ovens were being constructed, and if this could be confirmed, the article would conclude with a prosaic account of how much more efficient this was than the previous method of disposal of the dead. All of this would appear as if it were news of a recent improvement to a system which was already established. They hoped they could add photographic evidence, which would be printed with the article. They thought that when printers did their work on the night shift, they did not study the content of the articles in the newspaper. Auerbach said that he would persuade Melchior to "turn a blind eye" when the additional copy reached the printers. If necessary, they would both behave as German officers giving direct orders that the printers carry out their instructions. In the aftermath, it would be impossible for the Germans to identify the source of the article. They would have their hands full in attempting to deny the truth.

Vlad Glast had joined the Home Army, but thus far, had only met one other member, Ludo. He regularly passed on to him anything he learned in his position in the Wobnungsamt. When he informed Ludo that there was a plan to reduce the size of the Ghetto by clearing buildings at one side, he was instructed to contact Franciszek. In due course, Vlad found himself in the upstairs room. Glast and his parents had known Auerbach as a prominent member of the Krakow business community. When he met Franciszek, he did not recognise the bearded man with tortoiseshell spectacles, until he spoke.

"Forgive me, I think I recognise you from the past."

Auerbach tapped the side of his nose and smiled.

"Possibly, but no need to remember anything like that."

Auerbach wanted to know which part of the Ghetto was to be closed, and whether it was intended to demolish it. Glast was able to say that he knew the plan was to offer the vacant premises to Polish families, and rebuild the external wall so that these homes would now be outside. When he described the

uildings to be vacated, Auerbach realised that they included
he flat occupied by Ruth and the family she lived with.

"Vlad, I think you are a new recruit, and it may be more
han you are willing to offer. But do you think you would be
villing to join me in a dangerous scheme to publicise specific
trocities carried out here? It is a long shot, but could be of
normous importance if we succeed."

There was something in Auerbach's voice and manner
vhich made it impossible to resist, and which was an inspiration
o the young man.

"I have joined the Resistance willingly. Anything I can do,
t whatever risk, I am willing to try."

When Ruth received another note from Stefan, she met
iim at the end of his working day. He had brought something
inusual and significant. It appeared to be a red leather spectacle
ase. As soon as it was opened, the lens of a small camera pushed
ut followed by a view finder.

"Keep this. If you are ever sent to a camp, you may be told
o undress for a shower. Leave this on top of your clothes. There
vill be someone to collect and use it."

"Stefan, you can tell me; if the shower is really a place of
leath, I would prefer to know."

Stefan looked into her face. She held his gaze as his eyes
illed with tears.

"I cannot say the words to you."

He told Ruth that there was a plan to take photographs of
nstallations at the concentration camp at Auschwitz. Viktor
vas sure he could get them safely removed from Krakow and
hen he would deliver them to Strasbourg. Ruth realised that
Melchior and his printing press would be involved. Stefan

would not say what would be photographed, but when the
were joined by Juliusz, he exuded bright confidence. "I know
the real German people. Viktor and I used to go there so often
We used to meet many Germans, some liberal in their views
some conscientious Christians. If these rumours are true and
we can get proof, it is so bad that the people will turn against
Hitler. They will have to."

Chapter 33: The Final Chapter

The Officers' Headquarters, Krakow

Emil was mildly surprised to receive the order to see his commanding officer at 10.00. The general had moved into a different building and Emil set off early in case he could not find the right part of it. The guard was expecting him. Emil was escorted to a hallway at the end of which were a pair of tall polished doors with gilt fittings. A stone coat of arms, including the head of a bear, glowered down from above the doors, the relic of some Polish nobleman, no doubt. The windows were placed high in the wall so that they offered no view out. Between these windows, a line of cherubs had been painted, their soft forms and colours contrasting with the pair of red swastika flags below. There was a handsome stone fireplace which, in happier times, would have provided a focus of warmth. There was not even a fire-grate now.

Emil understood that the general would be behind the double doors. He must wait in the hall. The guard appeared uncertain as to whether he should stand there with Emil.

"Thank you, Corporal. You may go."

The guard marched away. Emil studied the floor which was made from small stones, cut smooth and highly polished. His boots also glistened as he looked down, wondering why he had been summoned. Could anything concerning his meetings with Auerbach have reached the general? Minutes passed. He became more anxious and took a seat on a hard lacquered bench outside the doors. They were not sound-proof. The general was on the telephone.

"I am merely expressing my concern for the unit here. It is not a personal matter."

There was a long gap while someone continued to speak with the general. Then his voice again.

"It's your decision, of course. There is no need to explain further. I must implement it."

The conversation ended, with the general responding wearily, "Heil Hitler."

There was another pause before Emil was ushered in by a clerk who immediately saluted and left the room. Emil had a good working relationship with the general, finding him to be efficient and generally supportive of Emil's suggestions to achieve better transport to the Eastern front. He was a big man with a closely shaved head, displaying a pronounced bulge above his brows. This gave him the appearance of a gorilla. He conducted meetings with a warmth uncharacteristic of the German army. He never criticised junior officers in the presence of others and tried to bring out the best in all of them. Normally, his wide smile and big teeth added a childish element to his features, but on this occasion, there was no such expression. Rather he seemed to be embarrassed and upset.

"Heil Hitler!"

"There is no easy way to say this, Colonel. You are to be transferred to the Eastern theatre. I must give you the orders, and they are, of course, final. I will be sorry to lose you and have tried to argue that you are indispensable here, but whatever I say, allegations have been made by the SS. You cannot stay in Krakow. I have tried to persuade them to keep you in a

Transport Depot in the East, but they insist that you join the main force at the front."

It was intended to be a death sentence. Emil knew this better than most officers. He was a man in control of his words and actions, but the look of astonishment on his face was more effective than any denial or exclamation of anger. The general paused and felt the need to offer some explanation.

"The SS say that you have links with Jewish people in Poland. They have no living evidence. It concerns a missing Jew formerly living within St Xavier's School. When she was to be investigated, she disappeared. Someone must have given her warning."

"I cannot see how I could ever have been thought to know that anyone was under investigation. I have no connection to the SS or Gestapo."

"When she was eventually captured, you were trying to find out what had happened to her. I said there are no living witnesses. A Polish man would have said that you had been seen in the school buildings with this woman, but his body has been found in The Vistula with his hands tied behind his back. He is the man who had the woman arrested and this killing is the work of a resistance group. You have spent time in a bar which has recently attracted suspicion and is under surveillance now. The decision is not mine. My duty is to inform you that you will leave with a convoy in two days' time. I wish you well, because for me, your work has been efficient and well-organised. Frankly, you will be hard to replace. Your staff car will no longer be available as from now. You will need to get the warmest clothing you can. The furrier in Karmelicka is the best place. I need hardly tell you that."

Before he met Ruth, Emil had adopted a fatalist attitude to his future. He had endured enough to discourage optimism, false confidence, even hope. He had suffered a failed marriage. He had committed himself to a military machine which had become increasingly vicious after he joined it. He had been proud to be a German while his nation became dominant and then, when she became a monster, he felt shame and frustration because he could do nothing to oppose it. When he found and loved Ruth a new hope grew in his heart, but their relationship had been stamped out. His trajectory had been downward despite every high aspiration. There was no point in arguing with the General. Emil was reduced to military discipline, standard good manners and his own sense of propriety. He would do his duty and accept what might befall him. He spoke slowly.

"This is likely to be our last meeting. If I may, I would like to thank you for your leadership and also your support. It has been a pleasure to serve under you in Krakow. I will do my best at the front, but I have no experience as a fighting soldier or leader of troops in the field. If care and attention are needed, these I can offer."

The General leaned forward. "Between ourselves, Colonel, and this goes no further than this room, I would like your assessment of the likely outcome on the Eastern front."

Emil, shaken and hurt by the transfer to the East, wrenched his mind back to the big picture, and after a moment, answered in clear terms.

"We will not defeat the Russian army in Russia. They have the option simply to retreat to the East. We cannot bring sufficient supplies, certainly not through the winter. I fear the very worst there."

"What is to be done?"

Emil now expressed the conclusion which he had been thinking over for the past three months.

"I hope that sufficient numbers at the very top of the Wehrmacht will see this, then say it in the Councils to which they belong. We should concentrate on the defence of Germany. We could recognise the rights of the Poles to retain their country, and ally with them against Russia. Then, our enemy would suffer the long lines of communication if they were to attack us and we could avoid defeat. We might make peace with the West too. Good German life could go on, and the waste of lives such as my own could cease. If I can say this to you, General, might you say it to others?"

"I invited your assessment. I have heard it, but it does not follow that I share it. We are both honest men. But unless someone is willing to take such a risk by asking my private opinion, I do not ask you to imagine that I dare step out of line to oppose the High Command myself!"

Emil returned to his own quarters. He bolted the door. He was not given to self-pity, nor to a soliloquy about the cruelties of the world, but now, he knelt and spent some time in a deep fit of despair. He put his thoughts together as if he were writing a report or perhaps a prayer.

I only have one life. I have done with it all that I can, my very best. Like most human lives, it has not followed the course I wanted. I do not believe that it has been what I deserve. At this time, I cannot expect to return from the East. I lament the loss of Ruth, her probable death at the hands of my compatriots, and my inability to stand out against them. I cannot even help in delivering a film of Auschwitz atrocities to the Strasbourg printer. I have achieved nothing. These injustices and defeats test my old Christian Faith. I cannot understand God's Will or his intentions on earth. If it is incomprehensible, I fall back on training as boy and man. I will do my duty. Perhaps, also,

I can recover the same simple Faith I had before these disaster overtook my people.

Emil stood up. First, he must get a message to Auerbac that the bar was under surveillance, and then he would functio as a soldier, while inwardly railing against those who gave th orders. He would not survive.

In the Ghetto

Before the Feast of The Passover, Mina became serious unwell. The parents were very anxious about her. They neede money for medicine, and Ruth gave to Marta the ruby neck lace, Bruno's first present to her, so that Sigmund could se it to pay for what was needed. The parents were very grate ful. The family celebrated the ritual of the Seder evening a best they could. Following the tradition, a place was set fo the prophet Elijah, who foretold the coming of the Messiah A small quantity of wine was produced, and some of the usu foods appropriate to the Passover meal were shared. Sigmun spoke to his family, including Ruth, about the celebration of th Exodus which allowed the Jews, led by Moses, to escape thei captivity in Egypt.

"We celebrate this tonight. We hope He will rescue us also.

He recited the familiar phrases of the Haggadah:

"This year here - next year in Israel; this year servant next year free." These traditions and prayers were well know to Ruth. She wondered whether this evening, her parents woul follow the same practises, assuming that they were alive an free to do so. They would be thinking of her, just as Sigmun and Marta were thinking of their son. She concentrated he thoughts on her family and on little Bruno, who now belonge o Halina, praying to the one God accepted by both Jews and Christians. She felt the need to belong to a group, a family, a circle of friends, and a religion. Later, she tried to say this, to explain to Marta how she felt, that all humans have this need to belong, but Marta did not really understand.

"Of course, you belong and we thank you for being with us, for all you have done here". It was a gracious response, but Ruth's observation was intended to convey something much deeper.

Weeks and months passed. Late spring brought warmer temperatures. The cruel cold diminished, but the meagre food and sad surroundings, even the repulsive smells, sapped human strength. Over these months, Ruth's spirit faded away. She had intermittent moods of utter despair. She knew of no positive developments in the war. She could see no better future for herself. Her mind returned to her decision to remain in Poland when her family had finally fled France for England in 1938. She had failed to foresee the danger to her adopted country. Ruth concluded that her life was over, whether she lingered on in the ghetto or died. What had she achieved? She had enjoyed music; she had helped others to participate in its pleasures. She had loved all her family and Bruno. Should she include Witold Lutoslawski and Emil? Had she inspired love? In her heart, she knew that all of these men had loved her. She also realised that the other Witold, Zeleski the pilot, had worshipped her with all the ardour of a schoolboy. She concluded that these emotions were not achievements. Her life was wasted. But when going to sleep each night, Ruth would think of little Bruno. In her troubled mind, she developed the conviction that he represented her only contribution to the world. He was her hope.

The camera

Mina seemed to be getting better, and more like a normal child of twelve. She depended on Ruth and loved to sit beside her. Her confidence was returning. It was not to endure. One summer morning, before Sigmund was lined up to set off to work, there came shouts and the barking of dogs.

"'Raus! 'Raus! Get out! Get out! Schnell! Schnell! Quick. Now!"

There followed the sound of doors being broken down and more dogs barking, the sullen crowd in the street, and the march out to the station. The train steamed in, barbed wire on the cattle trucks. Dead were removed to make space for the living, standing ready on the platform, soon to die. The crowded, fetid train contained human misery and fear. The platform at the dreaded camp. More dogs barked and guards shouted or brandished whips. Some wore the striped uniforms of the inmates and wooden clogs instead of shoes.

"Men that side, women and children the other line."

"No, the other line!" The whip flashed and stung. A couple separated.

Marta was wailing and clinging to Sigmund, but he could only instruct her to do what the guards were saying. Mina went with her mother and tried to stay close to Ruth. They were to disrobe before a bath. Ruth took her clothes off, and placed the red spectacle case on top of them.

"Arms up, Raise your hands above your head!" A few precious stones fell from armpits.

Amongst many other women, and with no shame in her nakedness, Ruth walked steadily into the long building indicated by the guards. Mina followed her, in tearful distress. Ruth would not be hurried by the shouts of men nor the barking of dogs. One of the first into the enclosure, she experienced a strange smell. She pushed out of her mind any thought as to how this aroma had been generated and why it now lingered in the space. More women, some with children, entered. Others were older and more emaciated. As the numbers increased, Ruth was pushed into close proximity with their bodies. All were crammed tightly together, an experience as repulsive to Ruth as it was to all of them. Mina was whimpering beside her and trying to clasp her hand. Ruth allowed this but did not bend down to speak or look into the child's face.

Ruth was making a final effort to escape fear. She was determined to keep in mind only what had real importance to her. She sought peace, and peace was coming. "Lacrimosa, Pacem".

She was thinking of her son, as she very often did. She always felt confident that Little Bruno was thriving. She prayed for him. "Keep him in your care, O Lord God."

He must now be talking, speaking Polish with Halina. Had she known where he was and how he had grown, she would have been overjoyed. For at this time, mid-afternoon, Little Bruno was in an orchard. He was sunlit and smiling on his grandfather's shoulders, reaching for the green cooking apples which Halina would bake and offer as dessert to the family, for the third time this week. It was a picture of peace. Halina joined them and took the basket from her father while he set the infant on the grass.

There is no pathway by which the experiences or emotions passing through the mind of one distant human can be transmitted to another. A realist would say this applies even if one is the natural child of the other. It remains impossible even when a prayer is uttered at the point of death. But as she brought all the intensity of her mind to concentrate on Little Bruno, a sense of childlike peace came to Ruth, whether from the sunny orchard or not. The pair of heavy doors closed with a thick thud. Bolts were thrust across them. Ruth heard all this, but kept her mind on her own thoughts, which she maintained the power to control. For little Bruno, all would be well. She experienced a sense of certainty about him. He was happy. She had made her choice. There was a movement on the roof. Gas flooded in. Heavier than the air, it killed first those at the lower level, the children, the small, and the aged. Some died in silence. Others choked loudly. Many cried out in anguish. Ruth ignored the screaming distress within the chamber. Now, death racing up at her, Ruth continued in her prayer for her child. Peace came to her. As she lost her life, no one could ever know this, but at the same time, the boy walked towards his home between Halina and her father, holding the last green apple in both hands.

Epilogue: The Adler

"O Shepherd of Israel, who dost neither slumber nor sleep, we are the people of Thy pasture and the sheep of Thy hand. Enfold us safely in Thy love."

Jewish funeral prayer.

It was a grey day of constant drizzle in October 1939 when Josefz saw the Adler being driven through the streets of occupied Krakow. He stole a bicycle and followed it. Having learnt where it was kept, he returned the bicycle, knowing that Auerbach would want him to do so. He had joined the Polish resistance, called The Home Army, and a few weeks later, the Adler was well concealed behind a false wall in a dilapidated garage on the outskirts of Krakow. Two German officers and their driver had gone missing, but Josefz and Stefan kept all the uniforms and the officers' cigars. Later, he repainted the bright green coachwork in drab German khaki. Number plates stolen from a different staff car completed this stage of Auerbach's preparations for his second escape route.

When the furrier delivered Emil's message of warning, Auerbach reacted immediately. He left his bar, telling the staff he had food poisoning. Juliusz disappeared from Schindler's works, and prepared the car for the journey. Glast joined them. They waited for one more day until Stefan arrived with his newspaper article and two photographs. These were horrific. One showed the gas chamber when the doors were opened

after use. The second showed a line of cattle trucks besid
the Auschwitz platform. Tucking all of this into an insid
pocket, Auerbach thanked Stefan. "You have done all you car
It is our turn now." Stefan went back to his place among th
Schindlerjuden. The others began their journey to the prin
works of Melchior Neuman. Stefan had told Juliusz somethin
about a plan to expose the truth about Auschwitz. Auerbacl
told him only that they were going to Strasbourg, following hi
usual practise of saying no more than was necessary.

Leaving Krakow presented no difficulty. Josefz was cor
rectly dressed as the military driver, and in the back, Vlad Glas
and Auerbach wore the stolen uniforms of senior officers. O₁
the main road towards Lodz, there was little traffic. The Adle
swept past the occasional farm cart and civilian truck. Josefz
who had been anxious in the busy streets of Krakow, now bega₁
to relax. He was enjoying driving this car for the first time sinc
he had recaptured it in 1939. He had missed the accustome
freedom of the open road, the new autobahn in Germany an
the country roads through Poland. He concentrated on th
pleasure of building speed on the straight sections and carefu
control of the momentum when driving downhill or tackling ₁
bend. The Adler was satisfying to Juliusz, always dependable
an unfailing friend.

It was also in this car that Auerbach had commence
their romance. For the first few years, Josefz had been a simpl
chauffeur. He admired Auerbach's personal charm as well as hi
business success. He became increasingly devoted to him an
then developed a new emotion, a different longing. Occasionall
he had some reason to believe that Auerbach felt the same fo
him, but nothing happened. Then, when they made a trip t
Germany which was completely unnecessary, Josefz had bee₁

overcome with delight when they reached a fine Munich hotel, and he understood what Auerbach was asking. "Yes and yes," he had replied, and later repeated.

Josefz continued as chauffeur, deferential and efficient throughout the working day. He enjoyed the secrecy. To the outside observer, he was the mere servant and the man in the back was in charge. But at night, it was different. Only rarely, when away from Krakow and after a joyful experience in a splendid hotel, Auerbach would take the seat beside him in the car. He would reach across and pat his thigh. "A beautiful night," he might say. They would look across and smile to one another. No one knew.

The Adler's easy progress came to an end at a checkpoint some miles outside Lodz. If Colonel Emil Mendler had been with them, he would have leaned out of the window and given a firm order to let them through. The guards might then have waved them on, suspecting nothing. But they wanted Glast to get out of the car. Before he complied, Auerbach spoke in German.

"This is urgent; there must be no delay."

"I am sorry, Sir. We have our orders."

Auerbach cursed in German and told Josefz to drive on. He did so. The Adler accelerated through the barrier. The guards were slow to start firing. They had nearly reached a bend when the machinegun bullets struck.

Josefz was steering to take the corner at maximum speed when the rear tyre was blown out. The car slewed out of control. It ploughed off the road onto open ground where a clump of trees brought the heavy vehicle to a sudden halt. Josefz, gripping the steering wheel, was uninjured. The machine gun had stopped but he heard the sound of a motorcycle starting up. Jumping out, he opened the passenger door. Auerbach was dead, his mouth contorted and his eyes staring. Vlad Glast had a shoulder injury and was struggling to move.

The motorcycle and side-car skidded to a halt on the road. Two guards approached, weapons ready. Following his Home Army training, Josefz was standing behind a tree, his knife drawn. When the Germans looked into the car, Josefz stabbed both of them with a ferocity fuelled by fury and shock. He added further blows with the knife even when they were finished on the ground. Then, slowly recovering his normal character, because he heard a cry from Glast, he helped him out of the vehicle and sent him back towards the motorcycle. Josefz entered the car for the last time, breathing in great gulps of anguish. He closed Auerbach's eyes and kissed them. What more could he do? Overwhelmed by anger and grief, some words of a psalm came to him.

"He will give His angels charge over thee… He will deliver you and bring you to honour."

He took the helmets from the Germans, and they set off on the motorcycle. Glast was slumped painfully in the side-car and would need help from a Home Army doctor in Krakow.

He did not know about the newspaper article and photographs, now obliterated in blood. He returned the motorcycle combination to the Adler's hiding place, and awaited another chance to avenge the death of Auerbach, a man who he would always regard as the love of his life.

Jewish Prayer of Remembrance

In the beginning of the year and when it ends, we remember them. When we are weary and in need of strength, we remember them. When we are lost and sick at heart, we remember them.

So long as we live, they too shall live, for they are now a part of us as we remember them.

About the Author

William Wood has been writing all his life; as a busy barrister, Counsel's opinions, as a Q.C., detailed skeleton arguments and as a Judge, conscientious judgments. But, in the background, novels were forming in his imagination. He has a keen interest in history, literature, music and religion. These have combined to create Fate and Faith, set in the period which, in the opinion of the author, must have been the most dramatic in European History, World War 2.